"Hi, Tom. Good of you to come

It was the voice from his myst
now coming from a woman sit

"How did you get in here?" Surprise gave way to anger,
and Tom felt distinctly vulnerable, with nothing but a
towel around his waist and an unknown woman in his
hotel room.

She shrugged. "Hotel-room doors are good. But
manageable."

"Then how about you manage it again and get the hell
out?"

She laughed; then her eyes hardened. "You don't really
want me to do that, Tom. You want me to tell you why
you're here and what you've gotten yourself into. You'll
want to get dressed, however. You'll find a Glock nine
millimeter in your overnight bag. Standard Bureau
issue. I knew you hadn't traveled with one."

He flipped open the travel bag, and sure enough,
a black handgun lay atop his clothes. Hefting it, he
popped out the clip and counted off twelve rounds.
Although he knew nothing about her, she apparently
knew a great deal about him. As a former undercover
agent, that was not a situation he found palatable. But
she didn't seem stupid enough to arm a would-be
opponent. Which meant she didn't see him as an
opponent....

"So why am I here?"

RACHEL LEE
WILDCARD

MIRA®

ISBN 0-7783-2129-0

WILDCARD

www.MIRABooks.com

Printed in U.S.A.

WILDCARD

Prologue

Akhetaten, Egypt
1329 B.C.E.

Tutu watched the wanton destruction with a heavy heart. His ruler and patron, Akhenaten, was dead, along with the Pharaoh's beautiful wife, Nefertiti, savagely murdered in a religious coup, their bodies hacked to pieces and fed to desert jackals.

Tutu himself had escaped the bloodletting, thus far, only because he had been out of the city at the time. But when they found him, they would kill him. Of that, Tutu had no doubt. The royal chamberlain could not be allowed to survive. Tutu had studied too much, learned too much, even if he had not been at Akhenaten's side to make use of that knowledge when it most mattered. He must die, and what he had learned must die with him.

Tutu cared not for his own life. He was an old man, and death would claim him, one way or another, soon enough. But the knowledge must live.

Hiding amidst the rocks above what had once been

the workers' village, Tutu could not help but chuckle at
the irony of it all. Had Akhenaten not grown up with a
Hebrew, he might well have kept his birth name, Amenhotep the Fourth. Like his father and his grandfather before him, he would have ruled in the city of Thebes. He
would have remained in the good graces of the priests
of Amun. He might still be alive.

Instead, Tutu and young Amenhotep had grown up
and played with a boy whom Tutu's mother had plucked
from a reed basket in the Nile. Tutu and the young
prince had hidden in the shadows as his Hebrew friend
listened to the wisdom of his people. Afterward, the
three would sneak away together to discuss in secret
what they had heard that day. Secrets had shaped
Akhenaten's life from childhood, and in the end they
had consumed him.

Perhaps it had been all his fault, Tutu thought, not
for the first time. Would young Amenhotep and his
friend have tumbled onto the hidden codes by themselves? Probably not. Writing and its mysteries were
Tutu's gift—and his curse. As fluent in Hebrew as he
was in Egyptian, even as a child, Tutu had transcribed
from memory the stories he had heard. The Egyptian
stories he wrote in the royal picture script. The Hebrew
stories he wrote in their own language. That had been
both his triumph and his downfall.

For once Amenhotep had ascended to the throne,
Tutu no longer had to conceal his fascination with the
Hebrew scrolls he had written down as a child. The

scrolls that had begun to reveal coded mysteries beyond Tutu's wildest imagination. The scrolls that now lay in a leather bag at his feet. Tutu had shared those mysteries with his two boyhood friends, and their fascination had spurred further study and the discovery of more mysteries.

It was those mysteries that had led Amenhotep to abandon the priests of Amun, change his name to Akhenaten and build the city that was even now being laid to ruin.

The mysteries of the Light. Tutu was now their sole surviving guardian. Akhenaten was dead. Their childhood friend had vanished into the desert, a fugitive wanted for murder. If the mysteries were to be preserved, it was up to Tutu.

With a sad sigh, he took a last look at the once beautiful city that had been his home for the past decade. Then he picked up his precious leather bag and the lone waterskin he had been able to scavenge from the home of a long-departed workman, and crept around the northern rim of the city. It would be a long walk down the Nile to the camps of the Hebrews. But they would offer him sanctuary in his last days.

And, perhaps, he would find among them a young man or two whom he could teach. If only the Light would grant him the time.

1

Miguel Ortiz sat on a bench in the Parque Centro-América and watched the morning traffic build—shopkeepers and businessmen en route to their daily labors, diplomats to their offices, tourists peeking out of their hotels like so many ants looking for honey. The sun was well over the horizon, already warming air still heavy from last night's tropical rain. A couple sat on a nearby bench, and Miguel nodded to them. Almost time.

It seemed he had spent his entire life preparing for this day, although in truth he had never imagined himself doing such a thing until four years ago. Had it been that long since the day he'd come home from school to find his father hanged from a lamppost outside their house? He had looked up into his father's face, bulging and purple, tongue distended, and in that moment he had known what his future would be.

His father had been an innocent man, a Quiché farmer eking out an existence from the impoverished earth. The gringos hadn't cared. Miguel's uncle had died defending the family secret, but not before he had killed two of the gringos who had tortured him. In Miguel's country, blood cried out for blood. His uncle had taken gringo blood, and they had taken the blood of Miguel's father. Today, he would take theirs. It was the way of the world. His world and, probably, his children's world. If he lived long enough to have them.

That vision of the future had dimmed in the past four years. He had once imagined himself with a wife, working his father's farm, raising children. He had once been so foolish as to imagine that his father's optimism was not misplaced, that the peace accord would stand up, that his country would know stability, that he would someday walk into town and not see men in uniform with machine guns hanging from their shoulders. In his youth and naiveté, that had seemed possible.

That vision had been torn apart as he'd stood on a dirt street beside a drying puddle at the base of the lamppost, a testament to the moment of his father's death. Blood cried out for blood. Nothing more. Nothing less.

He reached inside the shopping bag beside him and fingered the stumpy stock of the AK-47. The wood was rough where he'd sawed it off. He'd considered sanding it smooth and decided against it. Life was not smooth. It grated on the nerves and left splinters in the mind. A weapon should be no less. And do no less.

The couple were also armed, he with another AK, she with a 9 mm pistol and a block of plastic explosives in her handbag. The guerilla lieutenant had provided the C-4. The use of gringo explosives was a delicious irony. Miguel didn't know their exact provenance—that a corporal in Georgia had sold them to a wild-eyed friend who sought to restore the purity of the white race, to be sold and resold again by those who lived and died by a warrior creed, until what looked like a block of gray clay had made its way to the Guatemalan highlands. He didn't know the details, but he had learned enough about the ways and means of killing to recognize U.S. Army issue. It was perfect.

It was perfect, because the guerillas had also taught him about his country's history, about the endless cycle of violence that had nearly bled his people white, touched off in 1954 when the American CIA—to protect the profits of the United Fruit Company—had instigated and funded the coup that had replaced an elected president, Jacobo Arbenz Gudman, with a military dictator. In the years since, the gringos had continued to fund a reign of terror, training the death squads at the School of the Americas. Over two hundred thousand of Miguel's countrymen had died. All so American children could have their bananas.

That was the official story.

The truth, Miguel knew, was something else altogether. Gudman would not only have nationalized Guatemala's farms and thereby ensured a better quality of life for the Quiché Mayan people. He had also been working to authenticate and publish a document that would change the world. The gringos could not permit that. Everyone known to be associated with the document had been killed, including Miguel's grandfather.

Now, today, Miguel would strike back. Today's operation would not be the first blow. It might not even be the largest blow. But it would be Miguel's blow.

He heard the heavy rumble of the engine before he saw it, and checked his watch. Right on time. The armored limousine, bearing the gringo ambassador, passing through the streets like a Roman governor through a slave nation. *Well,* Miguel thought, *this is not a slave nation. And you are not welcome.*

He rose from the bench and lifted the shopping bag, striding casually, as if he were on his way to work. And, in a brutal way, he was. The couple saw him and got to their feet, as well, walking arm-in-arm, two young lovers out to greet the new day. Miguel stood at the corner and lighted a cigarette. He made as if to put the lighter in his pocket but dropped it in the bag instead. Shaking his head, he set the bag on the sidewalk and stooped, watching the limousine and the couple from the corner of his eye.

The timing was perfect. Just as they'd rehearsed it.

The couple had almost crossed the street as the car approached. The woman touched her forehead and stepped back from her partner, as if she had left something behind. Miguel gripped the stock of the AK-47 and rose, just as the limo slowed to avoid the woman. He fired, knowing the bullets would not penetrate the glass, but also knowing the spiderweb of cracks across the windshield would cause the driver to pause momentarily before his training took over and he gunned the engine. In that pause, the woman moved with well-drilled speed and precision, looking as if she were diving for cover behind the limousine, when, in fact, she was slapping the plastic explosive to the underside of its frame.

Now her partner drew his weapon from beneath his business suit, and the car was riddled with enfilading fire. The limousine surged forward, the driver reacting exactly as he had been taught to do. *Get out of the kill zone. Protect the principal.*

Miguel and the man held their fire as the car passed, so as not to hit each other, then opened up again as it pulled away. The rattle of rounds being discharged, the comforting recoil, the ping and whine of bullets ricocheting off hardened metal, were exactly as he'd imagined.

As was the fireball, moments later, when the plastic explosive detonated beneath the fuel tank. The heavy, almost hollow *crump* reached his ears a split second later, followed by the rush of heat. But he was prepared for that, as well, knowing he and his comrades had been protected from the blast itself by the limousine driver's training to speed away from the shooting.

They were already advancing on the burning vehicle, weapons at the ready, as the doors popped open. The woman fired first, two Teflon-coated 9 mm rounds cutting through the driver's Kevlar vest like hot knives through butter, shredding internal organs as they went. The ambassador was the next to crawl out, and by then Miguel was only three meters away, waiting for him. The ambassador was raising his hands, his eyes pleading, as Miguel smiled and sighted his weapon on the man's forehead.

"Vaya con Dios," Miguel said bitterly.

Then he squeezed the trigger.

A white Honda squealed into the intersection, the lieutenant at the wheel. Miguel yanked open the passenger side door and climbed in as the couple piled in back.

"Vámonos!" the lieutenant said, stepping on the gas even before their doors were closed.

"Sí," Miguel answered. *"Vámonos."*

"Sangre para sangre," the lieutenant said, glancing in the rearview mirror as they sped away.

Yes, Miguel thought, remembering his grandfather, his uncle, and his father. *Blood for blood.*

2

As the primary returns were posted, Terry Tyson jumped from the sofa and let out a whoop that almost deafened Tom Lawton.

"Yes!" Terry said. "He's got it!"

Grant Lawrence had indeed sewn up the Democratic nomination for president, with solid wins in Florida, Texas and Louisiana pushing him over the top.

Beside him, Miriam reached for a napkin to dab champagne from her slacks. "Terry!"

"Oh," he said, looking down. His ebony features fell. "Sorry, honey."

She smiled back at him and laughed. "Hey, I'm excited, too. But you just about blew out poor Tom's eardrums!"

Tom joined in the laughter, finding it more difficult than it should have been. Here he was, in the home of his Bureau mentor, having spent the evening basking in the obvious warmth that passed between her and Terry. It had been an evening of good food, lighthearted banter and ready smiles. No undercover role-playing. No reading between the lines for veiled threats. None of what he'd endured the past three years living in the underside of the Los Angeles glitter. He ought to have been a warm puddle. But the old instincts, the quiet, life-or-death whisper in his mind, wouldn't go away.

The fury wouldn't go away, either. It had gotten him suspended. Now it gnawed at him remorselessly.

Miriam had seen it, of course. So had Terry. They understood. They'd both been there, she with the FBI, he as a career homicide detective in Washington, D.C. They knew the signs. But they were too considerate and too experienced to offer casual bromides. Instead, they had simply fed him, welcomed him into their living room and allowed him to sit quietly as they watched the primary election returns and held hands like teenagers.

"I hope," Senator Grant Lawrence was saying on the television, hands raised to quiet a crowd of ecstatic supporters, "I hope tonight shows that the American people can rise above their outrage and see that it is not only the ends that matter, but also the means by which we achieve those ends. That it is important not only to do the right thing, but to do it in the right way. And if the American people grant me their trust in November, I can promise you there will be a reckoning. Not a time of vengeance, but a time of justice. Not an orgy of violence, but a veneration of principle. Not a feeding of hate, but a nourishment of hope. That, my friends, is the American way. And America will *lead* the way!"

His words and the passions of the moment ignited a cheer that drowned out further speech. Endlessly, they chanted, "Lawrence! Lawrence! Lawrence!"

"Damn, he's good," Terry said, pumping his fist.

"He's more than good," Miriam said, grinning from ear to ear. "He's amazing. And what's more, with him it's *not* an act. He's the real deal."

Tom gave her the required nod of agreement. Amidst the mess in L.A., he'd taken a private moment to smile at her handling of the Lawrence kidnapping case. She, together with Terry and then-Tampa-detective Karen Sweeney, had rescued Grant's children and saved him from a sniper's bullet. Detective Sweeney had moved to Washington, where she was now Terry's partner and—as the tabloids spared no ink to remind America—Lawrence's girlfriend. There was no doubt in Tom's mind which way the votes in this room would go.

And perhaps the man truly was as worthy as his words. He had faced down his chief Democratic opponent, Alabama Senator Harrison Rice, who had repeatedly called for continuing the U.S. war on terrorism in the Middle East. Rice had made those arguments even more forcefully yesterday, after the murder of the Guatemalan ambassador.

Tom had half expected Lawrence to rise to the bait, to use the assassination as a reason to reverse his policy and thus bolster his image on national security issues. Certainly no one would have faulted him for doing so, and in fact many pundits had predicted exactly that.

But Lawrence had not wavered. His response had been brief and direct.

"The murder of our ambassador," he had said, "while barbaric, is a reflection of the violence that has torn that country apart. There is no reason to connect this crime with the recent attacks on U.S. bases in Iraq. The solution to war is not more war. The solution to war is a just peace. And, as president, I will work toward that just peace."

That kind of backbone impressed Tom. He wished Grant Lawrence had been his Special Agent in Charge back in L.A. Things might have gone differently. A little girl might not now hate him, and he might not have broken his boss's nose.

Then his fists tightened, and he told himself he was just being wishful. Grant Lawrence was probably just another political chameleon. Like his former boss, with his eye on promotion, not on the lives that would be affected.

Tom forced his attention back to the television as Lawrence finally quieted the crowd and resumed speaking.

"As joyous as this night is," Lawrence said, his voice now softened, "I must pause to acknowledge the grief of Mrs. Kilhenny and her children. Nothing I can do or say will ease their loss. I met Bill and Grace Kilhenny a month ago, when I went to visit Guatemala to see for myself the conditions that prevail there. He was a skilled diplomat, a gracious host and a brave man."

A long moment of silence passed, both in the Lawrence campaign headquarters and in the apartment. In the space of that minute, the senator had swept away the trappings of power and politics and attended to the pain of one woman. Even Tom was reluctantly moved.

Tampa, Florida

Grant Lawrence looked out into the sea of faces and finally found the one he really wanted to see. Karen. She was standing near a side door, smiling. He wished she could be up here with him. But that would be tantamount to a public proposal of marriage, and that was a step they weren't ready to take.

She was, after all, a cop. It wasn't merely her job. It was a big part of her identity. If he won this thing—and tonight even that dream seemed within reach—they could not be together. She couldn't function as a homicide detective with a Secret Service retinue. And the country wouldn't stand for a First Lady who held a job regardless. He knew it. She knew it. It was the bitter cloud around this silver lining. He had wanted to bow out of the race, to remain in the Senate, so they could be together. She had steadfastly refused to let him do it. She said she loved him, and her country, too much to allow it.

And so here he was. And there she was. The gulf between the podium and that door seemed insurmountable.

It was with that thought in his mind that he looked again at his supporters, then at his prepared text, and pushed the text aside.

"Friends, we have work to do. Not just for the next

eight months, but for the next four years. That work will not be easy. Justice, peace and prosperity are not easily won. These past months have tested our commitment, but they are only the beginning. Greater tests lie ahead. But I am sure that if we commit ourselves to facing those tests together, to meeting those challenges, to giving wings to our dreams and life to our ideals, we can transform both ourselves and this nation. We can be, in the words of Abraham Lincoln, that last, best hope. Tonight I say to you, I am committed to that last, best hope. Join with me. Stay with me. And together we will go on to victory!"

The roar was almost deafening. He turned and saw Jerry Connally's smile. His old friend stepped toward him, extending first a handshake and then a bear hug. Grant chose the bear hug, for this bear had been at his side throughout his eight years in the Senate, in the lean times, and in the worst of the ugliness that politics and life can offer. This night was Jerry's as much as it was Grant's.

"Wow, boss," Jerry said, almost yelling in his ear to be heard above the crowd. "I don't know where you got that from. But you'd better bottle it for safekeeping."

"Thank you, friend," Grant said.

"Thank *you*," Jerry said. "But the best is yet to come. For all of us."

"Let's hope so."

"By the way, boss, there are about two hundred people in the lobby that couldn't fit in here. You should make your way out there and let them know they're not on the outside looking in."

"Right," Grant said. "You're right. Lead the way."

"Wasn't he amazing?" Miriam asked.

"As always," Terry said. "If the country doesn't elect him this fall, they're passing up one hell of an opportunity."

For his part, Tom simply nodded and forced a smile. Yes, Lawrence's speech had been an effective piece of political rhetoric. Whether it was any more than that remained to be seen. He watched as Lawrence left the stage and waded into the crowd. The man certainly seemed to enjoy people.

Tom could still remember a time when he'd felt the same. Lately, people were to be avoided. Even here, with Miriam and Terry, he avoided any real contact. Contact only led to betrayal and hurt.

His thoughts were interrupted by a sound like popping corn, emanating from the television.

"What the…?" Terry said, looking at the screen.

"God, no," Miriam said, eyes wide.

The camera caught it all in stomach-turning detail. Lawrence's smile faded in an instant, replaced by a blank look of shock as he slid to the floor. Tom Lawton had seen that look before and didn't need to hear the reporter's next words.

"My God, he's been shot. Grant Lawrence has been shot!"

3

"I want Tom Lawton on my team," Miriam said firmly.

"No," Kevin Willis replied. "I'm sorry, but no."

She gave him a look of disgust and pressed on. "Tom is the smartest investigator I've ever worked with. He thinks outside the box. That's exactly the kind of mind we need on this case."

In that sense, she was right. It was all too easy for an agent to fixate on a suspect to the exclusion of other evidence. Kevin knew that as well as anyone in the Bureau. In the mid-nineties, early in his career, he'd been assigned to the Atlanta field office, putting him among the dozens of agents who'd responded to the Centennial Olympic Park bombing. He'd witnessed firsthand the near ruin of an innocent man before investigators finally stepped back to reexamine the evidence.

Grant Lawrence was a media darling. He had been for years, and the kidnapping of his children had only pushed his star higher in the public consciousness. The firestorm over his shooting was already under way, and there would be pressure for a quick, clean solution to the case. Exactly the kind of conditions under which investigators were most likely to develop tunnel vision.

So yes, in that sense, Tom Lawton was exactly the kind of agent the Bureau needed on a case like this. But on the other hand, the psych evaluation was clear as day.

"Look," Kevin said, "I know you like Tom. You've mentored him ever since he joined up. Heck, I worked with him for six months in Dallas before he was sent out to that mess in L.A. I liked him then. I like him still. But the simple fact is, he assaulted his superior. The guy needs plastic surgery, for crying out loud. Did you read Lawton's psych evaluation? The report is four paragraphs long, and the phrase 'distrust of authority' appears four times. He's on suspension for a reason, Miriam."

"Can you blame him?" she asked.

"Hell no! The way things went down out there, any one of us could be in the same boat. I'd have done the same damn thing he did. But if I use him on this case, the director is going to be stepping all over me."

She sighed heavily and nodded reluctantly.

"I feel for the guy, Miriam. I do. But right now he's too damn volatile. He needs time to recover. You're his friend, for crying out loud. You of all people should realize that."

She looked away, the hurt evident in her eyes. He hadn't meant it to come out the way it had, even if it was the truth. But there it was.

"You're right," she said, turning back to him. "He *is*

my friend. I've read the reports on L.A. And his psych sheet. But I know Tom Lawton better than anyone. Better than that doctor. Better than you. What he *needs* is a way to prove to himself that he's not a screwup. Which you and I both know he's not."

Kevin nodded. He'd never gone through what Lawton had, thank God, but he'd had his share of cases gone bad. After every one, he'd felt exactly what she was saying. He'd wanted to get right back at it. Do it right. Regain his confidence. The Bureau recruited Type A personalities. Goal oriented, driven to excel. The kind of individual for whom failure was almost a worse fate than death.

But he'd had enough trouble just getting Miriam on the case. She knew Grant Lawrence personally. Like any other law enforcement agency, the FBI had a clear rule about agents who were personally involved with a victim, witness or suspect. They were off the case, period.

He'd fought for Miriam for the same reason she was fighting for Tom Lawton. He'd mentored her. He knew her capabilities *and* her limitations. And he knew her well enough to know that she would not stay away from this case, regardless.

Ultimately, his argument had been simple. Special Agent Miriam Anson was a consummate professional, and if she were on his team, working the case officially, she would exercise professional judgment and restraint. If she were left to pry into the case on her own, she would have fewer inhibitions and might cause more damage. His bosses had bought that argument, with the caveat that she was to work under his personal supervision. And that she would be his responsibility.

That was good enough, then and now. Except that now she was pushing him out on a limb with Lawton. He could understand it, much as it irritated him.

"Okay," he said, "here's the deal. Tom works with you. No one else. Hell, I doubt there's anyone else he trusts, anyway. And he's all you get, for the same reason—I doubt he'd trust anyone else I put with you. He's your responsibility, Miriam."

She nodded. "Fair enough."

Kevin looked at his watch. "How soon can you get him in here?"

"Five minutes. He's downstairs in the cafeteria."

Kevin shook his head, then laughed. "You knew what I was going to say, didn't you?"

She didn't join in the laughter. "You trained me, Kevin. Let's get to work."

Tom was the last person to enter the conference room, and he had no illusions about finding a chair. Instead, he squeezed into a space along the back wall. He caught Miriam's eye and gave her a quick nod. He would thank her properly later. Any piece of the action right now was better than staring at walls and waiting for his next appointment with the psychologist.

"Here's what we have so far," Kevin Willis said, standing at the front of the room with a notepad in one hand and a remote control in the other. "At twenty-two nineteen hours last night, someone fired three shots in the lobby of the Hyatt Harborside in Tampa. Two of those shots struck Grant Lawrence. The other struck a campaign staffer named Ellen Bates. Ms. Bates was wounded in the left arm and is in stable condition after surgery.

"Senator Lawrence was not so fortunate. One bullet hit him in the chest, the other in the midtorso. He's still in surgery. The doctors are saying fifty-fifty."

Tom saw Miriam's face sink at that statement, although he knew she was already aware of Grant's condition. Karen Sweeney had called within an hour after the shooting, and Terry was already on a flight to Tampa. Still, hearing it described in the cold, clinical language of a briefing had to be hard to bear.

"Lawrence had just finished his victory speech after the Florida primary," Kevin continued. "Apparently he'd gone out into the lobby to shake hands with staffers who couldn't fit into the main ballroom. Powder residue on the victims and two bystanders put the shooter within three or four feet, but it was a tight crowd. So far, we haven't found anyone who can identify the shooter or even give us a firm description."

Tom saw heads nod around the room. It made sense. In close like that, with bodies packed in tight, a hand with a gun could easily slip beneath the arm of someone in front. *Pop-pop-pop.* Victim goes down. The shooter slips away in the panic. It was the nightmare scenario for protective services, worse even than a sniper. It was the reason the president never waded into a crowd.

"What happened to his security?" an agent in front asked. "Why'd they let him get into that situation?"

More nods from others who'd had the same training and followed the same line of reasoning Tom and the questioner had. It wasn't rocket science. This was a basic breakdown in procedure.

"It was a spur-of-the-moment decision by Lawrence," Kevin said. "He didn't want the people in the lobby to feel left out. That fits with his profile. He's the type who will stop and talk to people on the Capitol steps. I doubt he gave it a second thought. But his security team should have. We'll need to talk to them, but you all know how the Secret Service is. They're going to want to take care of their own."

Just like the FBI, Tom thought. Or any other police agency. It was a mind-set as old as the human species. You look out for your own kind, because they look out for you. When they didn't, it got very ugly, very fast. As he knew from personal experience.

"We did catch a break, though," Kevin said. Fifty sets of eyes instantly became alert. "The hotel has good security, including video cameras in the parking garage and covering the sidewalk in front of the lobby. So we ought to have the shooter on tape. The guys in Tampa are trying to cross-match the news footage of the event with the video of people leaving the hotel. With any luck, that will leave us a short list of suspects. Then we'll split them up among our teams and run them down."

The brute force method, Tom thought. Standard Bureau procedure. It reminded him of a joke about a collection of law enforcement types looking for a beaver in a forest. The NSA put a surveillance camera in every tree. The CIA sent in an agent dressed as a beaver, who returned a week later scratched, dirty, breathless and pregnant. The L.A.P.D. sent in two officers, who returned in ten minutes with a bloodied, beaten raccoon that was ready to admit it was a beaver. As for the FBI, they rounded up every animal in the forest and held them for six months while a forensic veterinarian examined their dental impressions.

It had been the Bureau's modus operandi since the reign of Hoover. Overwhelm the problem with manpower and science. It was effective. It was also slow. In most of the Bureau's investigations, that wasn't an issue. When you were going after a John Gotti or a Ted Kaczynski, whose crimes weren't daily front-page news, you could afford to take your time and build a case brick by brick. But that wasn't the situation here. The media, not to mention the attorney general, would be demanding daily briefings, with each one detailing new information and positive progress toward an arrest.

The brute force method was not designed to achieve that. When it was misapplied toward that end, the Bureau inevitably ended up with egg on its face. Fifteen hundred Arab-American detainees were only the most recent case in point. Tom could see the writing on the wall, and the message wasn't promising. He began to feel sparks of anger in the pit of his stomach. By sheer force of will, he battered them down.

Willis continued the briefing, dividing the task force into teams, handing out assignments. Tom paid only cursory attention until Willis looked at Miriam.

"Miriam, you and Tom will eliminate the wacko groups. I want to say we've left no stone unturned. Dig around on the Net. Get a list from our domestic surveillance guys. Crazies who've written against Lawrence. Run their files. I'm sure you'll find a bunch."

"No doubt," Miriam said. "He's liberal, Catholic, handsome, single, a dad whose kids were kidnapped, running for president while dating a cop. Put it all together and he's probably the darling of half the fringe organizations in the country."

"Probably," Kevin agreed. "And it's probably a waste of time. But I don't want conspiracy nuts coming along to say we didn't look. So look."

In short, Tom thought, he and Miriam were supposed to run down bullshit. On the case, but safely out of the way. It made sense. Miriam was too close to Grant to be in the middle of things. And Tom had no doubt where he stood in the Bureau's hierarchy of competence.

Then Willis spoke again, and this time his eye fixed on Tom. "I want everyone in this room to remember that at this time we are acting in a *support* capacity to the Florida offices, which are heading the investigation. If you find anything, it goes through me to them."

In short, no running off on your own. Tom gave Willis the nod he was looking for, but his neck felt as stiff as if it hadn't moved in centuries.

Watermill, Long Island

"He might have been *what?*" The man tried to suppress his anger as he listened to the voice on the phone.

"He might have been caught on videotape," the caller said. "Word is the hotel had good security, and the FBI's getting the tapes."

"And you can make sure that doesn't happen?" the man asked, clearly expecting an affirmative answer.

"No," the caller replied. "I can't. They know those tapes are out there. If the tapes vanished, that would just pile more shit on the doorstep. Besides, he can be sacrificed. We knew that from the start."

"So long as there's no trail," the man said.

"I can handle the trail," the caller replied. "I have that part covered. Don't worry."

He hung up in disgust. What an absurd statement, after calling on his daughter's wedding day, with two hundred guests arriving in an hour, to tell him an assassin he'd paid for might have been caught in the act on videotape, and then to say, "Don't worry." There was too much at stake for him not to worry.

"Daddy, are you ready?"

He turned and looked at his one and only daughter. This was the last afternoon that she would truly be his.

In two hours, she would belong to another. A fine young man, of course. He wouldn't have permitted anything less than the best for his girl. But still… The old bromide about not losing a daughter but gaining a son just didn't work for him. Not when it came to her.

He'd held her as a baby, taught her to walk and ride a bicycle, tended skinned knees and later skinned hearts, watched her graduate from high school, then college, then law school, quietly opened doors as she'd begun her career, and all the while she had been the one pure, abiding joy of his life.

He rubbed his nose briskly and nodded. "Yes, darling. I'm ready."

She saw his face, read his thoughts, and came to him with open arms. Their embrace was tight.

"Oh, Daddy. I will always love you first."

"I know, precious. I know."

If only it were true. If only anything were true.

"Lovely ceremony, Edward," Harrison Rice said, extending a hand. "Your daughter is a stunning bride."

"Thank you, Senator. I don't quite know how to feel about it, but…thank you."

Rice held on to his friend's hand for an extra moment while flashbulbs popped in the fading evening light. Some were wedding photographers. Others were society press on hand to cover "the wedding of the season." The rest, and that was most of them, were covering Rice's campaign…again. Or still, depending on one's perspective. He pressed his face close to his friend's ear and whispered, "I know exactly what you mean there."

Edward Morgan met his eyes for a moment and nodded. "Yeah, I guess you would."

For Rice, the past forty-eight hours had been an emotional whirlwind. It had begun with the assassination in Guatemala and its aftermath, as news camera crews chased him across Mississippi, Louisiana and Texas to secure him as a guest on one talk show after another. He'd had to cancel a scheduled campaign appearance, although his staff had assured him that he would get far more mileage out of the TV time.

He supposed they were right. The speech probably wouldn't have made enough of a difference, even if he himself would have found it more reassuring. He always preferred a live audience to the blank eye of a camera. But he'd had too high a mountain to climb yesterday. Lawrence had been a lock in his home state of Florida. Rice had known he would have to win Texas and split the other two Southern states to have a chance. He hadn't. Grant won decisively in Texas, Louisiana and Florida, easily giving him enough delegates to lock up the nomination.

And Rice's campaign had been over. For about an hour.

Unlike most Americans, Rice had not been watching as Grant Lawrence was shot. He'd been sitting with his wife, taking a few minutes of silent consolation, away from the press and the cameras and his staff and even his friends. Some moments should be private, and that had been just such a moment. Until a staffer began pounding on his door, shouting, "Someone shot Lawrence!"

Rice had emerged in time to see the first of the now endless reruns of the attack. He'd had to turn away. While they had been rivals in this campaign, he and Grant had been Senate colleagues for years. They had been guests in each other's homes on numerous occasions. Rice had never felt as if he was on Grant's short list of true confidantes, but he'd liked and respected him. He'd watched Lawrence cope with the death of his wife, and, years later, the brutal murders of his lifelong nanny and a former girlfriend that culminated in the kidnapping of his children. The man had endured enough. And now this…

Now Rice was expected to carry the Democratic banner, the Grant Lawrence banner. His campaign had gone from dead to full steam ahead in the few seconds it had taken for a would-be assassin to squeeze the trigger of a handgun. Rice couldn't help feeling sick about it, even as the object of his lifelong ambition loomed nearer than ever.

"You look like you need to talk," Edward said, too quietly for anyone else to hear.

Rice realized his thoughts must have been showing on his face, a trait he'd picked up from his mother, a former stage actress in Birmingham. Edward had, intentionally or not, reminded him that appearances are everything in the world of presidential politics.

Rice nodded. "It'd be nice to catch up."

"After the reception," Edward said. "We'll go sit in the den, drink a couple of beers and pretend we're back in college."

It was, Rice thought, the nicest invitation his old friend could possibly have made. It was certainly better than brooding about the rest of his life.

4

Washington, D.C.

"Coffee?" Tom asked, holding out a foam cup.

Miriam looked up and smiled. "You read my mind." She took a sip and pushed a stack of papers away. "What a waste of time."

Tom sat and sipped his coffee. It was Bureau issue: too strong, too bitter. If he let himself think about such things, it was probably a subtle tribute to the Bureau's founder and the man for whom this building was named. John Edgar Hoover had also been too strong, too bitter. And his ghost still walked these halls.

"What did you expect?" Tom asked. "There was no way Kevin could put us in the middle of this. We're damaged goods. So we get to waste time while the rest of them do the real work." He eyed the stacks of files with distaste. "Prove there was no conspiracy to assassinate Lawrence. Helluva job, proving a negative. And we get it because I freaked in L.A."

"And because I know Grant personally," Miriam reminded him. "It's not that bad. Face it, Tom, like it or not, somebody's got to do it or we'll be hearing conspiracy theories for the next fifty years. It's just…"

"What?" Tom asked.

He'd spent enough time with her to recognize the subtle cues that flickered through her eyes. She wasn't thinking about the case.

"Terry called while you were out," she said. "Grant is out of surgery, but it's not promising. The bullet in his chest took a lung. The other one perforated his liver and spleen. He still hasn't regained consciousness. They don't know if he ever will. Karen's a wreck, and apparently there's a big debate about whether she should even be allowed in to see him. Dammit, Tom, you'd think in the twenty-first century it would be okay for a president's wife to have a job! You'd think it would be okay for Grant and Karen to get engaged, get married."

Tom nodded quietly. He didn't bother to remind her that Karen would be seriously hampered as a detective with a couple of Secret Service agents always at her side. Besides, Miriam Anson didn't open up often. On the few occasions when she had, he'd quickly decided the best course of action was to simply sit and listen, offering the occasional question more as a way of letting her know it was okay to continue than because he needed more information. It was a technique he'd learned while trying to help his father work through the death of Tom's mother, and again two years later, when the last shreds of his father's confidence had turned to dust during the trial. Now Tom often used the same technique in his work.

"Grant's daughters are a mess, of course," Miriam continued. "Karen's doing her best to comfort them. I think about what I'd be like if it were Terry. They say helplessness is the most depressing thing in the world."

"It is," Tom said.

He knew from experience. He'd never met Karen Sweeney, but simply knowing she was a career homicide cop told him a lot about her. She would want to fix things. To do something…anything. To help the doctors. To help the Tampa cops and the Bureau. Something to make it better. But for now, all she could do was to sit in the hospital with Grant's daughters. And pray. And wait. Like Tom and his father had done in those last days. Watching his mother fade away. Like Tom had done as his father slipped into a dark and dangerous obsession.

For a moment Miriam's eyes shimmered. Then they hardened. "Damn it. Where is it writ large on the cosmos that the world has to be such an ugly place?"

It was a question cops had to ask themselves far too often. A question Tom had asked countless times over the past three years and almost nonstop for the past month. A question for which there was no answer.

"Like this garbage," Miriam continued, holding up one of the files on her desk. "Why on earth would people believe this stuff? Commit themselves to this kind of rubbish?"

"Hey," he said, "why would people commit themselves to the kind of shit we do? Just because we're on the right side doesn't mean we're always doing the right thing."

The anger in his question silenced her. For an instant, regret pierced his fury. "Miriam, I'm sorry. I'm just… I'll get over it, all right?"

Miriam looked at him; then a small chuckle escaped her. "Miracles happen."

"Right. Now, let's get on with this chickenshit. Who knows? Maybe for once there really *is* a conspiracy."

"Wouldn't that be something?" Miriam said, trying to shift her mood and possibly his.

"This whole conspiracy thing…" Tom shook his head. "I know they happen. I mean, we've got a stack of files to choke a horse here, and these are just the incompetent idiots we've managed to get wind of. People conspire all the time in business. Take Enron as an example. But to go after a politician…that's a different can of worms."

Tom leaned over the desk and caught her gaze, holding it tight. "If there's a conspiracy to kill a major contender for the presidency, what have you got?"

She hesitated, not quite sure where he was heading.

"You've got a coup," he said. "You've just influenced the entire outcome of the election. You've made sure that only people you can live with are running for the office."

Miriam nodded, still not sure where he intended to go with this.

"It wouldn't be the first time," he said. "Look at the Kennedy hit."

"Oh, damn, Tom. You can't…"

He shrugged. "I can. I'm probably one of the few still-living people in the world who *has* read the entire Warren Report. It's suspicious as hell. Anyway, my point is…if there was a conspiracy, we'll find it." He waved at the pile of files. "I'll start here. You take those."

"Just remember," she said, "if you crawl into rabbit holes, you're crawling through rabbit dung."

Tom nodded and flipped open a file as she left the office. The Bureau had files on thousands of fringe groups. Radical environmentalists. White supremacists. Terrorist cells. Anarchists, even today. Drug and crime cartels.

When Hoover had interviewed for the top spot in the unnamed investigative branch of the Justice Department, he had promised his boss, Attorney General and later Supreme Court Chief Justice Harlan Stone, that the agency would be divorced from politics. It would investigate crimes and not political opinions. That was what Stone had wanted to hear, and Hoover had been given the job.

In fact, Hoover had headed the General Intelligence Division in 1920 under Attorney General Mitchell Palmer, and Hoover's index card files had provided the information for the infamous Palmer Raids of 1920. In those raids, the Justice Department picked up thousands of alleged alien radicals across the country. Most were in fact citizens. Fewer than six hundred were ultimately deported.

Four years later, despite his words to Harlan Stone, Hoover had wasted no time in setting his agents to work

developing files on suspected communists, labor leaders, and other groups and individuals whom he deemed
to be anti-American.

That practice had swelled into the COINTELPRO
excesses of the 1950s and 60s, until Congress and an
irate public finally called for an end to domestic espionage. There were some who said the lack of such domestic espionage had enabled Al Qaeda terrorists to
escape notice and kill three thousand Americans.

Tom knew better. The Bureau still kept tabs on violent organizations and suspicious resident aliens. As a
congressional inquiry had shown, there had been
enough information floating among the various agencies to prevent the 9/11 attacks. Had that information
been collated and presented in a single briefing, the
plot and the plotters would have been obvious. It had
not been a failure of data collection but rather a failure
of data management. The pieces of the puzzle had been
spread across too many desks in too many agencies.

The file in Tom's hands was supposed to be part of the
new-and-improved data management system. Cross-in-
dexed on a secure database, the idea was that an agent
could follow hyperlinked threads between various groups,
looking for motives and capabilities that matched a given
pattern. At Miriam's request, an agent had searched for
individuals or groups with both the motive and means to
commit murder in order to keep Grant Lawrence out of
the White House. The results were the scores of files on
his and Miriam's desks, and the one in his hands.

The Idaho Freedom Militia was archetypal in its ordinariness. Its founder was Wesley Aaron Dixon, a West Point graduate who had grown disillusioned with army life and left for a sheep ranch outside Boise. The file photos were unremarkable. Dixon looked about like Tom expected of a sheep rancher: grizzled and lean, with a slight middle-age paunch.

The group's ideology was apparently cookie-cutter Western individualism: the government in Washington was too powerful; the Supreme Court was counter-democratic; the nation should return to its federalist roots; government was inherently bad, and so on.

One sentence was highlighted, a quote from a letter to the editor Dixon had written in 1998: "Every person should be trained and ready to defend himself and his community against the excesses of Washington, and to strike blows against a government which conspires daily to undermine his private property and his family."

With that one sentence, Dixon had earned an FBI file for himself and the Idaho Freedom Militia. Such was the tidal wave of information through which Miriam and Tom were wading, for no other reason than to establish that the FBI had, indeed, left no stone unturned.

An hour later, Miriam returned. "Find anything?"

"Typical stuff," Tom said, finishing the file. "Except for a letter to the editor, it's pretty much mainstream libertarian."

Miriam leaned over to see which file he was scanning. "Except for the part about women."

Tom scanned down to the passage. It was a copy of a personal letter to a former militia member. Apparently the man had turned the letter over to the FBI after having been dismissed from the organization. From the context, the man had been kicked out because his wife had taken a job.

"The proper role of the woman," Dixon had written, "is to bear and care for the children and the home. When a man allows her to abdicate that role, he allows her to betray God's plan for womanhood, abdicates his own role as head of the house, and undermines the Divine balance of the family."

"Everyone's entitled to an opinion, I guess," Tom said. "Even a stupid one."

"Yeah, well, Dixon kicked this guy out of the militia, which is more a favor than a punishment, as I see it. But he also blackballed the guy around town. Guy lost his job, couldn't get another. He finally had to move to Oregon and start over. All because his wife took a job."

Tom shook his head. Having grown up in small towns, he could see how it had happened. Close-knit communities were a two-edged sword. They could rally around someone in times of grief, as the townspeople had done with him and his father after his mother died. But they could also cut someone out of the herd over the most trivial matter. Or, as had been the case with his father two years later, the not-so-trivial matters.

"So why did this group get flagged?" Tom asked.

Miriam shook her head. "Damned if I know. I didn't see anything that connects Dixon to Grant Lawrence.

But the computer spat it out, so we have to go through it. No stone unturned, right?"

"Yeah," Tom said, looking at his watch. He took three more files from the pile. "Look, it's almost ten. I'm going to make this my bedtime reading. And you need to get some sleep, Miriam. Sitting here all night stewing isn't going to do the Bureau, Grant, Terry or me any good."

"You're right," she said, reaching for a handful of files to take home with her. "Life will be better in the morning, right?"

Tom forced a smile. "At the very least, it'll be a different day."

Watermill, Long Island

Edward Morgan flipped through the channels until he hit on an all-sports network running classic NFL films. This particular episode was the famous 1968 "Heidi Bowl" game between the New York Jets and the Oakland Raiders, so named because the network had cut away from the final minutes of the game so as not to overlap its scheduled broadcast of the movie *Heidi*.

"Oh, God," Rice said, looking at the screen. "I remember that damn game. Freshman year. In fact, we had a bet on it."

"Twenty bucks," Morgan said. "I got stuck with the Raiders, even though the Jets were my home team, because Joe Namath was an Alabama graduate and there was no way you were going to root against an Alabama man."

Rice nodded. "Cost me twenty bucks, too."

"I seem to remember you got that money back in the playoffs," Morgan said. "And we made a killing when the Jets won the Super Bowl. You had half of the brothers betting the Colts."

Rice laughed. "Pledge year got real easy after that. They all still owed us money."

They fell silent for a few minutes, watching the game film. It had been a bizarre time for Harrison Rice. Most of his high school friends had been drafted and were headed for Vietnam. Rice's father, a banker in Birmingham, had forced his son to forgo football in his senior year and focus on his schoolwork. While obeying his father had hurt at the time—Debbie Mays had dumped him for someone who could get her a letter sweater—it had paid dividends. His grades had shot up enough that he could follow in his father's footsteps at Yale, and the student deferment had kept him out of the rice paddies.

As the country had torn itself apart, Rice and Morgan had pulled all-nighters, studying economics and finance, Morgan poking fun at Rice's Alabama drawl, while Rice needled Morgan about his silver spoon childhood. Rice was a big man, and had been even then. Morgan was slight and half-a-head shorter. They were in many ways as different as night and day, and yet in the late nights pouring over expectation curves and compound return formulae, they had forged a bond.

Rice had gone back to Birmingham after college to work in his father's bank, then moved into state politics. Morgan had gone on to Harvard Business School and a stellar career in international finance. But they'd always kept in touch, had always been the anchors to which each could turn when the pace of achievement became too frantic and one of them needed to get away and decompress. Just like tonight.

"What a shame about Lawrence," Edward said.

"Yes," Rice agreed. "I wanted to win. But not this way. Never this way. Christ, he's got two little girls who are probably already scarred for life from all the shit that's happened. And now this."

Edward nodded silently and seemed about to speak, then stopped and looked at the television. It was what he had always done when there was something he wanted to say to someone but was afraid of offending him.

"Oh, come on," Rice said. "You know that doesn't work with me. It never has."

"Well, it's just…that's exactly it. The girls. Their mom is dead. And all the mess last year. Why put them through the hell of a presidential campaign? Why not at least wait four years for life to settle some? I'm not saying he deserved what happened. Hell, no. Nobody does. But why take the risk?"

Rice could see his point. He'd had the same thought last night. Once the wave of sympathy passed, he was sure the press would pick up the same theme. A psychiatrist would probably say it was a way of dealing with the sense of collective grief. Blame the victim. *Nihil mea culpa.*

"Well, let's just hope he pulls through," Rice said. "The girls need him. And frankly, the country needs men like Grant Lawrence. I don't always agree with him, but I can't question his convictions or his courage."

Edward shook his head. "You're not talking to the press here, Harrison. It's me. Don't tell me a part of you didn't jump for joy when you realized he was out of the race."

"Of course it did," Rice said. "And that part of me makes me sick. I don't like to think I'm the kind of man who could feel that way."

"None of us does," Edward agreed. "But we are. At some level, we're all looking out for number one."

"So what are you saying?" Rice asked, anger rising in his belly. "That I should be celebrating because a friend of mine was shot? Sorry. I can't do that. It was wrong."

"Whoa," Edward said, holding up a hand. "I'm not saying that at all. All I'm saying is, you didn't pull that trigger. You didn't make it happen. And yes, it's a damn shame. But it's also an opportunity."

"A curse, you mean. Even if I win, I'll be living under his shadow. Every decision I make will be weighed against what people think Grant Lawrence would have done. It's almost not worth it."

"That's bullshit, Harrison. And you know it." He

paused for a moment. "Look, remember that high school game you told me about, the one where you finally got to play because the starting quarterback got hurt?"

Rice nodded. It was the only time he'd played in three years of high school football. Homecoming game. Junior year. Brad Mellows had sprained an ankle halfway through the fourth quarter, and the coach had nodded to Rice. He remembered the churning in his stomach as he'd strapped on his helmet and jogged onto the field. They were three points behind and driving down the field. On the first play, he'd almost tripped over his own feet as he'd handed the ball to the fullback, but big Buck Ledger had bulled his way to a first down.

Rice had called an option on the next play, and as he'd swept around the right side and prepared to pitch the ball to Gary Thomas, he'd seen a crease form in front of him. He'd tucked the ball in, turned upfield and burst into the open. Seventeen yards later, he'd crossed the goal line, winning the game and, briefly, Debbie Mays's heart.

"Nobody said, 'What would the other guy have done?' then, did they?" Edward asked. "No, they talked about what *you* had done. Stepping up to make a play when the team needed you."

"Yes," Rice said.

"So it's the same thing here, Harrison. You have to step up and make a play for the country. And not the play Grant Lawrence would have made. He might be a great guy, but he's not always right and you're not always wrong. You have to make *your* play, just like you did in that game."

Rice nodded. "Well, you're right there. I'm not going to stand by while these damn terrorists blow up our bases and murder our ambassador. They're not going to kill our people and get away with it."

"Nor should they," Edward agreed. "That's an issue where you were right and Lawrence was wrong. We do need to continue what we've started in the Middle East and create a real peace. And if you do that—put an end to those fundamentalist fanatics and let those people have peace and hope and prosperity again—I guarantee you, no one will be talking about what Grant Lawrence would have done. They'll be talking about what Harrison Rice *did*."

Rice nodded slowly. Trust Edward to get him out of his funk and back on the right track. It was time to step up and make a play.

Later that night, after Rice had left, Edward picked up the telephone and dialed.

"How did it go?" a voice asked, without a greeting.

"He was feeling guilty, like you said."

"No reason he should," the man said. "He's the right man for the job."

"Yes, of course," Edward said. "But I understand his feelings. He and Lawrence are friends, after all. Anyway, he seemed to be feeling better when he left. More like his old self."

"And he's on board?"

"Yes. I think we can count on him."

"Make sure it stays that way," the man said, then disconnected to end the conversation as abruptly as he had begun it.

Edward Morgan was no fool. His own life was on the line here, as well. Failure was not acceptable. There was too much at stake. Harrison Rice would be president, *must* be president. The men Morgan worked for could count on Rice to do the right thing. American resolve in the war on terror was wavering in the absence of concrete progress. Left to their own devices, the people would want their sons and daughters to come back home. Grant Lawrence had already laid out his proposed policy for disengagement, and even the Republican nominee was backing away from his predecessor's rhetoric.

Only Harrison Rice was resolved to stay the course. A course that, day by day, brought Morgan's colleagues closer to their goal. No one could be permitted to stand in their way. Harrison Rice must be president. And, once elected, he would do his masters' bidding.

5

Tom sat propped up in bed, the reading lamp on the nightstand competing with the flickering light of the muted television. On the screen, Bruce Willis was using a POW camp murder trial as cover for a mass escape, even if it cost a black pilot his life. Down the hall, judging by the quiet murmurs since the ring of the telephone ten minutes ago, Miriam was talking to Terry. Tom tried to ignore the movie, the barely audible sound of Miriam's voice and the all-too-audible noise in his own head, as he paged through the files he'd brought home.

Colin Farrell, the black pilot's attorney, had just discovered that the court-martial was a ruse, and that his client was to be sacrificed to protect the escape. The pain of betrayal was evident on the actor's face. Tom didn't need the dialogue to know what was happening. He had seen that look before.

"It's a DEA operation, Lawton. All you have to do is stay out of the way."

He'd read somewhere that it was possible to be an honest drug dealer but impossible to be an honest undercover cop. It had taken him months to gain the trust of a midlevel trafficker, and over the next two years, Tom had been able to pass along intelligence that had allowed LAPD detectives to close three homicides, and DEA and Customs officials to seize a half-dozen shipments.

And all without compromising his cover—or the twelve-year-old girl who had become his best informant.

She was his subject's daughter, an only child, just as Tom had been. One of the homicides he'd closed had been the murder of the girl's mother, cold retribution by a rival trafficker. Tom had seen his own childhood mirrored in the bond between the girl and her father. He'd watched them work through the grief, just as he and his father had done. Like Tom, she'd seen enough of Daddy's "business" to know he did bad things. Unlike Tom, she'd had a kindly uncle figure to talk with and share her concerns. Someone she thought she could trust.

"The DEA thinks they've gotten all they're going to get, Agent Lawton. This guy has killed two people that we know of. Including your partner, John Ortega. Carlos is bad news, and they're taking him out. And you will get out of the way. Understood?"

John Ortega. He'd been Tom's best friend at Quantico and probably the reason Tom had stuck with the difficult training rather than giving up. Whenever he'd felt low, John was there to cheer him up with an ancient *Cheech & Chong* imitation that kept Tom holding his sides too tightly to bang his head against the wall. John Ortega, who'd been sent to L.A. two months before Tom had, and had been the first to penetrate Carlos Montoya's L.A. network.

When Tom had heard he was being transferred to L.A., he was elated. He had looked forward to working with his old Quantico buddy. When he learned that John was in a deep cover operation, it made perfect sense. John always was an actor. And then, only two months after Tom reached L.A., John Ortega had been found dead in a Dumpster, his face and hands cut off, teeth crushed. He had, in the words Carlos Montoya would later use in a private conversation, "become a nobody."

Tom had remembered John's death and nodded obediently to his SAC. Tom had told Carlos he had to attend his brother's funeral back in Ohio on the day that Carlos was supposed to meet a new contact. Carlos hadn't objected. After all, this was only a first meeting with a new contact. It was in a public place. Carlos said it would be a fine day to take his daughter to the beach.

Tom couldn't say, *No, don't take your daughter!* He'd set up the meeting, and even suggested the time and place. Any objection would be suspicious. And in this business, suspicion alone was enough to get you killed.

Instead, he'd sat in the surveillance van and watched as things began to go horribly wrong. Carlos might not have had any formal training, but he had a lifetime worth of street smarts. He'd spotted the first tail—a young agent who had too little tan and too much curiosity to be the surfer he was portraying—within five minutes. So he'd given his bodyguard a subtle signal and taken his daughter for a walk down the beach, toward the rocky cove where lovers snuck away in the moonlight and behind which his bodyguard had parked a second car.

Tom had stiffened as he stared at the monitor. "He knows. Let him go. Pick him up another time," he'd said. But his warnings fell on deaf ears. Instead, the contacts had decided to move in then, approaching Carlos, following him over the sea-weathered rocks and into the cove. Out of sight of the cameras.

Tom had heard the rest. The agent's too-casual greeting. The wariness in Carlos's voice. The girl asking if she could go down to the water. Her father saying the riptides were too strong. The overeager scene commander giving the order. The shouts. The gunshots. The girl's scream.

Always, always, the girl's scream.

In the next three minutes, Tom's life had gone to hell. He'd tried to get out of the van, but the SAC had planted himself squarely in front of his seat and ordered him to stay put. "Fuck that," Tom had said, grabbing the man by his shirt front and pulling him down as he rose himself and lowered his head just enough to drive his forehead squarely into the SAC's face. He'd heard the satisfying crunch of cartilage and bone in the instant before he'd shoved the man aside and bolted from the van.

Tom had sprinted across the sand, arriving in time to see Carlos's eyes glaze over, an agent pulling the girl away as she beat on his chest, screaming for her father to wake up. Then she'd seen Tom, and the yellow FBI logo on his navy-blue windbreaker.

There had been no question of trying to approach her, hug her, explain who he was and what he'd done. Her dark eyes stripped bare two years of trips to the zoo, walks in the park, shared entries in her diary, and exposed them for the lies they'd been. He'd simply turned and climbed back over the rocks, walking numbly down the beach under a flat, haze-dimmed sun....

A knock at the door shook him out of his reverie. The anger that never quite died surged again, burning away the guilt and grief. At least for now.

"C'mon in," he heard himself say.

"Good movie?" Miriam asked, glancing at the screen.

"It probably would be if I were watching it," Tom said, holding up the file in his hands. "Was that Terry?"

She nodded. "Grant is stable, at least. And there's brain activity, although he's still not conscious."

"Sometimes the body just needs time."

"That's what the doctors told Karen," she said. "They can't say how long, of course."

Tom nodded. "Any word on what's happening with the case down there?"

She smiled. "Now why would you think I'd know anything about that?"

"Because I know you," he said. "Detective Sweeney

still has contacts in Tampa. So you told Terry to keep an ear to the ground down there."

"Are you suggesting I don't trust official channels?" she asked. "That I think Kevin might let us spin our wheels on the sidelines and not tell us what's going on? Perish the thought."

"So what did Terry say?" Tom asked, knowing she suspected exactly that.

Miriam put a hand above her eyebrows. "They have this much of the top of a head in the news footage. Male. Blond. Short hair but not remarkable. Same head, from the back, on the hotel street video as he's leaving the scene. His body is obscured by a woman leaving behind him, an underling on Grant's campaign staff. She was across the lobby when Grant was shot and doesn't remember who was in front of her as she left the hotel."

"In short, useless," he said.

"That's my guess, and Terry agrees. Of course, the SAC in Tampa is trying to run this guy down through everyone who was there. But I'd be stunned if they found enough to ID the shooter." She sighed. "So how about you? Anything in those files?"

"Yeah," he said. "They need to reprogram their damn computer. We might as well be sifting the Sahara looking for a particular grain of sand."

"That bad?" she asked.

He held up the Idaho Freedom Militia file. "Take these guys, for example. You know what the connection was, why the computer spat this out?"

She shook her head, and he continued.

"Wes Dixon, the guy who runs this outfit? Turns out that after West Point he married a girl he met at a social there. His wife's maiden name is Katherine Hodge Morgan."

"So?" Miriam asked, arching an eyebrow.

"Exactly," Tom agreed. "So Katherine Dixon-née-Morgan's brother is Edward Thomas Morgan. He's some banker in New York or London or wherever he is this week. Whoop-de-doo, right?"

"Except?"

"Except that he was a college fraternity brother of Senator Harrison Rice."

Miriam laughed. "It's like that game, Six Degrees of Kevin Bacon. Grant Lawrence is running against Harrison Rice, whose old college buddy is a banker named Edward Morgan, who has a sister named Katherine, who married a young army lieutenant named Dixon, who later formed this Idaho-militia thing…so…"

"So," Tom continued, "the new-and-improved computer spits out the Idaho Freedom Militia as possible suspects in the Grant Lawrence shooting. And that's the kind of absurd horseshit we're wading through."

"Yeah," she said. "Okay, well, do the usual checks in the morning. Then we can sign off on the file and move on."

"To more absurd horseshit."

"Probably," Miriam agreed. "But they say the system is better than before. Used to be we couldn't get from

A to B in those files without a compass and a road map and a Saint Bernard. I suppose we should take their word for it."

"If this is any indication," Tom said, tossing the file on the floor beside the bed, "we can get from A to pi just fine. But A to B is still impossible."

"Hey," she said, "it's still a government operation."

The bitter irony was not lost on him as she said good-night. He put the rest of the files aside and turned up the sound on the movie, just as Bruce Willis stepped forward to assume responsibility and forfeit his life to save his men. Hollywood heroism. If only the real world were as tidy.

Then, suddenly, he jumped out of bed and went to fling the door open. "Miriam?"

"Yeah?" It sounded as if she were in her bedroom.

"Do you know somebody who can get us a copy of every bit of video, TV and security tape there is on that night?"

She popped her head out the door of her room. "Tom, you know we can't go there."

"I know."

"As long as you know that." She pulled her head back in, then stuck it out once more. "I bet we can have it by noon tomorrow."

He was grinning for real as he closed his door. He would bet she was calling Terry right this minute.

Then, flopping back down on his bed, he picked up another file.

Savannah, Georgia

Father Steve Lorenzo loved the smell of peach blossoms. His daily midmorning jog was one of his few self-indulgences, and he made it a point to cherish every moment of it. The warm spring sun on his face, the comfortable burn in his thighs, the sound of his steady breaths and, this week, the smell of peach blossoms. His seminary training had taught him to live in prayer, to seek God in every moment of the day. Sometimes that was hard, but this was not one of those times. Only God could create a morning such as this.

The day hadn't begun so wonderfully, of course. The alarm clock had seemed especially rude, probably because he'd been called out late last night to visit a parishioner who'd been injured in an accident. The man's injuries had not been as severe as he had feared, but Father Lorenzo had given him the Anointing of the Sick regardless. It was no longer reserved for persons on the brink of death.

After the alarm clock had intruded into a comfortable dream, he had risen to shower, shave and perform the same morning ritual that had anchored his days for nearly thirty years: celebrating morning Mass at his parish. Of course, with the priest shortage, he'd had to drive across town to a neighboring parish to celebrate Mass for them, as well. It was a small sacrifice, and he understood the need for it, but it did eat into his morning jogging time.

But the last hour had been his own. He'd left the rectory and headed for the waterfront, taking an easy pace past stately, antebellum mansions. It was the same route he jogged each day, four and a half miles at a comfortable eight minutes per mile. He no longer trained for races, though he'd done his share of ten-kilometer events and even a couple of marathons. That had been years ago, when he saw running as a mission, a contest between his body and his will. Now it was simply a joy.

Running was a solitary practice, and he'd more than once had to apologize to some parishioner who had seen him, waved and received no reply. The outside world existed only in soft focus, enough for him to avoid traffic and obstacles as his attention turned inward. Because of that, he almost missed the dark-haired man who waved to him from a park bench.

Almost.

In an instant, he became aware of the slight twinge in his right ankle, a pain that usually disappeared into the biological magic called "runner's high." The rhythm of his breath broke for just an instant, allowing the beginnings of a stitch in his side. He let out a soft curse and pressed on for the last half-mile to the rectory.

He didn't need to be told what to do. He took a quick shower, changed into civilian clothes, told the parish secretary that he would be out for lunch and headed across town to a small diner near the university. Although he occasionally filled in at a nearby parish, he doubted any of those parishioners would recognize him without the clerical collar. Few people did, even from his own congregation, so fewer still would know a priest they had seen only once or twice.

The man was waiting for him, sitting in a booth away from the window, perusing the menu as if he actually cared what the lunchtime offerings might be. Father Lorenzo knew better. He doubted if the man would even eat.

"Hello, Father," the man said as Lorenzo sat.

At least we'll speak English, Lorenzo thought. Most of their discussions in Rome had been in Italian, and while Lorenzo was modestly capable in his ancestral language, he was by no means fluent.

"Hello, Monsignor."

"I see you remembered," the man said, with no trace of a smile, no trace of expression whatever on his strongly Roman features.

"It wasn't complicated," Lorenzo replied. "If I ever saw you in town, I was to come here within the hour."

"Yes, well, for some things it is better not to use telephones. Even e-mail might be read by others, on my side of the Atlantic or on yours."

Lorenzo nodded, hoping against hope that the overly dramatic words were merely preamble to a routine request. It would not have been unlike this man to do that. He was, after all, given to hyperbole. Still, the steady look in the man's eyes did not convey the sense of over-inflation. This was serious.

"It seems our old enemies may be closer than we

thought," the man said. "We have intercepted some… disturbing communications."

The man didn't have to identify the enemies, nor the subject in question. Father Lorenzo had no doubt to whom and to what he was referring. Theirs was a cause to which he had dedicated himself in a solemn oath, even if at the time he'd deemed it ridiculously unlikely that the oath would ever compel him to action.

He was, after all, merely a parish priest of no great account. He had never imagined for himself a bishopric or cardinal's red. He had never wanted such positions or the political responsibilities that accompanied them. He was content to serve God in the small ways, and his sabbatical in Rome two years ago had been simply an opportunity for a prolonged pilgrimage in the host city of his faith, a chance to breathe the same air and walk the same ground as Peter, Paul and countless other saints.

Instead, he had made the acquaintance of this man. A casual acquaintance, at first, born of the coincidence that this man had been born and raised in the same village from which Lorenzo's great-grandfather had emigrated. It was one of those curious quirks of fate, destiny or Divine Providence—depending on one's perspective—of which life was made. Over a dinner that would have pleased the Almighty, coupled with an Italian wine that might have been vinted by the angels themselves, they had discussed cousins, old family stories and, of course, their mutual vocation.

Like Father Lorenzo, this man had been gravely troubled by the emerging scandals in the American Church, and by the ways those scandals might undermine the Church's mission and message. And, like Lorenzo, he saw an undercurrent of political prejudice in the timing and persistence of the media frenzy accompanying those scandals.

But unlike Lorenzo, he had expressed the belief that something could and should be done about the situation, and not only in terms of reforms within the Church.

"This is an ongoing battle that has raged for millennia," he had said. "Sometimes openly, but most often in the shadows. The Church needs warriors. It always has. It always will."

Their conversations had continued over the course of Lorenzo's year-long sabbatical. Step by step, the man had offered a view of church history that differed from the official accounts in both substance and tone. It was a story of conflict, of a struggle against misguided but dangerous heresies within and ruthless enemies without.

Had he been at home, in the relative religious sterility of the everyday life, Lorenzo would have thought it absurd. But caught up in the fervor of Rome, where he could attend morning mass at St. Paul's Cathedral and noon mass at the Basilica of St. Peter, where he could gaze at the Sistine Chapel, where every prayer seemed uttered from a half step closer to heaven, it had struck a chord. More and more, he had found himself nodding as he listened. More and more, it had made sense. In Rome.

Now, in a diner in Savannah, it seemed almost silly. And yet the man's eyes were every bit as intense as they had been eighteen months ago, when Lorenzo had been walking through the catacombs. The man not only believed, he had the kind of moral certainty that Lorenzo found only rarely. A moral certainty in the faith, practice and future of the Catholic Church. The kind of certainty a priest could not easily ignore.

"The murder of your ambassador in Guatemala," said the monsignor, shaking his head. "It has created serious problems. Problems we cannot afford to ignore."

Lorenzo was familiar with the problems of Guatemala, having been posted to a mission there early in his career as a priest. For eight years, he had watched the people struggle with poverty, disease and war. Although they might not have understood all the reasons why, they knew the military dictator who ruthlessly wiped out one village after another was a CIA puppet. Anger was widespread, and the U.S. a common and, to Lorenzo's mind, justified target of that anger.

Still, Lorenzo had no idea how that connected to the monsignor's stated mission in life, or to his own vow.

"The rebels' success will encourage others to make bold moves," the monsignor said. "More people will die senselessly. It will be difficult for our allies to keep an eye on things that need watching. And our enemies will use that confusion to find what they are searching for and get it out of the country. That cannot happen."

"The fabled Kulkulcan Codex," Lorenzo said, his heart sinking.

"It might not be a fable," the monsignor replied. "They have good information. They may be close to finding it. If it says what they think it does…"

He didn't have to finish the sentence.

When Pedro Alvarado and Hernando Cortez led the Spanish conquest of Central America, they had found and destroyed the Mayan libraries, thousands of volumes setting forth the history, culture, religion and literature of that great people. Some archaeologists believed that as much as two thousand years of recorded history had been obliterated by the "cleansing" fire of the invaders.

Only a handful of texts had survived. The most prominent of those, the *Popol Vuh,* had been translated into Spanish from the Quiché *Chichicastenango* by a Dominican priest, Francisco Ximénez. Unfortunately, the *Popol Vuh* was only a fragmentary record of the Quiché Maya and their creation story. But even those fragments had disturbing correlations to the Bible. And when the Spanish had arrived, they'd also found symbols of the cross and stories of a god-man who had been sacrificed for his people.

Cortez had initially taken advantage of the legends that said the bearded, white-skinned god would return from the East, playing them for all they were worth, accepting as his due the title of Quetzalcoatl/Kulkulcan. But in the end, he was racked with guilt, wondering if he had betrayed God by playing God, wondering if he had stepped into a prophecy about Christ himself.

By themselves, the stories could be dismissed as native folklore and often were. But among the remaining poetry about Kulkulcan found in the Mayan book of prophecy called the *Chilam Balaam*, the Church found cause for greater concern:

> When there shall be three signs on a tree,
> Father, son, and grandson hanging dead on the
> same tree

The lost volumes, supposedly written by disciples, were rumored to have described the historical figure of Kulkulcan in detail, including his arrival in the early second century and his teachings. If copies of this Mayan codex existed, and if they said what they were rumored to say, Kulkulcan, also known as Quetzalcoatl to the Aztecs and Viracocha to the Incas, was none other than the firstborn son of Sara, the daughter of Mary Magdalene. None other than the grandson of Christ, descendant of a marriage the Church had denied for two thousand years.

Kulkulcan—a priest who claimed to be the son of the only god, who taught monotheism, peace and justice, who condemned human sacrifice and whose arrival catapulted a people to hitherto unknown heights of civilization—could well be the grandson of Jesus of Nazareth.

"What do you want me to do, Monsignor?" Lorenzo asked.

"Go back to Guatemala."

"Are you mad?" Lorenzo asked. "Need I remind you that Americans are not popular down there right now? That was why I was removed in the first place, and it's gotten much worse in the last fifteen years."

The monsignor shook his head. "You still have friends there among the people. They will remember you. They will trust you."

He leaned forward and looked into Lorenzo's eyes. "Find the codex, Father, if it exists to be found. And if you find it, guard it with your life."

6

"Anything?" Miriam asked as Tom scanned the computer printouts spread across his desk.

"Maybe," he said.

She'd been watching his growing excitement for the past hour and a half. She recognized the signs, the subtle cues of a born predator that has caught whiff of prey. These were the same facial tics, the same body posture, the same gleam in his eyes that had first attracted her notice. He had not been just another eager beaver law school grad who had signed on with the FBI. He'd had that air of a relentless hunter about him, even then.

"What do you know about sheep ranching?" Tom asked.

Miriam looked at him. "Are you back on that Idaho militia thing? I thought we'd dismissed them as cranks."

Tom shrugged. "I decided to run the financials on all the groups. No stone unturned, eh?"

"I suppose," Miriam said. "I'd feel better if I knew we were turning over stones in the right garden."

"Well," Tom said, "that's just it. Most of the groups we've looked at are unfunded nutcases. Many of them aren't even groups at all, judging by their financials. Turns out most of them are some lone wacko with a Web site and an inflated sense of his own importance."

"But you found something in the Idaho financials?" she asked.

Tom nodded. "Maybe. I mean, have you ever been to a sheep ranch?"

"No," Miriam said. "Have you?"

"Once, as a kid. School field trip."

"And?"

"It was a small operation, like Dixon's," Tom said. "A lot of grazing land. The rancher showed us how his dogs rounded up the sheep, and the shearing shed, and so on."

"And your point is?" Miriam asked.

"Why would a sheep rancher need a fleet of five Hummers? One, I can see. But five?"

"Employees? I dunno. Something to bounce over the pastures and round up the strays?"

Tom shook his head. "He'd use a horse or dogs. An SUV wouldn't be agile enough. A sheep rancher might use a Hummer for riding his fences, or for towing, but neither of those is an every day or even an every week chore. As for employees, from what I can see, Wes Dixon doesn't have a huge operation. It's a small ranch. So why *five* Hummers?"

She held up her hands. "You've got me, Tom. Maybe he bought them for his militia?"

He shook his head, studying the printouts again. "Maybe. But they wouldn't be all that useful for your run-of-the-mill citizens' militia group, and a Hummer is an expensive SUV, even if it's a base model rigged out for ranch work. He took out a loan for two hundred fifty thousand dollars to buy a fleet of five. And guess where he got the loan?"

Miriam's heart skipped a beat. "His brother-in-law's bank?" she asked.

"Bingo. Now, there's no big surprise there. Edward Morgan is a nice brother-in-law, so he pulls a string or two to make sure his baby sister's husband can get a loan for some new ranch equipment."

"Why would he need to pull strings?" Miriam asked. "Couldn't Dixon get a loan?"

"Like I said, the ranch is a small operation. And, judging by Dixon's tax returns, not all that successful. I'd guess it would be hard to find some local Idaho banker to spring for a quarter million on a fleet of monster SUVs for a small-time sheep rancher. I'd be surprised if Dixon could get fifty grand to buy new stock at this point."

Miriam nodded. "So Dixon's wife talks to her brother, and voilà. New Hummers for all."

Tom looked at her, once again shaking his head. "Not exactly. And that's the interesting part. Dixon's wife talks to her brother and gets a *loan* for new Hummers for all." He paused for a moment. "But there's no record that anyone ever bought them."

"When was the loan?" Miriam asked, sensing where he was going with this.

Tom flipped through the printout. "Eighteen months ago."

"So this wasn't an ordinary car loan," she said.

"Nope. The Hummers weren't put up as collateral. In fact, I can't find any security for the loan. Morgan's bank just issued a check for a quarter million. And Dixon never bought the Hummers."

"Payments on the loan?" Miriam asked.

"Not a one."

"Dixon's credit report?"

Tom held up another printout. "The loan isn't even mentioned. Apparently the bank never posted it to the credit bureaus."

"So what you're saying," Miriam said, "is that Wesley Dixon got an unreported loan for a quarter of a million dollars from a major New York bank with no collateral, and he's made no payments."

"And has no fleet of big, shiny new Hummers," Tom added.

"So where's the money?" Miriam asked.

"Not in his personal accounts. And I can't find it in his business accounts, either. Or in the militia's. Or any record that a sum like that passed through any of those accounts. But I'm no bookkeeper."

She'd picked up the scent, just as Tom had. The scent

of prey. She reined in her excitement. "You know this is a long shot, Tom. It's a hundred to one—hell, a *thousand* to one—that this means what we think it might mean."

Tom nodded. "But if it does, we might just have found the money that paid for the hit on Grant Lawrence."

"That's a stretch," Miriam said. "Eighteen months ago... Would someone plan an assassination attempt that far in advance?"

But someone might, she knew. Her pulse accelerated. If someone wanted to make sure all the trails were really cold, they might well plan that far in advance. And Edward Morgan *was* a lifelong friend of Harrison Rice, who was now the Democratic nominee for president.

"It's a helluva stretch," Tom agreed. "And it's probably exactly what I said last night. Horseshit. This Morgan guy wanted to bail out his brother-in-law's failing business, so he jimmied up a loan to slip Dixon some extra operating cash. That's probably all it is, right?"

"If it's even that," Miriam said. "He probably got the loan for the Hummers, discovered his barn was about to collapse or some such crisis du jour, and had to spend the money on that instead. And he kept it off the books to dodge the IRS."

"It's horseshit," Tom said.

"It's absolute horseshit," Miriam agreed.

There was a long moment of silence. She knew what

he was thinking. She was thinking the same thing. Yes, this was probably a waste of time and Bureau resources. But then again, their entire assignment was probably a waste of time and Bureau resources. At least this had a vague hint of illegality. Banking and IRS regulations, sure, and probably an innocent, well-intentioned, charitable violation, at that. But it was still far more interesting than the rest of what they'd read. And within the purview of the FBI.

"So you're going to run it down?" she asked, forcing herself to sound casual.

"Damn right I am," he said. "Any luck on those videos?"

She glanced at her watch, and both brows lifted. "Listen, we need to go to lunch."

"Now?"

"Sure. Then we'll be ready to dig into those files again."

He grabbed his suit coat and without another word followed her. Miriam never did anything without a reason.

Rome, Italy

Monsignor Giuseppe Veltroni sat on a stair at the Trevi Fountain, watching the tourists. They came in all sizes, great and small, all colors of the human rainbow, and speaking the babel of dozens of languages. At this time of evening, however, the fountain was even more crowded than usual. The most irritating thing was the tour guide using a megaphone to speak to his flock in

Japanese. The Japanese didn't bother the monsignor, but the volume did. It nearly drowned out the soothing sounds of cascading water.

He himself was clad like the rest, or nearly so, in civilian clothes of slacks, windbreaker and jogging shoes. The air was chilly for spring. While the tourists looked comfortable, the monsignor was not. A creature of the Vatican, he vastly preferred his cassock. Even a clerical suit was preferable to this open-throated shirt. He missed his collar and felt deceptive without it. But privacy was his primary concern in this public place.

A pigeon alighted beside him and cocked its head, indicating a demand as clearly as if the bird had spoken. "I'm sorry, little one," the monsignor murmured. "I have no food."

Moments later the pigeon departed, joining its fellows across the fountain, where a young boy was scattering bits of cannoli. The flocking birds alarmed the child's mother, and she whisked him away, leaving a trail of pastry crumbs in their wake.

Monsignor Veltroni returned his attention to the fountain. Begun by Bernini, it had been finished by Salvi, who earned most of the credit for the fantastic beauty of Neptune riding a seashell chariot drawn by winged steeds. The monsignor especially liked the winged horses. They appeared to rise right out of the fountain itself along with the water, as if emerging from the sea, and to his mind they carried a message of hope. *Out of the darkness and depths we shall rise into the light....*

The monsignor very much hoped he would rise into the light, which was the reason he was sitting here on this hard marble step, surrounded by people who tossed coins into the fountain to ensure their return to Rome.

A man sat beside him, a dark man, weathered hard by deserts and the suns of many years. They were a contrast, these two, the monsignor soft and pale from his duties, the other hardened and darkened by his. Yet they were players in the same game.

"You have difficulties," the man said in flawless Italian.

Veltroni wondered how many languages the man spoke, having heard him converse in no fewer than four. Rome was an international city, and this spot a tourist attraction, so Italian was as private as any language they might have used. Certainly no less so than English, Veltroni's only other language of competence.

"You requested a meeting to tell me something I already know?" Veltroni asked.

"No," the man said, shaking his head. "I requested a meeting to offer you my assistance."

Veltroni let out a short, silent, derisive laugh. "Thank you, but no thank you. The Church prefers to handle such matters itself."

"The Church," the man said, "doesn't even know about this matter. We both know your group is not recognized by the Vatican. I doubt the Pope knows you exist."

"The Holy Father has many responsibilities," Veltroni replied. "He cannot have his finger on everything."

"We both live with secrets," the man said.

"You more so than I, apparently," Veltroni murmured, "as you seem to know all of mine."

These meetings always troubled him for that reason. More than once had he tried to pry open the wall of stone that shielded Nathan Cohen, if that was indeed his name. He had found very little. Certainly not enough. The man beside him was too much of a mystery, placing Veltroni at a distinct disadvantage. In this game, information was power.

"Like you, I am but a humble man of God," Cohen said.

That part might have been true, though Veltroni knew this man was no rabbi. He doubted the man was even Jewish, although he sometimes presented himself as such. Rabbis operated within the structure of the Jewish community, and while that structure was not as rigid as the Catholic Church, neither was it anonymous. For a while Veltroni had wondered if the man was Mossad—Israeli intelligence—but discreet inquiries had ruled that out, as well.

"You don't believe me," Cohen said.

It was not a question.

"No," Veltroni answered. "But you already knew that."

"You tried very hard to locate me after our last little chat," Cohen replied. "Your people are good, but… well…mine are better."

"And who are your people?" Veltroni asked. "You're

offering to help in a confidential matter known to very few. I'm not such a fool as to believe that help would come with no strings attached. If I were to accept your offer, I'd want to know who I would be beholden to."

Cohen looked up at the clouds for a moment, as if he were considering what to say, although Veltroni had no doubt he had long since rehearsed every possible move and countermove in this verbal sparring match.

"Is it not enough to say I am a man who thinks the world would not be improved by the chaos that would arise from these discoveries?" Cohen asked.

"No," Veltroni said. "I am far too old to believe in convenient altruism."

"You are a cynic, my friend."

"I am a realist," Veltroni answered.

"The defense of all cynics and depressives," Cohen replied with a quick chuckle. "You don't *see* the glass as half-empty. It simply *is* half-empty, correct?"

"Mockery is a dangerous game, Mr. Cohen. Even a dog tires of being poked with a stick. And I lack the saintly patience of that species."

"Please, Monsignor, let us not devolve into boys, strutting about the schoolyard with our chests out. That would demean us and serve no one but your enemies."

Veltroni was not accustomed to being lectured, nor to being patronized. His temper flared, his jaw clenching for a moment, before he bit back his reply and forced himself to take a long, slow breath. Wading into battle with an unknown enemy was the height of folly, and he was no fool. But signing a blank check to a stranger was equally foolish.

"It seems," Veltroni said, "that we have little more to discuss. I cannot consider your offer unless I know what is involved. My superiors—and I do have them, even if my organization is not a formal organ of the Church—would not permit it. We could sit here and joust all day, but, as I said, I am not blessed with saintly patience."

Cohen watched Veltroni rise and walk away. Another man might have regretted the course of the conversation, but Cohen had expected nothing more. Veltroni might lack patience, but Cohen did not. The Guardians had waited over three thousand years for a conjunction of opportunity such as now existed. A few more weeks were but a drop in a vast river of time.

Veltroni was not yet desperate. But he would be, and sooner than he knew.

1

Fredericksburg, Virginia

Tom and Miriam reached the door of her house just in time to keep the courier from departing.

"I'm Miriam Anson," she said to the courier. "I believe that's for me."

"Identification?"

She showed him her Bureau ID. His eyebrows lifted, but he said nothing, merely had her sign a receipt. Then he was off, whistling, and Miriam and Tom entered her home with the box.

"I take it Terry came through," Tom said as she dropped both the box and her keys on the dinette.

"You betcha."

"So this is lunch?"

"Well, whatever you can find in the fridge is lunch. Unless you want to eat videotapes."

The thrill of the hunt was rising.

"Pastrami and homicide," he said, returning moments later. "Extra mustard."

She opened a bottle of water. "You want to tell me what you're looking for? We already know no one caught the assassin on camera."

"Well, it's really quite simple." He used a key to cut the tape on the box. "I want to know what the Secret Service was doing during the shooting."

She raised her brows. "Conspiracy involving the Secret Service?"

He shrugged and pulled a stack of videocassettes from the box. "We're supposed to disprove a conspiracy, right? Well, I'm about to disprove one angle everyone is going to be screaming about."

She nodded slowly. "Maybe," she said.

"Right. Maybe. No one's expecting us back, I hope."

"Tom, at the moment I don't think Kevin much cares if we fall off the edge of the earth, as long as we don't get in the way of the 'real' investigation."

"My thought exactly."

He held up the tapes and gave her a crooked smile. "Shall we?"

Tom and Miriam were still hard at work in her living room later that night. It had become their base of operations. She had dragged in a whiteboard on an easel she'd packed away in a closet, some dry erase markers, a folding table and the torchère from her bedroom, which made the entire room nearly as bright as day.

They had watched the videos repeatedly and were

now assembling a time line on the white board, listing who was where when.

Finally Miriam tossed her marker down in frustration. "I don't see anything out of line."

"I do." As he stood looking at the time line, Tom pointed out each item he mentioned. "Okay, we've got one agent on the podium with him."

"Right."

"One in front of the podium on the ground floor."

"Right." She flopped on the couch.

"And two near the back of the room, right?"

"Right."

"And none, absolutely none, outside in the lobby."

"Well, Grant wasn't out there."

"Hmm." Tom closed his eyes and pictured again what he'd seen on the tapes. "Wrong," he said.

"Wrong?"

"Wrong. Most definitely wrong. There were nearly two hundred people in the lobby, and a constant flow of people in and out of the ballroom. Nobody was checking credentials at the ballroom door?"

"Campaign staffers were," Miriam said. "Senior people were allowed in, and the rest were in the lobby. I'd guess that's standard procedure in these things."

"Maybe." Tom opened his eyes and sat on the other end of the couch. "It's possible. But Terry says they're running down a bunch of threatening letters, right?"

She nodded. "That's what he's hearing. Shop talk. Lawrence's protection team was busier than hell with all the hate mail. But he was the frontrunner. Terry didn't sound like anyone thought it was unusual."

Tom nodded. "The protection detail should have been more alert."

She leaned toward him. "Tom, you can't second-guess them. It won't do any good. There were four agents there. Five counting the supervisor in the video room. That should have been enough. Those guys know their jobs."

"Sure." He rubbed his chin. "On the other hand, 'those guys' let someone change the parade route in Dallas. Did you know Kennedy's limo nearly had to stop when it took that hard left turn onto Elm, and even so, it almost hit the curb? He was a sitting duck. And that was strictly against Secret Service regulations at the time."

Miriam let out a sigh of exasperation. "Tom, things happen. Unforeseen things. It doesn't make a conspiracy."

"I'm not saying conspiracy. I'm just saying that somebody screwed up."

"Okay. Okay." She pushed her hair back from her face. "I'll go with that. Security *was* a little lax. But in crowds like this…" She shrugged.

"You're a good devil's advocate, Miriam." He smiled.

"How am I supposed to take that?"

"You make me think more clearly. That's how."

Surprising her, he reached for the remote and switched on the TV and VCR again. He hit Rewind, and a bewildering array of images flashed before her eyes. Apparently this was one of the security tapes, in full living color.

Suddenly a picture froze on the screen.

"What do you see?" he asked.

"Jerry Connally and Grant embracing."

"And where's the agent?"

"Left rear."

"Right." He skipped ahead. "And now?"

"Grant's coming down the steps from the stage with Jerry."

"Right. And the agent is still on the stage." Tom jumped forward again. "Still not following them." Forward again. "He's still on the stage. If I remember correctly, the other agents in the room stayed where they were, too. Except for the guy in front of the podium."

Another picture showed that agent turning in the direction Grant and Jerry had gone. The next showed him take a step in that direction. The agent on the podium never moved a muscle.

"Now," said Tom, "call me crazy, but I want to know why that agent on the stage never moved. You know the protocol for protection teams in a crowd, Miriam. A moving box, with the principal in the middle."

"The crowd had been vetted, Tom."

"Maybe. Maybe."

He switched tapes to one with film of the lobby outside the ballroom. Grant and Jerry appeared in the doorway, stepping out into the crowd. The Secret Service agent was holding the door, eyes on Lawrence.

"It looks innocent enough to me," Miriam said. "Do me a favor and don't replay the shooting."

"I won't. But it's *not* innocent. The agent is looking at Lawrence, see?" He pointed. "They're trained not to look at the principal but at the crowd."

"Lawrence is passing him, Tom. It's a glance. He's a human being. I'm sorry. I just don't think there's enough here to hang the security detail out to dry."

After a few more minutes of discussion that went nowhere, Miriam went to bed. Tom replayed the news video that Jerry had sent. Only one of the news crews had been in the lobby…giving the world the unforgettable images that were still being broadcast.

Nothing.

Finally, to give his head a chance to clear, he picked up his files and drove back to D.C., where he could work on the Dixon conundrum without disturbing Miriam.

Like any good agent, he'd found an irregularity, and he was determined to run it to ground. So far he had only a probably illegal loan from a major bank to a slightly off-the-edge sheep rancher in Idaho who funded a private militia group that so far seemed to consist of five men and their dogs.

Which wasn't a hell of a threat to the security of the United States. After Waco and Ruby Ridge, the FBI wasn't about to ride in with guns blazing over six wackos with some semiautomatic weapons.

But the money…a quarter of a million dollars… That was too much to ignore. And for a while it silenced a small girl's cry of betrayal.

It was the links. And he'd long ago learned that few

links in life were purely accidental. Like attracted like. Harrison Rice had attracted Edward Morgan, whose sister had attracted a military cadet named Wesley Dixon—a man who by all accounts was destined for stars on his shoulders until he went…nuts?

Not nuts. If he was nuts, his wife would have left him and his brother-in-law wouldn't have risked giving him a shady loan. Ergo, Wes Dixon wasn't nuts, and nothing about him and his apparently crazy turn in life had caused a break between him and the powerful establishment he'd once belonged to.

That had Tom's nose twitching like mad. If Dixon still had an in with the power elite, then he must in some way be useful to them. The question was, was he still on the A-list, or had he been demoted?

That was surprisingly easy to learn, thanks to all the security put in place since September 11, 2001. It didn't take much effort to get his computer to spit out the records of all Dixon's air travel in the last two years.

It was a pretty picture. It seemed he regularly traveled to New York and Boston, and once to D.C. His wife often traveled with him, but not always. He maintained connections.

Tom sighed and rubbed his eyes, not wanting to admit that he was getting too tired to think clearly. Admitting that would mean going back to his room to sleep, a guest room in Miriam's house, a room with not one thing to identify it as his own space, even temporarily. Even in the bathroom, his toothbrush and razor were packed away in a travel kit. He was a man far from ready to move on with life, and far too close to his past.

So he got another cup of coffee from the machine, forced himself to drink it, then closed his eyes for a few moments as he tipped back in his chair.

Links. They were there. And for a quarter of a million, they meant something.

He returned his attention to the computer. By now the FBI had the names of all the agents assigned to Grant Lawrence's protection. And while they had probably only taken statements, since the Secret Service was virtually above reproof, one FBI agent, semi-suspended or not, was going to do some background checking.

It was another link, possibly accidental, but his nose was twitching like mad.

After all, those guys were trained never to look at the principal.

Actium, Greece
31 B.C.E.

Osarseph stood beside his queen and watched the Roman ships doing battle in the clear blue waters below. This was not what he, or his queen, had wanted to see.

Marc Antony, the handsome Roman general whose heart she had won, was watching with a knitted brow, leaning over to an aide, who relayed instructions to a signalman, who in turn stood on the cliff to wave flags in encoded sequence. It was a vain attempt to control what had spun badly out of control.

Since the murder of Julius Caesar, Cleopatra had steered a dangerous course through Roman politics. Ten years had passed since she had arrived in Tarsus and invited the young general to dinner. Since then, she and Antony had increasingly cast their lot together. That much, at least, had gone as Osarseph had planned.

Antony had all but guaranteed that, once he disposed of Octavian, Cleopatra would retain control over Egypt as a sovereign ally of Rome. Indeed, more than once he had hinted at permitting the Ptolemaic Dynasty to rule the eastern half of the empire, while Rome governed the west. With no other power sufficient to challenge her, and the throne of Egypt both secured and enhanced, Cleopatra would be uniquely positioned to permit Osarseph and the Guardians to bring mankind forward into a new age of Light.

Osarseph had no such hopes for Octavian. A hard-line Roman to his core, Octavian, if allowed to rule, would enforce Roman law—and, worse, Roman religion—throughout his reach. The prophesies had warned of a religion that would rise from Rome to dominate the world. Though by no means a superstitious man, Osarseph could feel in his bones the tingling of those prophecies emerging on this warm autumn morning.

Antony had hoped for a land battle, his army against Octavian's. Antony was the better general, and his nineteen legions were better trained and more experienced than Octavian's largely home-guard force. Weeks before, he had sent his twelve thousand cavalry on a raid to cut off Octavian's water supply and force his army into battle. The raid had come to naught, and the campaign had ground to a stalemate.

A stalemate that had favored Octavian's lies, for now Antony's own troops were hearing rumors of a Roman general who had abandoned Rome for Egypt and a queen-sorceress who held him in thrall. Day by day, desertion and disease bled Antony's once-proud legions. Finally he had been left with no choice but to meet Octavian in a sea battle. That battle was now proving why it had been Antony's last resort. His fleet was simply no match for Octavian's.

"You must prepare to escape, my queen," Osarseph said.

Cleopatra—intelligent, charming, attractive despite her hooked nose, perhaps the most powerful woman the world had ever known—nodded slowly. "So it appears. Tell them to prepare my flagship, with sails at the ready."

She turned to Antony. "We must go, my love. There is nothing left here to be won. We will fight that man at another time, in another place."

Antony seemed poised to refuse, though in the end he gave the orders. "You get away first. If they catch you, Octavian will kill you. I will stay with my men until you are safely away."

"No," she said. "We go together. As we have always gone. Together."

"I will permit no other course," Antony said. "I must see to my men. Arrange for their withdrawal. Many have abandoned me, but I will not abandon those who have stayed by my side. They deserve my loyalty, as they give theirs."

Osarseph knew this was not a battle Cleopatra could or would win. Antony was a soldier to his soul, and he would not leave his men leaderless. "Come, my queen. Let us away, and quickly."

By the time they boarded her flagship, the captains had finalized the details of the breakout. Octavian's ships, though greater in number, did not carry sails into battle. The excess weight merely slowed the oared vessels. But Antony and Cleopatra had insisted their captains be ready to raise sail. A freshening afternoon wind would be their deliverance.

If only for today.

Osarseph had no illusions that this was more than a temporary escape. Octavian would buy off Antony's legions, then hunt the couple to the ends of the earth, if necessary, to secure his primacy in Rome. And with that would come the end of Egypt. The Guardians would return to the shadows, forced yet again to wait for the course of events to offer opportunity.

The time would come. The prophesies guaranteed that. And with opportunity would come a new age for the world. Osarseph would not see that time. His grandsons, who were just now being groomed for the mysteries they would one day master, would not see that time. Instead, he and they would do what those who'd come before had done.

Preserve the mysteries.

Protect the Light.

And wait.

8

Tom Lawton might have banged his head on the desk, if head-banging would have shaken loose the ideas that were lurking at the edges of his mind. But it would only give him a headache and clarify nothing.

A review of the candidates' political platforms had revealed only minor differences, which wasn't surprising. Most of the Democratic candidates had the same stance on economic and social issues. The only real bone of contention was the situation in the Middle East, where Lawrence favored strengthening U.S. ties with Arab states, working with other nations to address human rights and economic issues, and hunting down terrorists covertly. Rice took a more direct approach, pushing for direct U.S. intervention in states that harbored terrorist camps, and driving what he called "the engine of democracy."

As Tom saw it, reasonable arguments could be made on both sides, and when push came to shove, their positions had more common ground than differences. It didn't seem like the kind of issue that would motivate an assassination.

Back to the quarter million bucks. Reaching for the mouse, he began a deep background check on the members of Dixon's militia, hoping he would find something he had overlooked earlier.

It was possible he needed to look back further than the last few years. Certainly there was nothing in the last three years that made any of Dixon's cohorts sound alarming. Nobody in the area had filed any reports about them with the police. A brief look at them by the FBI office in Boise had resulted in nothing of interest. The investigation had been terminated after only three days for lack of anything worth pursuing. It seemed they were just a bunch of good ol' boys who liked to play army on weekends when the weather wasn't too bad and their various businesses allowed them time off.

In fact, probably the most interesting thing about them was that they were all upstanding members of their communities. Two owned ranches, another sold real estate, a fourth owned an insurance agency and the fifth was a district manager for a lumber company.

This whole militia gig, on the face of it, sounded more like rich boys playing soldier to massage their male egos. Except for Dixon, the should-have-been general. And a quarter million bucks.

Only when he looked deeper did an odd pattern

emerge. None of these men were Idaho natives. In fact, while they had all moved to the area at different times over the last ten years, they had all sprung from places like Boston, New York, Philadelphia.

Curious, he looked up their parents and felt his hackles quiver even more. There was a congressman. A senator, a banker… Hell, all these men were blue bloods. They came from the kinds of families that produced successive generations of bankers, lawyers and politicians…not wanna-be soldiers who ran around the Idaho mountains with assault weapons.

Coincidence? Maybe. Maybe Dixon had known some of them in his former life, and they'd each decided at one time or another that life in Idaho was better than life on the East Coast. More pristine. Quieter. Cleaner.

Hell, it sounded good to Tom as he sat there staring bleary-eyed at a computer screen. A little mountain hideaway. Nothing but pine trees for miles. The silence of snow-muffled woods. Yeah, it would be a wonderful sort of lifestyle.

Tom's head was throbbing now, and he closed his eyes and rubbed his temples. None of this was making sense. Five guys decide they want a quieter life? Sure. That they come together in a sort of militia? Possible. Why not? These days, people all over the country owned weapons and practiced military techniques, especially since 9/11. And most of them weren't nuts. They were just afraid.

And he was trying to nail spaghetti to a wall, simply because he was too stubborn to accept that he'd been sidelined and told to waste his time. Cripes, he ought to be punching out every day at four and playing racquetball or something. He'd been set loose to bark up the wrong tree. Right?

Maybe. God, he was beginning to hate that word: *maybe*.

The phone on his desk shrilled, and for a moment he wondered where he was. Slowly reconnecting to reality, he realized he'd dozed off in his chair. The clock on the wall said it was 7:45 a.m., and already he could hear stirrings in the outer offices.

Shaking his head, he reached for the phone.

"You will be taken off this case," a woman's voice said. She had a European accent. French? German?

"What?" Tom asked. "Who is this?"

"I will call you later. Look him in the eyes."

The woman hung up, and for a moment Tom wondered if he had dreamed the conversation. It made no sense. Why would he be taken off a case when he was already so far on the fringe that he might as well be reading cereal boxes? And how would someone know what was about to happen with the FBI's handling of agent assignments?

He shook his head again and rubbed a hand over his face. A day's worth of stubble had emerged on his chin, and his eyes felt as if they were coated with sandpaper.

He dug into his desk and found the portable shaving kit he kept there for such occasions, then made his way to the rest room, trying to avoid eye contact with the freshly groomed, prim-and-proper agents who were just arriving.

After shaving and washing his face, he at least felt closer to human. He was headed back to his office when he ran into Kevin Willis.

"Tom," Willis said, studying him closely. "What'd you do, stay here all night?"

Tom nodded. "Running down the meaning of nothingness, in proper FBI fashion."

Kevin shook his head. "Well, I want to see you and Miriam when she gets here. We'll go over what you have and see if it's worth pursuing."

Tom heard the echoes of the phone call in Kevin's words. He fought the anger rising within him. "Sure. No problem."

"I'll be waiting," Kevin said.

Then, before he could get suspended again, Tom went back to his desk and ordered up a background investigation on all the Secret Service agents who had been guarding Grant Lawrence, including known family and friends.

An hour later, they had just finished briefing Kevin on their progress. Or, as their boss seemed to see it, the lack thereof. Willis had dismissed the Idaho connection with a wave of his hand.

"It's not case-related," he said. "If it's an illegal loan, it's the IRS or FDIC's problem. We can ship the file over to them, and if they decide it's an issue, they'll ask for one of our bean counters to pry open the can. But there's no connection to the Lawrence shooting, apart from the fact that this guy Dixon married a woman whose brother was a college fraternity buddy of Harrison Rice's. And that's just not good enough."

Tom studied Kevin's eyes and took a breath as he listened. A warning glance from Miriam said she had sized up her mentor and knew this was nonnegotiable. He nodded. "Okay. You're right. It's very thin."

"It's invisible," Willis said. "So what else have you found?"

"Not a thing," Miriam said, heading Tom off. "We've run through the usual collection of crazies. Yeah, a lot of people didn't like Lawrence. I'm told he received over two dozen death threats, and the Secret Service is running those down. But the names don't correlate to anyone in our watch-files. And I haven't found anything to indicate that the people in our watch-files have done anything unusual in the past couple of months. We could be missing something, but if so, I've no idea where it is."

Willis paused for a moment, then nodded. "Okay. Good job, both of you. Write up a report on this angle and have it for me by five, okay? It'll be appended to the rest of the investigation, once that's complete. And our asses are officially covered. No stone unturned and all that."

"That's it?" Miriam asked.

Willis shrugged. "I don't see where there's anything left to chase down. You've hit dead ends, except for Tom's possible tax and banking violations. And like I said, that's up to the IRS and FDIC to decide whether to investigate."

He flipped through a file on his desk for a moment, then looked up at Tom. "I'm also going to note that you did outstanding work, Agent Lawton. I don't know if it'll be enough to pull you off suspension for good, but I'll do my best. We both know what happened in L.A. was a one-time thing. High stress. Operation goes sour. Heat of the moment. I can't fault you as an agent, and I think you're an asset to the Bureau."

Tom suppressed an instinctive curl of his lip. "What you're saying is, I go back home and learn to like Jerry Springer."

"For a few more days, at least," Willis said. "It's hands down on this case."

"And me?" Miriam asked.

Willis handed her the file. "You're off to Guatemala. We've negotiated a deal with the government there to have our people involved in their investigation of the murder of our ambassador. Advice and counsel."

"I don't speak Spanish," Miriam said. "Don't we have a bilingual agent we can send?"

"We usually send someone from the Miami or Tampa offices, but right now we can't," Willis said, shaking his head. "I tried. Those that aren't working the Lawrence case are on drug cases and Hispanic street crime have been sent over to INS to run down illegal immigration cases. Homeland security run amok. Besides, you have people skills. That's important when you're going to be looking over their shoulders."

"When do I leave?" she asked.

He handed her a ticket. "Eight tomorrow morning. Sorry for the short notice. The deal just came through, and we want someone there while the trail is still warm enough to bother."

"Gotcha," Miriam said, rising.

"Good work, again," Willis said as they reached the door. "I know it sounds glib, but you probably saved us a whole lot of PR headaches down the road."

So that was it, Tom thought, returning to his desk to box up the files. They'd saved the Bureau some PR face. Big, fat, hairy, fucking deal.

"I hear Guatemala is pretty in the springtime," he said to Miriam. "Nice vacation for you."

"C'mon, Tom," she said. "We were chasing shadows and we knew it. What did you expect him to do? Put an agent on suspension and another who knew the victim personally in the middle of a high-profile investigation? It's the way it had to be."

"I'd still like to run that money down," he said.

She shook her head. "It's hands down, remember? Let it go. It's not our job anymore."

"You're right," he said.

"I'm going home to pack."

He nodded. "I'll finish boxing this stuff up and get it shipped back to the file mavens. See you tonight."

She nodded and left. Four minutes later, his phone rang. For reasons he couldn't explain, he knew who it was before he answered.

"Special Agent Anson is off to Guatemala," the woman said. "And you are back on vacation."

"Suspension," he said. "Not vacation."

"True. I'm sorry. And Kevin Willis never told you that he went to West Point, did he? Or that he and Wesley Dixon were classmates?"

"What?" Tom asked, suddenly sitting forward, the hair on his neck rising. "How did you—"

"There's a lot you don't know," she said. "And you're not going to find it out there. You'll need to come out here. To Idaho."

"Who *are* you?" he asked.

"There will be a ticket waiting for you at the Delta counter at Dulles Airport. Tomorrow afternoon. The flight leaves at 2:15 p.m. I'll meet you in Boise."

"Why should I...who...what the hell is this?"

"A mess," she said, her accent weighting the words. "A far bigger mess than you know." She paused. "But before you leave, wait for the reports on the Secret Service protection team."

Then, with a click, she was gone.

Languedoc, France
81 A.D.

Marie sat on the wooden bench her grandson had built for her and enjoyed the sunshine of the warm spring day. Her modest home, built of native stone, was surrounded by others like it. Her community.

Sometimes she found it hard to believe that as a young woman with a young daughter she had found the courage to come to this outer bastion of the Roman Empire for no other purpose than to bring the Word. They had been safe in Egypt; there had been no other reason to come this far.

Sometimes she found it equally difficult to believe how many disciples she, a mere woman, had found here. They surrounded her now like a loving family, caring for her needs as she aged. Wouldn't Simon Peter be surprised?

The thought made a little chuckle come to her lips, though she knew it wasn't quite charitable. Simon Peter had always resented that she was accorded as much respect as he, and at times more respect, as an apostle. It was during a bitter outburst after the crucifixion that Marie had known she must leave.

She had done her duty and had spread the Word. And her daughter, Sara, had done as much and more, once she'd achieved adulthood.

Marie hoped He would think they had tended the vineyard well.

But her grandson…her heart quailed a little as she thought of him, now a man almost as old as her Lord when He had undertaken his ministry.

Marie had always believed their work would continue here in the south of Gaul, near the warm waters of the Mediterranean. But for some time her grandson had been speaking of setting forth on a new ministry, to lands even farther away.

She knew it was selfish of her to wish he would remain, selfish to shed even a private tear that she would never see him again. He was determined. He would go. And she must once again bear the terrible rending of her heart at the loss of a loved one.

She ought to be proud of him and his desire to spread the teaching. She ought to give thanks to God that her daughter's son had grown so brave and true to the faith.

But inside, a quiet yet resentful voice questioned, *Lord, haven't I already given enough?*

Bowing her head, she awaited her grandson's arrival. Awaited the words she knew in her heart he was going to say. Awaited yet again a final farewell.

9

Boise, Idaho

Tom tried to remember the last time he'd been in the northern Rockies. It had been a lifetime ago, when his family had packed up the car for the trip to Yellowstone. He had just turned ten, and he recalled being awed by the huge expanse of blue sky that gave the region its nickname. Old Faithful had been a pungent, over-crowded surprise that he remembered mostly for having reeked of sulfur. In fact, the smell of sulfur was what he remembered most about that whole vacation.

Boise didn't smell like sulfur. In fact, it didn't smell like anything at all. For Tom, who had spent the last five years of his life breathing the noxious smog of L.A. and the beltway exhaust of D.C., taking in air that had no discernible scent was a novel experience. For a moment he simply let himself take it in, deep lungfuls of untainted air. Then he remembered why he was here and how far out on a limb he'd stepped when he'd decided to come.

He'd debated whether to tell Miriam where he was going, and decided against it. Kevin Willis had been her mentor at the Bureau, and she had been Tom's. Miriam was nothing if not loyal, and Tom had decided it would be unfair to trap her between competing loyalties. If his anonymous caller turned out to be a crank, or the woman's information turned out to be bogus, Tom could write all of this off as a much-needed vacation and no one had to ever know otherwise. Assuming the woman showed up at all.

He'd scanned the arrivals area upon stepping off the jetway but had seen no looks of recognition. Although he'd brought only a single carry-on, he followed the herd to baggage claim, in case he might see her there. But apart from the customary lip-locks of reunited lovers and the peripatetic scurrying of an overexhausted two year old too long pent up on an airliner, he'd seen nothing noteworthy.

So he'd made his way out to the taxi queue, thinking there must be a respectable Sheraton or Ramada somewhere in town where he could take a room, stretch out and think about whether and by whom he was being led by the nose. He flagged a cab and closed the door as a pair of unnaturally pale eyes met his in the rearview mirror.

"Where to?" the driver asked, taking a sip from an insulated mug and returning it to a cup holder at her side.

"A decent hotel," he said. "Downtown."

"The Grove is excellent," she said. "Not too pricey, great Italian restaurant. Gets rave reviews."

He nodded, wondering for a moment if she received

a kickback on referrals, before deciding he'd become way too cynical. She probably just wanted a nice tip in exchange for a good tip. "That's fine. Thanks."

"No problem, sir."

The ride was fairly brief and, by L.A. or D.C. standards, the streets devoid of traffic. Tom offered a prayer of thanks that his driver wasn't the chatty type who wanted to fill him in on all the nuggets of local history and entertainment. He wasn't in the mood to talk, nor to listen. He had no fear of flying, but the steady decline of airline amenities, coupled with the inevitable delays, had turned it into an exhausting mode of transport. He wanted a hot shower, a good meal and some quiet time to mull over his options.

He hefted his bag and passed the driver her fare, plus a ten-dollar tip, with a muttered "Thanks."

"Thank you, sir," she said, smiling as she pocketed the tip. She had a lovely smile, open and honest. The kind of smile that seemed destined for Hollywood, rather than driving a cab. "Enjoy Boise."

"I'll try."

He registered at the front desk, went upstairs and quickly concluded that she had not led him astray. The rates were cheap, by D.C. or L.A. standards, but the lobby was both spacious and tasteful, and his room immaculate. He tossed his overnight bag on the bed and dedicated himself to task one on his list: a steaming, pounding, relaxing shower.

After briskly rubbing himself down with a thick

towel, he felt almost human again and emerged from the bathroom to dress for dinner. He froze.

"Hi, Tom." It was the voice he'd heard on the phone, now coming from a woman who sat in one of the two armchairs, silhouetted against the sunset streaming in the window. "Good of you to come."

"How did you get in here?" he asked, surprise giving way to anger. "For that matter, how did you know where I was staying?"

"You told me," she said, reaching for the lamp on the table. She switched it on, and he recognized her as his cab driver. Except that she'd hidden her accent in the cab. "Or rather, I told you."

"That answers the second question," he said, feeling distinctly vulnerable with nothing but a towel around his waist and an unknown and now even more suspicious woman in his hotel room. "What about the first?"

She shrugged. "Hotel room doors are good. But manageable."

He nodded. "Then how about you manage it again and get the hell out?"

She laughed, and once again he saw that smile. "You don't really want me to do that, Tom. You want me to tell you why you've come out here. You want to know what you've gotten yourself into."

"And why all the cloak-and-dagger bullshit," he said.

Another laugh. "Yes, perhaps it was overdramatic." Then her eyes hardened. "Or perhaps not. You'll want to get dressed, however. You'll find a Glock nine millimeter in your overnight bag. Standard Bureau issue. I knew you hadn't traveled with one."

He flipped open the travel bag, and sure enough, a black handgun lay atop his clothes. Hefting it, he popped out the clip and counted off twelve rounds.

"The clip holds thirteen," she said, "but like a lot of agents, you only load twelve. Thirteen compresses the feed spring too much, right?"

Although he knew nothing about her, she apparently knew a great deal about him. As a former undercover agent, that was not a situation he found palatable. On the other hand, she seemed to see no reason to conceal what she knew. Nor did she seem stupid enough to arm a would-be opponent. Which meant she didn't see him as an opponent.

He reseated the clip and tossed the Glock on the bed, instantly memorizing the subtle wrinkles it created in the bedspread. He then gathered a change of clothes and returned to the steamy bathroom. When he reemerged, the gun and the wrinkles were exactly as they had been. In fact, he would have wagered she hadn't so much as left her chair.

"So," he asked, "why am I here?"

By way of response, she picked up the remote and switched on the TV, where Harrison Rice was addressing what the crawl described as an Arab-American gathering in California.

"Many of you may still have relatives in your homelands," Rice was saying. "And I want to assure you that the United States will not stand by while they are needlessly killed. A wise man once said, 'With the power to do good comes the responsibility to do good.' The United States has the power to help restore peace and stability, and to ensure real freedom, in that troubled part of the world. And if I am elected, the United States will do that."

She flicked off the TV and fixed her icy gray eyes on his. "That, Tom, is why you are here."

10

Guatemalan Highlands

Steve Lorenzo stood in the chapel sacristy, peeling off his vestments. Most of the villagers were at work with the sun in the morning, so he said daily Mass in the early evening, before dinner. He realized he'd gotten soft in the past twelve years. Even with the lightweight cotton chasuble, he was perspiring profusely. The afternoon rains had left the air thick and soggy, and the village chapel had no air-conditioning. He had grown too accustomed to the amenities of the United States, too insulated from the realities of life in much of the rest of the world.

"Padre?" a young woman asked, standing in the doorway.

Lorenzo searched his mind for her name, knowing he had been introduced to her upon his arrival two days ago. He was normally quite good with names, but the last week had been so hectic that his mind was still spinning.

"Perdone," he said. *"Cómo se llama?"*

"Rita," she replied with a shy smile. "You have too many names to remember. And it has been many years."

"You look familiar," he said. "But yes, it has been many years since I was here."

"You performed my Confirmation," she said. "In this chapel. Fourteen years ago."

Lorenzo's cheeks colored. His mind flashed back to this same face as a teenager, with bright, smiling eyes. "I'm so sorry. Rita. Now I remember. Your Confirmation name was María Magdelena, yes?"

"Sí, Padre," she said, her smile broadening. "Rita María Magdelena Carmena-Ortiz. Now Rita María Magdelena Quijachia."

"Of course, I remember now," he said. "I see you're married. How have you been, Rita?"

She nodded. "Yes, I am married now. My oldest son, Rolando, was your altar boy tonight."

Lorenzo laughed and shook his head, smiling. The years went by too fast. It was a feeling shared by most priests. One minute you were baptizing an infant. The next minute, it seemed, that same child was receiving First Communion. Then Confirmation. Then Matrimony.

Or a funeral, he thought, his smile fading. That was why he'd finally left this country. He had performed too many funeral Masses for children, killed by war or disease. At least young Rita and her children seemed to have avoided those dangers so far.

"How are your parents?" he asked, remembering the beaming couple who had stood beside their daughter at her Confirmation. "And your brother? Miguel, wasn't it?"

The smile dropped from her face as quickly as if a cold wind had blown through her heart. "My father is dead, *Padre*. Hanged by the army. And my brother will soon be dead, I fear."

"Oh no," Lorenzo said. "Come in, please. Sit. Tell me what happened."

"My husband will be home soon," she said, shaking her head. "I need to prepare dinner."

"I'm so sorry about your father," the priest said. "May his soul rest in peace. But your brother, is there anything I can do to help?"

"I wish you could," Rita said. "But there is nothing you can do. Your people will hunt him down. They will kill him. If he doesn't get himself killed first."

"Why would my people… What people?" he asked.

"Your government," she said. "They have offered a reward of eighty thousand quetzals. Someone will talk. And then they will come and kill him."

Eighty thousand quetzals? Lorenzo asked himself, doing the math. Ten thousand dollars. What would…?

The answer came to him almost as soon as he had asked the question.

"No," he said, shaking his head. "Not Miguel."

Rita's eyes glimmered with tears, though her face had set hard. "You will see, *Padre*. They will come and take us all. My entire village. You have come back in time to watch us all die."

Boise, Idaho

The hotel's Italian restaurant was every bit as good as advertised. Tom was enjoying a three-pasta meal of linguini in clam sauce, lasagna Florentine and penne with grilled chicken and vegetables. The selection had been Renate's idea; the woman had finally given him a name, though doubtless a phony one. She'd ordered grilled salmon served with angel hair in a white wine sauce.

She had suggested a bottle of wine, but he'd declined, saying he preferred to keep his wits sharp. That had drawn another of her patented laughs, along with the comment that a meal such as this was not complete without the fruit of the vine. She'd ordered a glass of the house chardonnay. The incident had served to reinforce his impression of her as European, although he hadn't yet been able to pin down her faint accent, and had no idea where she called home.

"So, is there more to Renate?" he asked.

She cocked her head. "In what way?"

"Well," he said, "a last name, for example. Most people have them."

She smiled. "Yes, there is more. Renate Bächle."

She pronounced it *Besh-leh*. Had he been sufficiently cosmopolitan in background, he supposed, that might have garnered him more information. But having grown up in a small town in Michigan and spent his entire life within the borders of the United States, he was still clueless as to her origins.

"Interesting name," he said.

"How so?"

"I don't know. It sounds French."

Again that laugh. "Well, it isn't. And if you're fishing for information, why not just ask?"

"Okay," he said. "Who are you? Who do you work for? What's your angle in all of this? And why me?"

"Hmm," she said, sipping her wine. "Let's work backward. Why you? Because you're clever, and you have nothing to lose."

"Meaning?"

"Meaning you're on suspension—and for good reason—and you're angry at the Bureau and the world because of that. You have no living family, and from what I've seen, only a couple of real friends, both of whom are out of town at the moment. So what else were you going to do? Sit around and grumble at the futility of existence? I figured you were...available."

"You obviously do your homework," Tom said, once again realizing he was at a distinct disadvantage in this working relationship. If it could even be called that. It felt distinctly uncomfortable to find that this woman might have had access to his very private personnel file. Or, nearly as bad, that someone at the Bureau had been bad-mouthing him. "Let me guess. CIA?"

"Please," she said. "Don't insult my intelligence."

"Meaning you're not CIA, or that you won't answer?"

"Oh, I'm definitely not CIA," she answered. "But

you have no need as yet to know exactly who I work for. It's sufficient to tell you that we both work for the same thing."

"Which is?"

"Justice."

He twirled pasta around his fork, thinking for a moment before replying. "You're aware, of course, that justice can have many meanings, depending on one's viewpoint."

"Very true. But in this instance, our desires for justice run parallel. Neither of us wishes to see the government of the United States chosen by a coup d'état."

He froze. She had so closely echoed the suspicions in his own mind that he wondered wildly if she was able to read his thoughts. "You have proof?"

"If I had proof, I wouldn't need you," she said bluntly. "But I think we both have information we can share, and that together we can find more. And when we do, Mr. FBI, the collar will be yours."

He eyed her with deeper suspicion. "Why?"

"Because I like to keep my profile low."

He doubted this woman's profile would go unnoticed anywhere in the world. Or that her strange eyes would ever be forgotten. "Why Boise?"

"Don't tell me you haven't been checking into Wes Dixon."

"How would you know?"

She smiled. "I have a crystal ball made by IBM. Now, shall we finish dinner and return to the room? There's much we need to discuss without being overheard."

At that point he was so damn intrigued, he would have skipped dinner and resigned from the Bureau just to hear what she had to say.

He was sure that was her plan. But he didn't mind falling in with it.

For now.

Guatemala City, Guatemala

Miriam Anson sat as close as she could to the rattling air conditioner as she listened to the briefing. So far, the Guatemalan police had made only marginal progress. The assassination had been carefully planned and well executed. At least four people had been involved, perhaps as many as six, depending on which witnesses one chose to believe. The armored limousine had been stopped by a blast of C4 on the gas tank. Both 9 mm and 7.62 mm rounds and shell casings had been found at the scene, and their distribution pointed to at least three shooters. Add a driver to get them out of the area and, yes, at least four assassins.

A very professional job, Miriam thought, even if the ambassador had made himself a relatively easy target. He had been an organized man, with a regular schedule. His driver chose one of three routes at random each morning, but a lookout with a radio could easily signal which of the three he was taking on any given day. They might have had three teams of assassins—one along each route—or they might simply have chosen a given route and waited each morning until the ambassador drove into the killing ground.

"Had anyone noticed anything suspicious in the mornings leading up to the assassination?" she asked via her interpreter. "Anyone sitting around that corner each morning?"

"No one has said nothing like that," the police commander replied in fractured English.

Miriam reminded herself not to read anything into his syntax. The double negative was both common and correct in Spanish, or so her briefing papers had said.

"Was it a busy intersection? A lot of pedestrian traffic?"

"Not too busy," he said. "But not…how you say… vacant, either."

Which might mean no one would notice people sitting at the corner, Miriam thought. But the 7.62 mm cartridges were AK-47 rounds. Even cut down, such a weapon would be too big to tuck under a suit jacket. That meant a bag of some kind. People would have noticed if the same three people were sitting at the same intersection with the same bags on three or four consecutive mornings.

"They would have been seen if they had been there more than once or twice," Miriam said. "So unless they got very lucky on their first try, I think we can assume there were three teams. One along each route. Assume each team had three shooters and a driver. Plus the lookout to tell them which route the limousine was taking that morning. That's thirteen terrorists. At least."

"*Sí*," the commander said. "We see it that way also.

The guerillas are becoming more organized. They could not have done this even five years ago."

Miriam turned the operation over in her head. Six gunmen with AK-47s, three with handguns and C4. Careful, precise reconnaissance. Attack plans rehearsed and based upon known protection procedures. Radio intelligence. It was a military-style operation, the type one might expect from special operations forces. Minimal exposure. Maximum chance of success. She had no doubt their escape routes had been planned with equal precision and efficiency.

"They're good," she muttered.

"*Qué?*" the commander asked. "Good?"

Miriam shook her head. "Not morally. I meant they're good at what they do."

"If you say so," he replied with a look of disgust.

As she saw it, they had made one major mistake. There were too many people involved. A lone assassin could keep a secret. A dozen or more could not. Someone would have talked. Eighty thousand quetzals was a fortune by village economy standards.

"Someone will talk," she said.

The commander nodded. "*Sí.* Someone will talk. And once they do, we will find them. We will find them all."

"And arrest them," Miriam said, not liking the tone of his voice. She hadn't come down here to ride herd on a vengeance committee.

"They will be punished," the commander said, a hard

edge in his voice. "We have no death penalty in Guatemala. We are a civilized people."

No official death penalty, Miriam thought. But there were two hundred thousand dead in the past half century of civil war.

"Thank you for the briefing," she said. "With your permission, I will return to my hotel. It's been a very long day."

"Of course," the commander replied. "You are much tired. Your interpreter is also your driver. He will take care of you here."

Pablo Jimenez was a better interpreter than he was a driver, Miriam thought ten minutes later, as he moved across three lanes of traffic without so much as a turn signal. If the water didn't turn her stomach inside out, his driving would.

"You are nervous, Special Agent Anson," he said. He offered a slight smile. "Do not worry. The driving here is very different from America, but it has its own logic. I won't get you killed."

"I'll hold you to that promise," she said.

"You don't trust the commander," Pablo said, nudging in front of a taxi to make a right turn, ignoring the horn blasting behind him. "I heard it in your voice."

"My job is to see these people arrested," she said. "That's all. No one wants a bloodbath, I'm sure."

"No. No one wants a Waco, or a Ruby Ridge." He paused at a traffic light and turned to face her. "I'm sorry, Special Agent, but please don't assume that we are savages. The commander attended forensic classes at your FBI academy in Quantico. I myself graduated from the University of Miami in Florida. My country has suffered much, and the suffering continues. But we are professional law enforcement agents. Not vigilantes."

"I spoke out of turn," Miriam said. "I'm sorry. Just color me the rude American."

"No," he said, pushing out into the intersection just as the light turned green. "Not rude. But your people are often arrogant. I was told you were sent here because you are good with people. I'm simply trying to help."

"Thank you," she said. "So help me. What should I expect to see?"

"It will be complicated," Pablo replied. "Most of the guerillas come from the highlands, small Quiché villages. But more and more come from the cities, as well. If I had to guess, I would guess that each of the teams came from a different guerilla cell. They trained separately. I doubt any of them knew the other teams. Only the planners and the operation commander would know everyone."

Miriam nodded. "That would make sense. Like the French Resistance in World War II. You can't reveal what you don't know."

"Exactly. And the leaders are too careful to boast about this with friends. One of the assassins will talk, yes, and someone will overhear it and decide he wants to be a rich man. He will come to us, and we will capture the assassin. But then the assassin will have to tell us who the leaders were, or the rest will go unpunished."

"And you'll have to move quickly," she added. "Once word gets out that someone has been picked up, the rest will go to ground very quickly."

"Yes," he said. "Or the leaders will silence the rest, to make sure there are no more leaks."

He parked in front of her hotel and turned to her. "There will be death, Special Agent Anson. I can almost guarantee you. But it will not be the police or the army wading in to annihilate a village. The guerillas will do it, sacrificing their soldiers to protect their generals. That is their way. It will be safest for everyone if we can capture someone quietly and he talks, and we are able to take down the rest in one quick operation. But that is, I think, too much to hope for. There will be death. In Guatemala, there is always death."

Miriam nodded. "All we can do is our best."

"And that we will do," Pablo said. "Please know, however, that I do not think our best will be enough for your tastes. You will have bad memories of Guatemala, Special Agent Anson."

11

Boise, Idaho

Renate paid for their dinner with a credit card. Tom did his best to eyeball it and see if there was some indication of what company she worked for. Unfortunately, it appeared to be a personal card, in her name only.

In her room, on a different floor of the same hotel, Tom sat in a surprisingly comfortable upholstered armchair near the window. Renate sat in a straight-backed chair on the other side of the small round table that most such rooms seemed to boast. She reached out and pulled open the curtains, letting in a red sunset. Her colorless eyes caught the light and for an instant seemed to flame. Had he been a superstitious man, Tom might have wondered if he was about to make a deal with the devil.

He wasn't superstitious, but he wondered anyway. "You know," he said, "I'm really uncomfortable not knowing who you work for."

"That's fine," she replied with an almost imperceptible shrug of her shoulder. "Remain suspicious. And do what you will with the information I give you."

"How do I know you're not misleading me?"

Her brows lifted. "I'd be astonished if you didn't check out everything I tell you."

Point, set, match, he thought. With a sigh, he leaned forward, resting his elbows on his knees. "Talk."

"You've followed an interesting trail in your search for those who might be involved in the shooting of Senator Lawrence. It's not an obvious trail. Certainly one that many others might regard as simply coincidental. But you think it might be more."

"What makes you say that?"

"The fact that you keep trying to find out where a quarter million dollars might have gone."

He pursed his lips, trying to conceal his reaction. Had this woman been monitoring every move he'd made on the computer? Even as he went into banking files that should have been off-limits to everyone except law enforcement?

"Do you know where it is?"

"I have my suspicions, as do you. But I think what you're missing here, Tom, is far more important."

"And what's that?"

"This goes deeper and spreads a lot wider than simply finding out who pulled the trigger, or even who paid him. You're dipping your toes into a swamp that is full of alligators. And if you aren't very careful, you'll become more than merely expendable. You'll become a target."

His pulse quickened, as much with excitement as uneasiness. To the tips of his toes he was a bloodhound, and finding a trail excited him as little else did. "That's supposed to frighten me off?"

She laughed quietly. "If I'd expected that, I wouldn't be here now. You need to understand this isn't about a political disagreement turned bloody. This is about money. And power. It's about people who can and do use others as you would use a paper napkin."

"How many conspiracy books have you read? Have they fried your brain?"

Again that quiet laugh. "You know better. You found the connection between Wes Dixon, Ed Morgan and Harrison Rice. And you wouldn't be here if you hadn't checked out my tip about Dixon and your boss, Kevin Willis."

Tom nodded. "They were at West Point together. Class of 1988. And they served in Iraq together during the first Gulf War. But there were close to a thousand cadets in that class, and a lot of them went to Iraq. Yes, it's a connection. But it's thin."

"Life is thin," she said.

He shook his head. "Do you have any evidence that SAC Willis and Wes Dixon had any contact after Iraq? I don't. What I have is a whole bunch of very loose, circumstantial spaghetti."

"But you're here," she said.

"I'm here because I'm on suspension and have nothing better to do. And because I suspect *you*."

She smiled. "Good. I'd be disappointed if you didn't."

He was beginning to dislike this woman and her head games. She'd been less than forthcoming, and she'd given him no reason to trust her. She was using him, without any doubt, and didn't even try to hide that fact. And all her platitudes about "justice" were not enough.

Tom let out a heavy sigh. "I'm thinking this is a waste of my time. You tease, but you don't come through. So do you have anything solid, anything *real,* beyond a pack of wild conspiracy theories, or do I hop on the next plane back to D.C. and spend my suspension learning origami?"

She nodded, as if considering the challenge, although he suspected she'd known exactly how this part of the game would play out. After a long pause, she reached into her bag and pulled out a file folder. She placed it on the table between them and flipped it open. On the top was yet another photo of the assassination in Guatemala City. But it was a photo that hadn't appeared in the newspapers. It had been snapped immediately after the shooting, and showed a man and a woman climbing into a car, with a third man, barely visible except as an outline, behind the wheel.

"The assassins?" Tom asked.

"We think so," Renate said, nodding. "These photos didn't get out to the press. And so far as I know, your government doesn't have them. If they do, they haven't acted on them."

"My government?"

She smiled. "Yes. Your government. And yes, that means I don't work for the United States."

"Okay," Tom said. "So what am I looking at? I won't ask where you got these photos, because you're not going to tell me anyway."

"You're right," she said. "You're looking at a young Guatemalan man named Miguel Ortiz, or so our sources say."

"And?"

"Look at the next photo, Tom."

This one had obviously been taken with a telephoto lens, and not in Guatemala. It showed a similar man, this time emerging from what looked to be a rooming house, with mountains in the background and a dusty Jeep parked off to the side.

"What am I looking at?" he asked.

"Miguel Ortiz, six months ago. Working at Wes Dixon's ranch. That's the bunkhouse for Dixon's employees."

Tom thought for a moment, looking at the two photos. It could be the same man, although the lighting, angles and settings were so different that it was difficult to be positive.

"Dixon has only five listed employees," Renate said. "I'm sure you checked that out when you were looking at the money angle."

Tom nodded. "It's a small operation."

She shook her head. "No, Tom, it isn't. His ranch

covers eight hundred acres. It's just that the rest of his employees aren't on the books."

He shrugged. "So he's hiring illegals and paying them under the table. It happens. It's wrong, but it happens. Hell, maybe that's what he used the quarter mil for. In which case we're wasting our time."

"He doesn't have to pay them," she said. "Not in cash, anyway. He trains them. The Idaho Freedom Militia is a cover for a mercenary training base."

"You're saying Wes Dixon trained the man who killed the U.S. ambassador to Guatemala."

"That's exactly what I'm saying," Renate said. "And that operation was scheduled to happen the day before your Southern sweep primaries. To goad Grant Lawrence into continuing the war on terrorism. And if that didn't work, they had a backup plan."

"Killing Lawrence."

She nodded. "Exactly."

Coincidence piled upon coincidence. Tenuous connection piled upon tenuous connection. And yet, when laid out this way, Tom had to admit that it *was* curious. Intriguing. Suspicious.

He looked up and met her icy gray eyes. "So who are 'they'? You said 'they' had a backup plan. I assume you don't think Dixon is behind all this."

"I think Dixon's a bit player," she said. "A cog in a larger machine. And no, I don't know who 'they' are. And no, I don't know why 'they' are so intent on continuing a war on terrorism that they would train the exact same kind of terrorists you're fighting against to murder an American ambassador, then try to murder a presidential candidate, all in order to ensure that war continues."

"That's a big hole," Tom said.

"You're right. And that's why I need you to fill in the blanks."

"And probably lose my job. If I don't get killed in the process."

She nodded. For an instant he saw genuine concern in her eyes. Then those eyes hardened again. This was a very dangerous woman.

"Exactly," she said. "That's what I'm asking."

Tom leaned in a bit, his voice quiet. "Why do I think I'm facing a Hobson's choice?"

"Excuse me?" she asked. "I'm not familiar with that phrase."

"Damned if I do and damned if I don't," he said. "You're not going to let me say no and walk out of here. Whoever you are, whoever you work for, whatever you're up to, you've revealed too much to just let me walk away."

"You flew to Boise," she said. "Under your own name. To the hometown of a suspect you've been told to ignore, on a case you've been told to drop."

"And word of that could get back to SAC Willis," Tom said.

She shrugged. "It could."

"You'd make sure it did."

She paused for a long moment. Finally she nodded. "Yes. I would."

Tom gritted his teeth and felt the hot anger surge through him. This woman spoke about people in power who used others like paper napkins. But she was using him in exactly the same way. Exactly the way his SAC in L.A. had used him. Exactly the way his father had used him.

He fought down the urge to reach across the table and squeeze her slender, pretty throat. "Goddamn you."

"This is the part where I'm supposed to say I'm sorry," she said. "Sorry for your situation. Sorry for having put you in it. Well, I'm not. I need you."

"Fuck you."

"Justice needs you."

"Fuck justice."

"And you need me," she said. "Not because I could hurt you if you say no, although I could. But because you need to stand up to The Powers That Be. You've been kicked once too many times, and you need to stand up and fight back and prove you're not a pawn in the world's giant chess game. That's why you joined the FBI to begin with. To make a difference. Well, here's your chance."

The worst of it was that she was right. Which was yet another reason to despise her. But there was something in those cold eyes. Something hidden deep beneath the layers of cynicism and manipulation. She didn't have the eyes of a fanatic, nor the eyes of a stone killer. They were the same eyes he saw in the mirror. The eyes of a hunter.

And he didn't see her as prey, nor as bait. She hadn't been lying. What he saw in her eyes was need.

He took a long breath. "So where do we start?"

She smiled. "Why don't you tell me what you found out about Lawrence's protection team?"

Watermill, Long Island

Edward Morgan heard the phone ringing as he came through the door. It had been a long, tiring, dreary day in the city, and he hadn't been in the mood to pore over the accounting practices of a proposed Dutch-South African pharmaceutical consortium. The two smaller firms had no choice but to merge if they were to remain viable, but even that would not be enough. The resulting consortium would need a heavy infusion of capital in order to modernize its South African production facilities.

Dutch accountants had audited the books of both firms, and their work had been checked by the bank's accountants. Morgan had to read and compare both reports, as well as the raw data behind them, before deciding whether to recommend that his bank underwrite the merger and vet the public stock offering.

There had been a time—back in college and business school, when he'd studied international finance—when he'd dreamed about the opportunity to work on such deals. Now, almost three decades later, it seemed a monumental waste of his time. He had far more important concerns than whether a few thousand Dutch and South

African chemists and sales reps and plant workers would keep their jobs.

He was installing a President.

He tossed his suit coat over the arm of a leather chair, placed his briefcase in its customary place to the left of his desk and reached for the phone.

"Morgan," he said.

"We have a problem." The accent was British, although Morgan knew that was only because the caller had been schooled at Oxford and Cambridge. "A serious problem."

Morgan sighed. There had been entirely too many of these calls lately. He'd practically had to write Rice's speech about the war on terrorism after his contact in the campaign had faxed him a copy of Rice's own draft. Then there was the growing mess in Guatemala. Now, apparently, there was more.

"What's wrong?" he asked.

"A young FBI agent has more zeal and anger than he has loyalty or common sense," the caller said.

"My sources say they're nowhere close to the Atlanta operation," Morgan said. And his source ought to know. "And if need be, we can sacrifice—"

"That's not the problem," the caller said, impatience evident in his voice. "This goes beyond Atlanta. It goes to Idaho. And to you."

"That line of investigation was terminated," Morgan replied. "As of yesterday."

"Well, as of *today*, that agent is in Boise."

"What the hell?" Morgan asked. Had his source been

wrong? Worse, had he been betrayed? If so, his source would soon discover that not even the full resources of the FBI could keep him alive.

"Apparently this agent is on suspension," the caller said. "He was reactivated, probably in a probationary capacity, then returned to suspension after that part of the investigation was terminated. Obviously he didn't agree with that decision, as he flew to Idaho today."

At least that was some consolation. Morgan recognized assets for what they were, and all assets were ultimately disposable if need be. But this particular asset had been very useful over the years, and he would have regretted having to kill the man, if for no other reason than that it would have been difficult to cultivate an equal or better source.

"So he's a Don Quixote, tilting alone at windmills," Morgan said. "Without official backing, what can he do?"

The caller let out an impatient huff. "He may be a Don Quixote, as you say, but the word is that he's a very gifted investigator. And a lucky one. That's a dangerous combination to have running loose."

"So I'll talk to my source," Morgan said. "The FBI will rein him in. They're big on loyalty and obedience. They don't like agents going off on their own. I'm sure they can handle it."

"I'm not," the caller said.

There was obviously something else, Morgan

thought. What he'd heard so far was a simple matter to resolve, and hardly an occasion for this sort of urgency. The FBI was both blessed and cursed by the inevitable product of any massive organization. It valued procedure and conformity over efficiency. Agents who broke procedure or who failed to conform—no matter how successful—were quickly and forcefully brought back in line or discharged. It would be a simple matter to arrange to have this agent's leash jerked, unless something else was involved.

"What aren't you telling me?" Morgan asked. Now impatience crept into his voice. "I have to know what's going on if I'm going to manage this. I'm exposed here."

"More than you realize," the caller said.

There was no mistaking the veiled threat. Just as Morgan was willing to sacrifice the operative in Atlanta, just as he was willing to sacrifice his source inside the investigation, this man was willing to sacrifice *him* if need be. He, too, was merely an asset.

"If there's something else," Morgan said, trying to affect a conciliatory tone, "it would help if I knew. I don't want to try to solve a problem, only to make a worse one because I'm acting on incomplete information."

"We think Bookworm has resurfaced," the caller said.

Shit, Morgan thought. This was beyond belief.

"Bookworm is dead," he replied. "We confirmed it."

The caller paused for a long moment, then finally spoke. "Do you want to stake your life on that?"

12

Guatemala City, Guatemala

"How are you doing, angel?"

Even through a long-distance connection, Terry's voice was a salve to Miriam's soul.

She sighed. "I'm tired, darling. It's been a long, depressing day."

"Bad airline food?" he asked.

She couldn't help but laugh. "Bad food, narrow seats, late connections. The usual Bureau accommodations here in steamy, rainy Guatemala."

"My international agent," he said, "living a life of adventure."

Miriam let out a snort. "I guess that's one way to put it. How are *you* doing?"

"Eh, I've had better days," he said. He, too, sounded tired. "They moved Grant from critical care to ICU today. He's going to make it. Still not awake yet, though."

"That's got to be killing Karen and the girls."

"Yeah," he said. "She's at his side all day, talking to him, until the girls get out of school. Then she goes to his parents' house and takes care of the girls, even though his parents would be happy to do it for her. She says it's so they can have time to visit him, too. But I think she just wants to be with the children."

"I think I understand," Miriam said. "At least he's alive through them."

"That seems to be what it's about," he said. "Catherine Suzanne has done more therapy for Karen than vice versa. That girl is scary smart. But I worry about her. She was always the quiet one."

Miriam's heart squeezed as she remembered the little girl's face in the window of a cabin in Maryland, pressed to the window, somehow knowing Miriam's team was out there, mouthing the word *"help."* Miriam and Karen had freed the girl, and killed her kidnapper in the act of trying to kill Grant Lawrence. Miriam had spent a lot of time with Grant and Karen in the year since, and she'd watched Catherine deal with her grief and anger in her own silent way. Belle, the younger daughter, had been willing to talk. Catherine Suzanne kept it all inside.

And now yet more grief had been piled onto her young shoulders. The fear of losing her father, as she had lost her mother. And dealing with Karen's grief, too.

"Life is fucking unfair," Miriam said softly.

"You're right about that," Terry said. "Those girls…geez, they'll be in therapy for life. But they're good kids. They're strong. And so is Grant. Karen says the doctors predict that there's no permanent brain damage. He curls his toes and grips her hand sometimes. If he'd just wake up…"

"He will," Miriam said. "I know he will. God is too loving to take him away from those girls. And Karen, too."

She took a breath, not wanting to get herself even more depressed. "So, any news on the case?"

"Nothing much," he replied. "They're all crapping their pants about a ballistic match on a gun that was used in a shooting in St. Louis. But you know how guns move around."

"Like water in a river," Miriam said.

The sad truth was that Pablo's commander hadn't been far wrong in his sideways slight at the United States. She might shake her head at the two hundred thousand killed in the fifty-year Guatemalan civil war, but easily ten times that had been murdered in the U.S. over the same period. Her country was awash in guns and fear, a dangerous and too often deadly combination. She had no right to be looking down on her hosts.

"You got quiet," Terry said. "Something wrong?"

"Just thinking that there's too much violence and death everywhere. Like I have to tell you that. You're a homicide cop, for crying out loud. You see it day in and day out. And I see how it wears on you. You don't need me getting all morose over it."

"Sweetheart," Terry said, his voice suddenly soft. "When I let myself think about those things, it makes me crazy. People do bad things. You and I try to catch them and get them out of society. But there will always be more people doing more bad things. We just do our best."

"My interpreter said that today," Miriam said. "He talked about the case. It's going to get ugly, he thinks. He said we can do our best, but that it won't be good enough."

"It never is," Terry said. "Not for the victims. Not for their families. Not even for the perpetrators. But it's all we can do."

"I guess so," she said.

He paused for a moment. "I hate to dump more on you, but do you have any idea where Tom is?"

"He's at home, I think," Miriam said, the hairs on the back of her neck prickling.

"Nope. I called there. Kevin Willis called me, asking if he'd come down here. I guess Willis had tried to contact him at our place."

"He didn't say he was going anywhere," Miriam said.

"Maybe he just needed a vacation," Terry said. "He's on suspension, after all. No reason he can't fly home, or go fishing, or whatever."

"Nope," Miriam said. "No reason at all."

"So that's what he's done, then," Terry said.

The tone in his voice was clear. If Tom was doing something else, she and Terry would not be the ones to blow the whistle on him.

"Yep, that's what he's done," she said.

"Okay, well, I'll call you tomorrow. I love you, angel. I wish I could curl up with you. I miss your smell."

"I miss you, too, darling. And I love you, too. Talk to you tomorrow."

Miriam hung up the phone, trying to imagine Terry's arms around her.

And trying to guess where Tom might be.

Watermill, Long Island

Bookworm has resurfaced, Edward Morgan thought, sipping his third—or was this the fourth?—tumbler of Scotch. He wasn't so foolish as to think the whiskey would light up a path for him to follow out of this morass. But at least it could numb the shock of those three words.

Bookworm.

Has.

Resurfaced.

It was impossible, but then again, Bookworm had made a career of the impossible. It was, after all, equally impossible that an agent of the BKA—Bundeskriminalamt, the German equivalent of the FBI—acting alone, could upset the plans of a dozen of the most powerful men in Europe. They were untouchables, insulated by layers of loyal or ignorant underlings, with connections reaching up to the highest positions of their governments. No one could get at them. No one could stop them.

And yet…Bookworm had. And what was more, she'd done it before any of them realized she existed.

In a way, Morgan admired her. Step by step, layer by layer, she had peeled back the protective cloak of secrecy. An informant here. Disparate snippets of information put together there. A ninja of the information age, she had silently crept into their lives, careers, ferreted out their peccadilloes and, most damaging of all, their plans. All without revealing herself until she was ready to strike.

Knowing what would happen if she pursued the case through official channels, she had instead grounded her plan of attack on the basest of societal impulses: the desire to see the powerful brought low. She had cultivated sources in the media and begun to leak information, tidbit by juicy, venomous tidbit, each independently verifiable, each laying the groundwork for the next, a toxic sequence of revelations calculated to elicit maximum public outrage.

The first stories had emerged in gossip columns of the sort that propagated in modern culture like rabbits. Their targets had at first ignored the reports, considering them the usual, almost complimentary, smears that accompanied great wealth and power.

Europeans were not like Americans; they did not expect their civic and business leaders to be paragons of moral virtue. An illicit affair with a well-known figure skater or actress was more likely to elicit admiration or, at worst, envy. Common men wished they, too, had the power to attract such beauty. Common women wished they, too, had the beauty to attract such power. It was part of the social contract. Lacking any exceptional qualities, the common man lived vicariously through the exploits of those who possessed those traits.

And so Bookworm's early attacks had gone unnoticed. But as the revelations began to shift from bedroom to boardroom, her targets began to sense a disturbing pattern. Moreover, it became apparent that someone had gained access to the kinds of information these men considered sacrosanct. She had burrowed into accounts, forecasts, plans and policies. She had crawled into their books. And thus they had named her Bookworm.

They had called upon Morgan and his associates to track her down. He was, after all, accustomed to digging into the private affairs of those who sought financing, looking for indicators of risk and reward. This was not so very different. Morgan had thought it a privilege to be invited into their inner circle, and he'd gone about his investigation with his customary ruthless efficiency.

Bookworm was good, and she'd had the resources of the BKA. But Morgan was also good, and he could call upon the resources of a more powerful and far-reaching organization. It had taken months to find her, but find her he had.

And, having found her, acting on their orders, he had orchestrated her death with equally ruthless efficiency. He had watched through binoculars as her car hit the patch of ice and—the steering column and antilock brakes disabled—slewed off the road and down the side of the mountain. Two liters of aviation fuel in her trunk and a tiny charge triggered by remote control had ensured the fireball that had destroyed any evidence of tampering. A tragic but all too common auto accident.

End of Bookworm.

And now she was back?

He had no doubt that she had indeed been in her car on that frosty day in the Black Forest. He had seen her face as she walked to the car, as she opened the door, again as she glanced at him as she was pulling out of the parking lot. Her car had been under continuous observation for the rest of her final journey. His team was good. They would not have missed her switching cars, nor would she have had any reason to do so.

Between the rumbling plunge down the mountain and the explosion, there was no way she could have survived. While neither he nor anyone on his team had approached the scene to confirm the presence of a body, he clearly remembered having looked back up the mountainside in case she'd been thrown clear. He'd seen no one, moving or otherwise.

Morgan took another sip of whiskey as he replayed the scene in his mind again and again, and every time he came to the same inevitable conclusion: Bookworm was dead.

That left two possibilities. Either his superiors did not trust him, or they were testing him. The former seemed unlikely. While he knew only snippets, he certainly knew enough to be dangerous. If they didn't trust him, he would be dead already.

Which meant this was yet another test, like so many he'd undergone in the past fifteen years. No one simply walked into their world. Candidates were scouted, watched, carefully groomed and protected, without even knowing they had been chosen.

Looking back over his career, he could see their fingerprints. Early on, he'd been transferred out of municipal fund analysis right before the savings and loan scandal exploded and left many cities and counties grasping at air, their bonds all but worthless. Most of Morgan's early colleagues had gone down with that ship, but he had been safely ashore. Or, more precisely, he had been offshore, learning the details of Caribbean banking laws to better help clients avoid the clutches of the IRS in the wake of Reagan's tax reforms.

And so his career had gone, each move a step out of a static or declining field and into an emerging one. At the time it had seemed like a miraculous ride, a series of fortuitous coincidences and opportunities. Now he realized he had been chosen, groomed and shepherded.

Moreover, each step in his career had presented increasingly gray ethical choices, from tax avoidance to dot-com speculation to creative accounting to invasions of privacy in the guise of background research. And, finally, to murder.

He hadn't begun his career as someone who could kill. Instead, his moral qualms had been eroded step by step as his superiors had guided his career. They had molded him, testing him along the way, and he had passed each test.

Now they were testing him again. But how? Midway through his fifth tumbler of Scotch, the answer came.

Tom Lawton was another Bookworm. They weren't saying the Bookworm he'd killed had returned from the dead. They were warning him that Lawton had the same skills, the same resources and, most dangerous of all, the same attitude.

As his eyes grew heavy, Morgan knew he could pass this test. Tom Lawton would be eliminated.

By whatever means necessary.

13

Boise, Idaho

Tom's cell phone started vibrating with an insistence that felt almost like a warning. He hardly needed to pull it out and scan the caller ID to know he was in trouble. Again.

Kevin's voice demanded, "Where the hell are you?"

"I'm on suspension," Tom reminded him. "I'm calling it a vacation."

"Don't tell me you've run off to pursue some lead on your own. I'm sure I told Miriam to tell you not to do any such thing."

Tom wondered why Kevin was even calling him, but even more, he wondered why Kevin would be wondering so quickly what he was up to. His gut tightened with suspicion.

But lying had become a lot easier for him since they'd sent him undercover. In fact, it had become a far-too-natural way to protect his skin.

"It's a personal problem, Kevin."

"Yeah? What kind?" Kevin's tone couldn't have been more suspicious.

"I just had to get out of D.C. Sitting around there was reminding me of all the things I'm not being allowed to do. So I packed up my rod and reel, and I'm heading for the mountains for some angling. Rainbow trout, I hope, but right now I'll settle for any fresh fish cooked in butter over a campfire, okay? And once I get into the mountains, you won't be able to reach me on my cell anymore, so don't panic. If you're lucky, a grizzly will eat me."

Kevin was silent for long moments. "Just don't do anything stupid, Tom. I value your skin more than you seem to think. But if I discover you're lying, you've just used up your last chance."

"I hear you."

Tom disconnected and looked at the cell phone in his hand. Then, with deliberation, he turned it off. If anyone else wanted to give him a hard time, they could yell at his voice mail.

He looked at the "personal problem" sitting across from him. Miss Cool, he thought. Or maybe Ms. Ice. Certainly Ms. Crazy. "I'm not buying into Armageddon. Are you some kind of religious nut?"

"Quite the contrary. I have no religion. If the word *Armageddon* makes you uneasy, then focus on *terrorism*. Because terrorism is the stepping stone."

His skin was starting to crawl, not so much because he believed she was a nut who was trying to take him in with her delusions, but because he was beginning to fear she wasn't. "Are you saying the assassination attempt was a terrorist act?"

She sipped her wine again. "You need to expand your world view."

"How so?"

"Not all terrorists are Islamic, or religious zealots of any kind. Not all terrorist acts claim multiple victims. In fact, not all terrorist acts are designed to create terror. The point is to move the pawns on the board in a certain direction."

"So who's doing the pushing?"

She shrugged, such a European shrug. "I have ideas—in this case, at least. But little proof."

"So what's the first step?"

"Now we play hide and seek."

Guatemala City

Guatemalans had a lot of reasons to hate *yanquis,* but most of the people Miriam had so far met on the street seemed to be friendly and outgoing.

From a guidebook, she swiftly devoured what she could of local culture. The Guatemala highlands had once been home to one of the world's most advanced cultures, a culture with a calendar so accurate that only lately had the rest of the world come close. The Maya remembered this, of course.

For whatever reason, they had chosen to abandon

their cities in favor of subsistence farming. Some said it was prolonged drought, others had other explanations. No one was certain.

The rest of her information, Miriam acquired from other sources at the embassy. With the assistance of the late ambassador's secretary, she was given access to historical evaluations of the country and current situation reports.

The Maya remained proud and kept many of their old ways, and quite frankly didn't seem all that eager to become part of the modern world. They did, however, continue to bear a simmering resentment against the authorities. This simmering resentment often exploded into bouts of outright rebellion, sometimes in individual areas of the country, sometimes in more widespread ways. Peace was rare in Guatemala.

The Spanish invaders, who became the upper echelons of money and society in Guatemala, were of a very different attitude. They very much wanted to join the third millennium, but only as long as their power position could be upheld. The death of hundreds of thousands of Maya over nearly forty years of war had helped to do that. It had certainly put the Maya back at their subsistence level, mostly in small villages scattered through the mountains.

A random collection of photos taken accidentally by tourists around the time of the bombing lent credence to the fact that the perps were Mayan. And there was certainly a new civil war under way here, though it had not yet erupted into broad-based fighting.

The act had been one of terrorism. The likelihood of searching the rough terrain of Guatemala and finding the one man pictured here was small. Yet that was what she and the Guatemalan police were supposed to do.

The police force in Guatemala had been created as recently as 1996, as part of the peace accord signed between the government and the leftist guerillas after forty years of constant war. The police were required to be civilians, completely detached from the army.

The history of the fledgling force wasn't completely stellar. Under Portillo, it appeared, they had even hidden evidence and delayed investigations. Then there had been the police-beating death of a thirteen year old that had managed to make its way into the international press.

Events like that, and a continuing rise in crime, had helped usher Portillo out of office. His replacement was working hard to turn matters around, and had even supported the police strongly enough that they had managed to solve some cold cases where witnesses had been threatened by the police themselves.

On the face of it, matters were improving.

Except that in most of the mountainous country the law enforcement units were small, incapable of controlling much of anything. Recently, when a thousand *indios* had attacked a police outpost over the murder of a local man, the officers and all government authority had simply been withdrawn from the region.

For the first time since arriving in this country, Miriam began to feel fear. If the killers had gone to ground among their own people—and they certainly had—then the police did not have the resources to find them. If the reward didn't bring them the information they needed…she feared the army might be called in. And that would probably lead to even more war and perhaps to another round of ethnic cleansing, for machetes were no proof against modern weapons.

Conflict that had begun with CIA involvement in the overthrow of Guatemala's democratic government still simmered, needing little more than a spark to reerupt.

Officially, the country would have it otherwise, at least as far as tourists were concerned. The power elite had no problem with showcasing Mayan ruins as tourist attractions, or ballyhooing Mayan handicrafts when the tourists arrived. But they weren't as proud of this heritage as their pamphlets would indicate.

Quite simply, the Quechua had never been truly conquered. Some, of course, had made the transition to the way the world was now. Her driver was a good example. But the vast majority had made no real change at all. They lived as their ancestors had lived since they'd abandoned their great cities of stone. They might adhere to Christianity on Sunday, but on Wednesday they would have no qualms about visiting the local shaman for a cure, a foretelling or reassurance.

The civil war had done nothing at all to heal rifts. They had instead become as wide as the Gulf of Mexico.

Closing the folders she had been perusing, she made her decision about the situation, then picked up the phone and called Washington.

"Kevin? Miriam. I've reviewed the situation."

"What's your assessment?"

"That we keep a low profile on this. I recommend we encourage the police to treat it as a crime, not as an insurrection, and that we support them with whatever forensic tools we have. We've worked together with the Guatemalan police before, in that tourist killing. So far we haven't left any hard feelings, and I'd like to keep it that way."

"So, for the sake of harmony, they're in the lead?"

"Absolutely. Things here are touchy enough. If I find any reason to believe we need to do more, I'll let you know immediately. But for right now, the smartest move we can make is to let the locals handle as much as they can. In fact, for the sake of stability in this country, we need to treat the police with the utmost respect."

"That's going to be…difficult to explain to some people."

"Well, tell them to accept it. This place is a tinderbox on the edge of ignition, and I'd rather not have history record that the FBI set it off."

"Has anyone suggested a motive yet?"

"Most of them are sticking to the notion that it's just another expression of hatred for the U.S. over what the CIA did."

"Most? You sound dubious."

"It might be that. It might be exactly that."

"But?"

Miriam hesitated. "I get the feeling there might be

something more going on. I'm going to put my ear to the ground."

"Do that. And keep me up to date."

Boise, Idaho

Renate Bächle certainly came prepared to deal with the issues. Before dawn, Tom was dressed in camouflage she had provided and riding with her in the direction of Wes Dixon's ranch. He stifled a yawn, thinking that he really needed to get his biological clock off the L.A. rhythm it had developed: late nights, late sleep-ins. Drug dealers, as a rule, weren't an early bird lot.

"We will have to come down to the ranch from the mountains in the west," Renate told him.

"Well, obviously we can't just walk up to the front door and ask him if he's running a mercenary training camp."

She flashed him one of her cool smiles. He wasn't sure how to read it.

"If my intelligence is correct," she continued, "we should get a view from above the camp."

"And if it's not?"

Again that look, and this time he was quite sure she was thinking he was an idiot.

"Then we may have to do some hunting."

Tom put one foot up on the dash of the battered old four-by-four Jeep they were in. It was a brilliant choice of vehicle, he admitted. It could be parked almost anywhere without drawing notice, even in the middle of the woods, unlike a rental. Score one, Renate.

Score two were the Remington rifles in the back, and the orange hunters' vests. Claiming they were out for target practice was a good cover. He suspected, however, that the orange vests were likely to remain folded and unworn. At least he hoped they were. He wasn't sure he wanted to walk into a mercenary training camp acting as if they'd stumbled into it by accident.

Because they might never get out of there…by accident.

But as time and the coffee in the foam cup drove the last of his need for sleep into the background, he began to ask questions.

"What's the plan?"

"We observe what we can from a distance."

"So you're not planning to wander into the camp?"

She glanced at him. "Not on this trip."

"It's always good to know we're reserving an option to get ourselves killed for later."

She didn't dignify that with an answer.

He pushed himself up higher in his seat and took another swig of coffee. "There's one item that's notably absent from our gear."

"Which is?"

"A camera. No record of what we see."

"If they find us, a camera would be hard to explain."

"If they don't find us, lack of proof is going to be hard to explain."

She looked at him then, this time longer, icy eyes as expressionless as a glacier. "The point of this trip is for *you* to see. It is proof for you, and you alone. Then we decide what we will do."

"Ah."

He shut up. She was making sense, because he knew damn well he was sitting in this Jeep with a lot of questions and a healthy dose of skepticism. Especially since this woman had no background she chose to share with him.

For all he knew, some drug dealer in L.A. had hired her to take him into the woods and get rid of him.

But there was still her intriguing knowledge that Kevin had been going to take him off the case. How had she known that?

That, as much as anything, was pulling him along here, and before he was done with Renate, he was determined to learn who her source had been.

Just as the first sliver of sun poked up in the east, she pulled off the rutted dirt road they'd been traveling for the last ten miles and into a thick stand of woods.

"We're here," she said. "Ready?"

For a mountain goat hike to see something he wasn't sure he believed existed? "Sure."

He climbed out of the car, feeling the first surge of adrenaline. This could prove to be fascinating.

The one thing he knew for certain was that it wouldn't be dull.

Guatemalan Highlands

Steve Lorenzo hadn't slept well, so he watched the sun rise from the little porch of his thatched house. Like everyone else in this village, he lived in what some spoiled Americans referred to as "instant urban renewal." They could not see the wisdom of structures that could be destroyed by a hurricane but rebuilt with minimal loss in a matter of days.

Steve recognized the wisdom, but then, he had lived in this village during more than one hurricane and had watched it come back from complete devastation in almost no time at all. Life returned to normal quickly when you lived at a very basic level.

But these thoughts were on the periphery of his mind. At the forefront were Miguel Ortiz and his sister Rita. If Rita was right about Miguel, then this village was about to face dire consequences.

He'd spent a lot of hours in prayer, begging God for some direction, for some idea how he could save these people.

God had remained silent, and Steve was feeling very alone.

Monsignor Veltroni had sent him here to find an ancient codex, but such a task seemed beyond the ability of one mere mortal, especially in a country where brushfire wars had a habit of breaking out at any time.

Nor had Veltroni given him the least guidance in how he was supposed to achieve this miracle.

And Miguel. His heart ached for Miguel, who had been such a warm and gentle child. The hanging of his father by the army must have twisted his spirit sadly. Steve wished he had been here to help the boy, but it was a vain wish. He had been yanked out of here beforehand, when the area had become contested, simply because he was an American. The archbishop had decided it would be better to insert a local priest.

The archbishop had probably been right. But that didn't ease Steve's feelings of guilt when he thought of Miguel.

Sighing as the light at last overcame the darkness completely, he went inside to put on his cassock and begin the day with a heavy heart.

God, he asked, *why do you put these, your children, through so much?*

The silence in his heart was the only answer he got.

So he stepped out his door and began to walk through the village greeting people. And from time to time, he asked if anyone had inquired about an ancient, hidden text.

He was trusted here. If anyone had heard anything, they would tell him.

Which was more than God seemed to be doing.

14

Boise, Idaho

The hike through the woods, though at times over challenging terrain, was just a hike. He and Renate made good time, Tom thought, considering that once or twice they had to play mountain goat on an outcropping.

The rifle he carried was irritating, however. He wasn't used to hiking around with one dangling from his shoulder, and no matter how he placed it, it annoyed him. Renate, on the other hand, was moving forward as if she was quite used to having a rifle slung over hers.

"Military background?" he asked her when they paused for a drink and a quick breather after a particularly rough patch.

"Who?" she asked.

"You."

She shrugged. "It's not relevant."

Closed as a clam. Boy, did that inspire trust. It was, however, a distraction from all the anger and sorrow he'd been feeling lately. And, remembering how he'd just recently wanted to bang his head on his desk with frustration over the impossibility of proving his theory, he decided hiking through the woods with a two-legged clam was actually a step up in life.

Hell, was he getting his sense of humor back?

They had hiked for another half hour over easier terrain when she suddenly turned to him and put her finger to her lips. He froze.

Carefully, she stepped back toward him and whispered, "Another quarter mile, if that. I don't know if they're bothering to keep sentries or if they've set up trip alarms."

"Talk about an oversight. I thought you were omniscient."

Her expression never changed. This woman needed a serious injection of personality.

But he took her warning to heart. Their movements became stealthier, easy enough on pine needles, which were the world's earliest soundproofing.

The thick pine forest helped in other ways, too, for there was almost no undergrowth to hide anything, including sentries and trip wires. At last he could see the light of a clearing ahead; as they approached it, ferns and other concealing undergrowth increased.

Finally Renate signaled that they should get down and belly crawl. This was something Tom hadn't had to do since his training days at Quantico, but at least he knew how to do it—and with a rifle. Slinging the weapon across his back, he squirmed after Renate through thick brush, aware that their progress was leaving a trail anyone could follow.

But after only a few minutes, her reasoning became clear. She stopped inching forward and signaled him to come up beside her. Gently parting the next foot of yellowed grasses, she showed him.

They were above whatever was going on at the camp. Well above. Sort of a hawk's-eye view without the hawk's eyes.

But it was clear enough for them to see a collection of hollow building shells, a target range and an obstacle course. And there was no mistaking the number of men who were down there. This was no five-member militia.

There were four teams down there, being led through their paces by men who appeared—to Tom's eyes, anyway—to be drill instructors. In only a few minutes it became very, very clear that this was paramilitary urban warfare training, not the ragtag band of bored soldier wanna-bes and their dogs that the FBI report had implied.

"Christ," he said under his breath, watching intently. Twenty-five to thirty trainees, he estimated. They kept moving too much for an accurate count, but it was clear as crystal they were undergoing unit training, the kind of thing that welded men together.

Renate pulled a pair of binoculars out of her hip pocket and passed them to him. Moments later he was looking close up at AR-7s, or…he revised that as a rattle of fire came from the range. Fully automatic M-16s.

And…cripes, was that man carrying an Uzi?

Then Tom began to scan the area and liked even less what he was seeing. A section was marked off with a sign that bore a skull and crossbones over the word Mines. There was also evidence of demolitions training.

Finally he rolled onto his back and passed the binoculars back to Renate. "Houston," he muttered, looking up into a deep blue sky, "we have a problem."

Watermill, Long Island

No answers. Edward Morgan absolutely, positively *hated* it when there were no answers. How could the FBI have no idea where one of its agents was, suspended or not? But his source in the Bureau said only that Lawton had gone fishing.

Morgan no more believed that than he believed the sky was going to fall at midnight. Now he had begun to doubt the information he was receiving from the same source that said Lawton had found nothing whatsoever of interest during the few days he'd researched radical domestic groups.

And it bugged him even more that Lawton's best friend had been sent to Guatemala, the seat of all present problems in Edward's life.

He poured himself another drink and decided he was going to call in sick to work in the morning. He needed to pool some resources, and he couldn't do it from the office. He needed backup information, and he needed it fast.

His hand hovered over the telephone for a few moments; then he glanced at the clock and realized it was still early in Idaho. Wes probably wouldn't be back at the ranch house for an hour or more. Edward could call his sister, of course, chat with her for a few, then ask her to have Wes call him.

But he didn't feel like chatting with his sister right now, and he loathed having to wait for phone calls.

He dropped his hand back on his desk and looked around his elaborate home office, a library in the English style, filled with books in leather bindings. Books he'd mostly read, unlike some of his friends. Alas, not one of those books had the information he needed right now.

Where was Tom Lawton? And how much did he know?

Guatemalan Highlands

As evening settled over the highlands, Father Steve Lorenzo made his way to the shaman's hut at the edge of the village. He didn't know about his predecessors, much less his successors, but he had always made a point of treating this woman with great respect, for that was what she received from everyone in the village. She attended their births and deaths and illnesses in much the same way he did, and she was believed to hold a power over such matters that he could not and did not claim.

If someone became seriously ill, Steve would give them the anointing for the sick. Then the *curandera* would give them the blessings of her faith. Steve did not object. He believed that God operated through faith, and who was he to tell God whom to work through?

Some hard-liners might disagree, but Steve and many other priests over the centuries, and even the Church herself, had concluded that God worked in mysterious ways and could take other spiritual paths. The modern catechism taught that if any man sincerely sought God, by whatever path, God would find him.

Paloma had a Mayan name that Steve could pronounce only with great difficulty, so she had told him to call her by the Spanish version of her name, Dove. The past fifteen years had aged her considerably, but her smile was still warm, and her greeting was genuine.

"We missed you, *Padre*," she said. "Those who came after you were not as friendly."

"Their loss."

Paloma laughed and offered him a fermented brew that was known in some places as pulque. Only the very old or the very young were allowed to drink it, because the supposedly uncivilized Maya had long since learned that they were prone to alcoholism. Except at the time of a great feast, no one else drank it, except the *curandera* or her select guests.

Steve politely took a sip and noted that she had remembered his distaste for alcohol. Only the tiniest bit had been poured into the earthenware cup. He smiled and nodded at her. For her part, Paloma drank nothing.

"I am surprised," she said, "that they sent you back to us."

"I'm delighted to be here."

"But they sent you for a reason."

Paloma always knew. She knew every single thing that went on in her village, and even things she couldn't know by normal means.

"Yes."

"You seek the book of Kulkulcan."

He nodded and put his cup down.

Paloma sighed, and twisted to stir the coals under the pot of beans and chili peppers that always simmered on the fires around here. When she looked at him again, her face was grim.

"You will not find it. Nor will any of the others who search for it."

"Others?" His heart slammed. What had Monsignor Veltroni failed to tell him?

"You do not know?" Paloma sighed again. "You may need more pulque than I have given you, *Padre*."

"I would rather hear the bad news with a clear mind."

She nodded. "You were always a good man. Someone has sent you on a very dangerous mission, and I can tell you now that you will not complete it. The book of Kulkulcan is not meant for eyes that are not Mayan."

"Why is that?"

"Because others would destroy it, or themselves, and probably both."

Steve was hardly the one to argue with that. He was all too aware of the sacred and historical texts that had been destroyed in the past. And knowing the suspected contents of this book, he was very certain his church would either burn it or bury it so deep in the Vatican archives that it would never again see the light of day.

"Then I shall not find it."

Paloma laughed, a surprisingly youthful sound from such a creased face. "But you must look, for so you have been ordered. So I will tell you the difficulties."

"Please."

Again her face grew grim. "There are many who seek the book, for they think it will give them power over others. Or because they fear it will give others power over them. Truth is a dangerous weapon, my friend. It can be used for both good and ill."

Given Veltroni's concerns, Steve could only nod.

"There are many seeking the book," Paloma repeated. "I do not know who sends them. What I know is that they are using our young men, stirring up trouble and war to cover their actions. Who will notice if some village shaman is tortured during a war? Who will notice the deaths?"

Steve began to feel like a very low life-form. "I'm sorry."

Paloma's eyes burned like hot coals as she looked at him. "Do not search too hard, *Padre*. I do not know where the book is. Only a small number have been entrusted with that secret, and they are guarded by the jaguar. You and your people may not believe in our spirits, but they are powerful indeed."

Her eyes grew glazed then, and he had the feeling she

was seeing the future. "Take care, *Padre*. Trust the jaguar, or it will eat you, too. Blood will run thick, but the jaguar can protect you."

Then, with a solemnity that touched him nearly as much as a sacrament, she passed him a small leather bag attached to a long looped leather thong.

"Wear this beneath your clothes, beneath your cross, so the jaguar will recognize you."

Steve hesitated only a moment before putting the pouch over his head and tucking it inside his cassock.

Paloma nodded. "Good. The One God who is known by many names watches over us all, but the spirits are strong, also. In these mountains, the jaguar is very powerful."

Later, strolling through the dusty village toward his own hut as night darkened the world, Steve found himself touching the pouch around his neck. From far, far away, he heard the cry of a jaguar.

There were times when Jesus seemed very far away.

Boise, Idaho

Nor did Tom Lawton feel divine companionship that evening. He and Renate had hiked back as they had come, then carried their luggage to their new motel, outside of town up in the foothills. While their new lodgings were not as posh as the Grove, their compensation was anonymity. Tom had checked into the Grove under his own name, using his own credit card. Renate had insisted that they check out that morning, and she'd checked them into this place using a false name and driver's license.

The room rate was reflected in the furnishings. The bed had a slight hump in it, the bathroom tap dripped and the plush chair had a fanny-shaped hollow that was nearly threadbare. On the other hand, no one was likely to bother him here.

Except for Renate.

She stood in the doorway between the adjoining rooms, having unpacked in less time than it had taken him to use the bathroom and make a futile attempt to shut off the tap. Now she wore crisp jeans and a cotton T-shirt with the logo of a popular brand of sunglasses. Despite what he knew of her personality, it was impossible not to notice that she was both beautiful and shapely, with firm hips and thighs, a slim but not tiny waist, and delicate but comely—

He jerked himself away from the thought. There was no room for it—in their working relationship or in his life.

"Unpacked already?" he asked, already knowing the answer but seeking distraction.

"I'm used to it," she replied.

He nodded toward the bathroom. "Well, I had other priorities."

"That's fine," Renate said. "We need to eat."

Pure business. There was no question that she expected him to attend to such details. She was used to having her way.

"You're the boss. Is takeout okay?"

"Yes," she said. "Chinese, please."

He found a telephone directory in a drawer beside the bed and thumbed through the well-worn restaurant pages. If he was going to eat Chinese—and her statement left no room for negotiation—he wanted Cantonese rather than the ubiquitous Szechuan brown sauce. He found a restaurant that advertised "authentic Cantonese cuisine" and called in an order from the limited menu given in the phone book.

"Thank you," Renate said when he had finished. She went to her room and returned with a twenty-dollar bill. "Pay in cash. No credit cards."

Obviously she intended him to pick it up, as well. At least she had deigned to pay for it. Tom tamped down his urge to rebel. She wasn't malicious or arrogant in her air of authority. She simply took it for granted that she was in charge. Which, he realized, she was.

"Aren't you coming?" he asked. "I don't know this town, or how to find this place."

She shook her head. "I have some work to do on my computer. Where is the restaurant?"

He read her the address from the phone book, and she gave him directions. Every cell within him screamed to tell her off, but he could find no justification beyond his own lingering anger at the world in general and bosses in particular. Venting that anger was what had landed him on suspension, and while that particular risk didn't exist here, neither could he afford to alienate the only ally he had at the moment.

"Fine," he said. "I'll be back in a half hour."

"That's good," she said. "I should be done with my work by then. We can talk over dinner."

"I can't wait," Tom said, hoping his sarcasm didn't drip as thickly in her ears as it did in his own.

Back in the Jeep and following her directions, he pondered the events in L.A. that had poisoned his emotions. He was as angry at himself as he was at anyone else. More so, in fact, because he knew he had made the lumpy bed in which he now lay. Yes, the case had gone sour. But he'd gotten too involved, and in the wrong ways. He'd tried to be a surrogate father for a girl whose real father was headed for prison or a grave.

Tom realized he'd been the wrong man in the wrong place at the wrong time. He wasn't a social worker, by training or profession. And his own experiences had only served to color his assessment of her life and needs.

He was a cop. His job, sooner or later, had been to ruin that girl's life by putting her father in prison. In the long run, that would be in her best interests. In the short run, she was sure to hold those responsible in contempt, especially if they had betrayed her trust in the process. It was not the kind of story that lent itself to a happy ending. One way or another, Tom would have ended up in the same situation: hated by a girl he'd come to care for very deeply.

It hadn't been his SAC's fault. It hadn't been the Bureau's fault. It had been Tom's fault, plain and simple, and he was determined not to repeat that mistake.

* * *

José Martinez watched the man climb out of the Jeep and walk into the restaurant. The parking lot was not well lit, but he got a clear enough look at the man's face to confirm that it matched the photograph he'd been given by Colonel Dixon.

Martinez had been called in from the field early in the afternoon and had spent much of the rest of the day sitting around while the colonel made and received one telephone call after another. Boise was a small town of a big city, the colonel had explained during a break in the calls. If Tom Lawton were staying at a hotel in town, even if under an assumed name, they would find him. Apparently the search had been complicated by the fact that Lawton was traveling with a girlfriend, who had rented the room in her name. In the end, though, persistence had paid off, and the colonel had given Martinez an address and his orders: *Make it look like an accident.*

José was out of his van and beneath Lawton's Jeep almost by the time his target entered the restaurant. The primary hydraulic brake line was easy to locate, even in the dark, and equally easy to penetrate with the awl from José's pocket knife. That afternoon, he had scraped the awl over a metal file, then over a slab of granite, until its edges were rough and irregular. There would be no clean cut, only a ragged tear of the sort that might have resulted from gravel or glass kicked up from the road bed. José would dump the pocket knife in a storm drain on the way back to the colonel's ranch.

José was back in the van when Lawton emerged from the restaurant with a brown paper bag stapled shut at the top. Apparently the FBI agent was hungry, for he paused after starting the engine and broke open a fortune cookie.

"Si lo dice que su vida será prolongada," José said quietly, *"es incorrecto."*

If it says you're going to have a long life, it's wrong.

15

Guatemala City, Guatemala

Miriam had almost fallen asleep when the pounding at her door began. She rose and shrugged on a terry-cloth robe, then opened the door to find Pablo wearing an expression that could only mean one thing.

"We've found one of them," Pablo said. "We must go now. Dress quickly, please."

His admonition for haste was superfluous. She was already pushing the door closed and scrambling for the pair of jeans she'd left at the end of the bed. Three minutes later, she emerged wearing an FBI tactical T-shirt, with her credentials clipped to her belt.

"Where are we going?" she asked as he pushed the elevator button for the roof rather than the lobby.

"A helicopter is waiting on the roof," Pablo said. "My commander wants you to be there to observe the capture, so you can see that we are handling it well. He is a very proud man."

The rotors were already turning when they emerged,

and Miriam held a hand over her face in a futile attempt to ward off the swirling dust as she and Pablo ducked under the blades and boarded the helicopter. They had hardly taken their seats when the pilot increased the throttle and pulled pitch, smoothly taking them up into the night sky.

"Where is this place?" Miriam shouted above the roar.

"Dos Ojos. It is not far," Pablo said. "About twenty kilometers outside of town."

Twenty kilometers, Miriam thought, doing the math in her head. About twelve miles. Less than ten minutes' flight time. So much for a briefing.

"We have already surrounded the village," Pablo said. "The tactical force went in by truck a half hour ago. My commander is there, waiting for you."

A Bureau tactical team would already have established a perimeter, put the target house under observation and be moving into position for the final assault. Miriam had no idea whether the Guatemalan police were as well trained, though she steeled herself to hope for the best and prepare for the worst. She was there as an observer only, and was resolved to watch and listen, rather than criticize. Still, she felt her adrenaline flowing, and began to go through the mental checklist imprinted by years of training and experience.

She had barely begun when it seemed as if the bottom had fallen out of the world. Her stomach rose in her throat, and the trees below suddenly seemed close enough to touch. The pilot was on final approach, flying NOE—nap of the earth—to buffer the sound and avoid peering eyes. He was doubtless a skilled flyer, but the constant lurch and roll as he navigated over or around obstacles left her stomach churning.

Ahead, she saw a jagged ridge looming larger by the minute. Just beneath the ridgeline, she could make out the outline of a Jeep and two men beside it. The road seemed too narrow for the helicopter to land, but the pilot slid it in regardless, the tips of the rotors clipping off twigs in the process.

Pablo bounded out of the helicopter, then turned to offer his hand, but Miriam was already on the ground. They had no sooner stepped off the road and into the trees than the pilot once again lifted the aircraft into the sky and, with a deft turn, headed back for the city. Pablo motioned for Miriam to follow him, and they climbed the last hundred yards to the commander's Jeep, overlooking the village in the valley beyond.

The commander gestured then into the back seat of the Jeep. "One of the men in this village was on a secondary team. He bragged to his girlfriend, and she told her parents. They never liked him, anyway."

"That's how it usually happens," Miriam said. "What's our status?"

"I have two entry teams in place," the commander said from the front seat, pointing to dark forms almost invisible in the shadows. "One at the front door, one at the back. He's staying with his sister and her children. Once we have him, our trucks will come in and pick up my men and the prisoner. We will be back in the city before the locals have time to respond."

"If everything goes according to plan," Miriam said.

"Yes," he said. "If everything goes according to plan." He rapped the dash with his hand. *"Vámonos."*

"Where are we going?" Miriam asked, as the driver started the engine.

The commander turned in his seat to face her. "In my country, Special Agent, we do not lead from the rear. Now that you are here, I'm going to move in to be with my men. You're welcome to come along for the ride or stay back here. But decide now."

"Let's go," Miriam said without hesitation.

The commander smiled and turned to his driver. *"Se oido. Vámonos."* He lifted his radio to his face. *"Vaya ahora."*

Go now.

Miriam heard the flash-bang grenade explode as they reached the edge of the village, but the words replayed over and over in her head: *If everything goes according to plan.*

Boise, Idaho

Tom had traveled only three blocks when he saw the van close up behind him, its high beams glaring in his eyes.

"Dammit," he muttered aloud. "It's not like there aren't enough streetlights."

Probably a drunk driver, he thought. Or kids. But the

van was glued to his tail as he made a left turn, and the hope that this was a routinely idiotic driver vanished almost as soon as it had arisen.

The traffic was thin at this time of night. He knew the correct way to react when being followed. Don't drive home, because that is likely to be more isolated, and it lets the attacker know where to find you again. Drive to the nearest police station or firehouse or, failing that, to a gas station, bank or other business that is likely to have outdoor surveillance cameras. In short, make sure the attacker knows that, whatever happens, he will be seen or photographed—and caught.

But Tom didn't know the city. He had no idea where the nearest police station, firehouse or bank was. There was a gas station two blocks up on the right, but the sign was off; it had already closed.

As Tom saw it, he had three choices. Return to his hotel. Escape and evade, trying to lose the van and very likely getting himself lost. Or stop, turn and fight.

Much as he leaned to the last option, he realized there were probably two or more attackers in the van. And he was unarmed, having left his Glock in his room. At the hotel, he would at least have Renate's support, provided he could get her attention. It would expose their lodging, but he suspected that was irrelevant. It was unlikely his pursuers had simply stumbled across him in the parking lot of a Chinese restaurant. They'd followed him from the hotel. They already knew where he was staying, but apparently they didn't know about

Renate. So he had nothing to lose—and Renate to gain—by leading them back there.

He pressed down on the gas pedal a bit. If they knew what they were doing, they would try to ram him as he made a turn, forcing him into a spin and immobilizing him. He needed to open up a gap between them, and while the van had the advantage of mass, his Jeep had better acceleration.

He reached the intersection and tapped the brake as he turned. Normally the light tap would have bled off enough speed that he could make the turn easily, but now it had no effect whatever. The SUV, with its high center of gravity, heeled to the left as he turned. For a moment he felt the right side wheels leave the pavement and was sure he was going to roll over. But the Jeep righted itself, just as the van bore down on him.

He stepped on the gas now, only a half mile from the hotel, and the only backup he could hope for. The van was closing in again. Turning into the hotel lot, he tapped the brakes and this time felt the pedal sink with almost no resistance.

With more time, he would have used the brake failure techniques he'd learned in driver emergency training—downshifting and using the parking brake—but he had no more time.

He felt the right wheels rise from the pavement, and pulled the steering wheel back to center, but it was too late. Directly in front of him, sitting atop a concrete

base, was the blinking sign for the hotel, and as the SUV
began to roll, he watched the sign turn upside down before the world went black.

José Martinez slowed as he passed, watching the target's SUV tumble and slam into the concrete base of the
sign. In the flicker of neon lights, he clearly saw the red,
goopy mass explode over the inside of the windshield.

He would have stopped to verify the kill, but the
screech of metal on asphalt, followed by the bone-jar-
ring crunch of the impact, had already brought the hotel's night manager out to see what had happened. Right
now, José was simply a passing motorist. If he stopped,
he would be memorable.

Besides, what was there to verify? The man's brains
were spattered over the inside of the car.

Misión consumado, he thought, driving away.

Dos Ojos, Guatemala

Miriam watched as the operation began to spin out
of control. The flash-bang grenades, intended to stun the
occupants of the house while the entry teams stormed
in, had also awakened the village. The sight of armed
troops—even *policía*—had an immediate effect on this
village that lay in the shadow of two volcanoes. Shouts
echoed in the nighttime stillness, and within moments
the crackle of small-arms fire began.

The commander, standing in the now-halted Jeep, his
radio to his face, was an easy and obvious target.

Miriam heard the buzz of bullets whipping past, and dove out of the Jeep onto the ground. Moments later, the commander crumpled atop her, his gurgling wheeze unmistakable evidence of a chest wound. She rolled from beneath him and felt for a pulse, but his eyes were already glazing over.

Pablo scurried around the back of the Jeep and squatted next to her, his eyes widening as he saw his commander lying on the ground.

"He's gone," Miriam said. She handed him the radio. "You're in charge."

"I don't know anything about this," he pleaded, pushing the radio back into her arms. "I do office work."

Miriam met his eyes. "Pablo, take a breath and look at me. I don't speak Spanish. Even if I did, I have no authority here."

Sputtering voices were already flooding the radio, as the entry and evacuation teams called out for orders. Even though she didn't understand the words, Miriam clearly heard the edge of panic creeping into their voices. The same panic she saw in Pablo's eyes.

"Tell me what they're saying," she said, handing him the radio. "Take a deep breath and translate for me."

He nodded, eyes still like saucers, and listened. "The trucks on the far side of the village have been hit," he said. "One is disabled. Another driver has been shot."

"How bad?" she asked. "And what's the status on the entry teams?"

As he relayed her questions, she crawled to the front

of the Jeep and tried to take stock of the situation. On both sides of the street, gunfire was winking from windows. One of the entry team members was down, lying near the doorway, though she could not tell how badly he was hurt. One truck had rumbled into the village, but its tires had been shot out, and the windshield was spiderwebbed with bullet holes. The other two trucks were apparently still holding on the far side of the village, for she saw no sign of them.

"Hurry, Pablo," she said. She searched her memory for the few Spanish phrases she'd picked up over the years. The only one that seemed to apply bubbled up from cartoons she had watched as a child. *"Ándale!"*

"The driver is dead," Pablo said. "The entry teams have the suspect. He is shot but will live. They also shot one of his nephews. They are ready to come out."

"Tell the other trucks to get moving," Miriam said. "Let's get the hell out of here before this gets worse."

Pablo relayed her orders, then shook his head. He crawled up beside her and pointed. "The disabled truck is blocking the only road. They say there's no room to get around."

"Tell them to push it," Miriam said. "Get it out of the way."

She listened as her orders were translated first into Spanish and then into action. The dark outline of another truck emerged from behind a building, easing up to the disabled truck and making contact. Then the engine revved and the disabled truck began to roll. But with the tires shredded, it dug in on one side and turned, crunching into the front of a house. The harder the second truck pushed, the more firmly the disabled truck became lodged.

"Shit," Miriam said. "Someone's got to get into that disabled truck and get it out of the way."

"They say the gunfire is too great," Pablo said after relaying her command.

"The entry team members have flak jackets," Miriam said. "Tell them to send someone out to move that truck or we're all going to get killed here."

For the first time, she glanced up into the Jeep. As she had feared, the driver had been killed in the same volley that had felled the commander. A hiss from the front of the Jeep told the rest of the story: the radiator had been hit. They would have to evacuate on the trucks with the rest of the men.

She watched as three members of the entry team emerged from the doorway. Two took up prone positions and began to pepper the windows from which fire had come. The third ducked low and dashed for the disabled truck, climbing over the hood to reach the driver's side. He pulled a body from behind the wheel and climbed in.

"Tell the second truck to back up," Miriam said. "He needs room to back out."

Pablo complied, and once the second truck had backed off, the entry team driver tried to pull the disabled truck out of the building. With the rims digging into the dirt street, it was agonizingly slow going. The truck rocked forward and back as the driver tried to free the wheels from the base of the building. Finally, spewing dirt from below, it lurched back out into the street and began to creep forward.

"Send the other trucks in behind," Miriam said. "Tell the entry teams to be ready for pickup. And tell them they need to get us, too."

The disabled truck finally lumbered off the street and into a gap between two houses. Moments later, the driver crept out from beside it. She signaled for him to stay low and wait for the trucks to reach him.

Miriam knew that disengagement under fire was considered the most difficult of all military operations, and in the circumstances, she was inclined to agree. Now that the *policía* were clearly trying to escape, the villagers redoubled their volume of fire. Unlike the truck drivers and members of the entry team, the villagers had cover. They could duck down below windows. Their attackers were in the street, exposed.

Two more members of the entry team fell, leaving only five still combat effective. Two were shoving the prisoner into the truck. The two prone in the street were trying to give covering fire in every direction. That left one man to gather the wounded. His courage was unquestionable, but it was only a matter of time before he, too, would be hit.

"We've got to go secure the wounded," Miriam said, rising and pulling Pablo by the sleeve. "Now!"

The night air was filled with angry shouts, pained moans and a persistent buzzing that made Miriam feel as if she had walked into a beehive. But she knew those were not bees flying past. They were bullets.

The man who had cleared the disabled truck joined them as they ran to the center of the village. Miriam felt a sting on her side but ignored it as she helped to heft a man whose knee was shattered. Gritting her teeth against his screams, she pushed him into the back of a truck. She looked back into the street, and saw Pablo and the other officer grab the last wounded man.

"Let's go!" she shouted.

Pablo nodded and climbed into the first truck. She was about to vault into the second truck when another stinging pain jolted through her leg. One of the soldiers reached for her, but the driver was already revving the engine and pulling away.

Miriam clutched at her leg and fought the urge to scream as she watched the truck recede into the darkness.

16

Boise National Forest, Idaho

Tom first became aware of a headache that felt as if a bomb had gone off in his head. Next he felt the movements of a vehicle under him, and the tightness of a harness across his chest and hips. Every so often, bright lights would flicker red through his eyelids, then vanish.

With minuscule movements, he tested his body for injuries and bindings. Nothing broken, no bindings on his hands or his ankles, but damn, the seat belt that held him was pressing on some pretty painful territory.

He heard a female voice mutter something beside him, then the vehicle downshifted, straining as its front end tilted upward. *Renate.* That much he remembered. That and Armageddon.

Cautiously he opened his eyes, but only the dim glow of the dash lights greeted him, enough by which to see Renate, not enough to hurt. She was driving a pickup, and he was riding in it. So far, so good.

"Welcome back," she said. "You're dead."

If his head hadn't been hammering so hard, he might have evinced shock, anger or confusion. Instead he decided he simply hadn't heard her correctly. "Concussion," he said, testing whether he was still able to speak.

"Yes," she answered. "You have a concussion, a couple of lacerations of no importance, and plenty of contusions. Your seat belt saved your life."

"What happened?"

"No brakes and a nasty man chasing you. You turned too fast into the parking lot and rolled the Jeep."

"Oh." He let his groggy brain absorb that.

"You'll be okay soon. In the meantime, I took care of business."

"What?"

"You went to the emergency room, unconscious. I went with you, of course."

"Sure." Vaguely he realized this was leading up to something.

"They checked you out, decided that you needed a scan because of the severity of the concussion, and took a few stitches to stop the bleeders. Then they left you."

This, he began to understand, was important.

"Of course, in the way of emergency rooms, they ordered you sent for a scan, but the line for the scanner was backed up, so you stayed in your little cubicle until I came to wheel you up to MRI. You never arrived."

"Oh." He wasn't sure he liked that.

"You weren't in any neurological distress," she said bluntly. "I was able to rouse you twice. So I dealt with it."

"How did you deal with it."

"You're dead now."

"That's the second time you've said that. Unfortunately, owing to the amount of physical pain I'm feeling, I suspect I'm very much alive."

She laughed then. "Good, your sense of humor is intact."

"I don't think I'm being humorous."

"Perhaps not. The point is, they forgot you for a long time, long enough for you to have a serious cerebral hemorrhage, which killed you. Your file clearly states time and cause of death, and that you were released to a funeral home. I found a John Doe in the morgue, similar enough. And since your face was smashed up…"

Pain or not, he was getting a very clear picture, and he didn't like what he was seeing. "Is that where we're headed now? To a funeral home?"

"Of course not! We're going to camp out for a day or two, so the word of your death can spread. Then we're going to continue our investigation."

"I see." He paused. "Did it ever occur to you that I might not want to be dead?"

She shrugged. "Right now, it's the best thing for you to be. What happened to you was no accident. You're supposed to be dead. Later, if you want your old life back, you won't have any trouble getting this explained away as a mistake."

If he wanted his old life back?

He wanted to press her further, to argue about her

high-handedness, to threaten to go back to D.C. right now and to hell with her.

But he kept silent, and it wasn't because of the headache. Concussed or not, he was so damned intrigued by this woman that he was going to stick around a few more days, at least, just to find out what the hell she was up to.

Or so he told himself.

Guatemalan Highlands

Miriam woke to flickering firelight and the wizened face of a Mayan woman. She caught her breath, suddenly frightened for her life, but then a European face leaned over her, and she saw a Roman collar.

"Rest easy," the priest said to her. "Our *curandera* is very good. She'll stop your bleeding, and then you'll feel better."

"Where is everyone?"

The priest's smile was not happy. "Your actions in Dos Ojos have set off the rebels. They're roaming the jungle right now, looking for targets of opportunity. You're safe here, but your helicopter won't be able to land anytime soon."

"And the others?"

"They made it safely back to the city."

She let her head fall back on the mat. "Thank you, Father."

"Don't thank me. I'm not sure I would have put the

village to this risk. Thank the *curandera*. She's the one who offered you shelter."

Miriam looked at her benefactress. *"Muchas gracias."*

The woman waved her hand as if it were nothing. Then she began to speak.

"She says," the priest translated, "that you would be wise not to become involved in the affairs of the Maya. She says that the Maya were once a relatively peaceful people, who warred for tribute and captives but never destroyed their enemies. Then something changed, and they began to war for territory, and to kill one another in large numbers. She says it has been thus for more than..." He paused. "I need to translate the numbers...more than a thousand years. They have been fighting the Spanish for centuries, and they will fight any others who try to take them from their land."

He sighed. The *curandera* grinned at him. "Paloma laughs at me. She knows I do not approve of killing and warfare. And she asks me, '*Padre*, how can you change our nature? You want us to be peaceful, but others will not leave us alone.'"

He nodded. "Unfortunately, there's a fair measure of truth in that. My name is Steve Lorenzo, by the way. And yours?"

"Miriam Anson. FBI."

"Well, Ms. Anson, I don't know whose harebrained idea it was to go into Dos Ojos like a conquering army, but it has stirred up some serious trouble."

"It wasn't mine," she admitted. "I was dragged out of bed to accompany them on the raid."

Father Lorenzo translated for the old woman, who nodded and muttered something.

"Paloma says always it is this way. They cannot simply arrest those who committed the act, but have to come in as if an entire village is responsible."

Remembering how the whole affair had begun, with flash-bang grenades and armored trucks, Miriam silently agreed. She couldn't say so aloud, of course, lest it get back to her hosts, but it did seem to be overkill for picking up one man…unless you believed everyone in the village was a rebel.

Paloma might have read her mind. She spoke again, and Father Lorenzo translated. "She says the vast majority of people in any village are simply ordinary people trying to support their families and feed their children. If they are left alone, nothing will happen. But now…" He shook his head.

Impulsively, Miriam reached out to touch Paloma's arm. The *curandera* looked at her, deep into her eyes, and it was as if something passed between them. Then Paloma spoke again.

"She says, Ms. Anson," Father Lorenzo translated, "that you are being used by forces you do not understand. She says you must henceforth stay in Guatemala City, for your own safety."

"Why does she think that?"

Father Lorenzo said something to Paloma, who answered. Then he looked at Miriam. "She has a gift, Ms. Anson. Sometimes she sees things others do not. More than that she will not say."

Watermill, Long Island

Tom Lawton was dead, according to the agent who had carried out the mission. Edward Morgan wasn't quite sure, however, since Wes had assigned a Guatemalan to do the deed. Morgan was never sure when any non-European handled a job.

Regardless, since Lawton had been in the area, Wes had decided to move his operation. Edward fully agreed with that. Protect and cover. Always wise when someone was sniffing around. If Lawton had gotten wind of what Wes was doing, he might have passed the word to someone.

So his first call was to his contact in the Bureau.

"Haven't heard a thing from Lawton since he said he was going fishing," was the answer. "Why are you so worried about him?"

"Because he's not following orders."

"Actually, right now I'd guess he's following them better than I'd hoped."

"Maybe so."

"I know so. If he was into anything, he'd be trying to use Bureau resources. Relax, will you?"

Edward hung up, reasonably certain now that Lawton was no longer a concern. One last phone call.

The hospital in Boise was at first reluctant to release

any information, but Edward wasn't used to taking no for an answer, and after a few minutes of pretending to be a worried brother, he finally got through to someone who was willing to answer his questions.

"I'm sorry, Mr. Lawton," said the woman. "Your brother is dead. He expired in the emergency room from severe head trauma. It appears that he was released to a local funeral home."

"And his personal effects?"

"Hmm…I show that a wallet containing credit cards, driver's license and…oh, yes! We don't ordinarily see this, but he apparently had an FBI badge case, as well. Someone from the local FBI office will be coming by to collect everything. We assume they'll get in touch with you. Unfortunately, the deceased had no indication of other family in his effects, or we would have called you sooner."

"Thank you. I just…" Edward pretended to be broken up and drew a couple of deliberately shaky breaths. "Thank you," he said again.

"You should contact the FBI," the woman said kindly. "They'll have everything shortly."

He hung up, and the one word in his mind was *Yes!* Now he could call his contact and tell them Bookworm was a goner.

Pine Flats, Idaho

As Tom's headache began to ease a bit, the throbbing in his arm and leg from the gashes and stitches began to set up a replacement ruckus. He was beginning to feel as if he'd been in a car accident, all right.

"Where are we going?" he asked.

"Someplace safe where I can stash you for a day or two to recover. Meantime, I'll go back and take a look at what Dixon is up to."

"Not alone, you're not."

"You can't seriously think I'm going to let you stumble around in the woods with a concussion."

"Concussion, hell. I'm already dead, so what difference would it make?"

"Oh, behave! You'd be a liability right now. Someone tried to kill you. Hence, it's likely someone saw us in the woods the other day. I want to know what Dixon is doing about it."

"And get caught by one of his sentries? You're out of your mind."

"I won't get caught."

"How can you be certain?"

"Because I'm going to take a flying lesson. It's amazing how much you can see from the air at a safe distance."

Tom slouched lower in his seat and wished the road were smoother. "You're awfully high-handed."

"I was raised that way." She slipped her hand into a bag beside her on the seat and tossed him a wallet. "There's the new you. Save your breath and get used to it."

He flipped the wallet open and found himself staring at his own face on a Colorado driver's license. The name was Lawton Caine. "Why Caine?"

"Why not? It was easy for me to say."

"Gee, thanks."

"Everything in there is valid, including the credit cards. If you need cash, the ATM card works, also."

"Who's paying for this junket?"

She shook her head and downshifted to climb a steep incline. "Maybe someday I will tell you."

17

Washington, D.C.

In a relatively brief space of time, Kevin Willis's life turned to hell. Word from the embassy in Guatemala indicated that Miriam Anson had been caught in a fire-fight in the jungle and had disappeared. Then, just as he was absorbing this bad news, he received word from the Boise field office that Tom Lawton had died in an auto accident. His effects were being forwarded.

Kevin gripped the phone hard, listening to the voice of the Boise SAC give him the bad news. Something in him suddenly rebelled. "Can you get your hands on Lawton's vehicle?"

"Uh, probably," SAC Fred Milgram answered. "But it was an SUV rollover, Kev. You know it doesn't take a hell of a lot."

"Check it out anyway. If Lawton cornered too fast, there may be a reason."

"Yeah. Sure. I'll get my guys to look into it." His tone suggested it wasn't going to the top of his priority list.

"Listen, Fred," Kevin said. "Lawton was in deep cover. I want that vehicle checked." He knew he was risking Fred's annoyance that he hadn't been included in that little tidbit, but Kevin was past caring. He couldn't do a damn thing about Miriam, under the circumstances, but he *could* find out what had been going on with Tom to some small extent. Even if it meant lying.

There was a pause while Fred must have run through a gamut of possible responses, most of them unpleasant. In the end, however, all the man said was, "Sure, Kev. We'll get right on it."

"Thanks, buddy. I owe you."

"Big time," was the very serious reply.

For a long time Kevin sat staring into space, wondering how the hell he was going to tell Miriam's husband that she had disappeared in the jungle. Wondering why the hell he had ever

All of a sudden he remembered Lawton talking about the money from Edward Morgan. The money that had seemingly never reached Idaho.

Leaning forward, he picked up his phone and punched in the extension of his best researcher. "Hi, Linda. Listen, I need you to follow some money...."

Boise National Forest, Idaho

From what Renate had said in the truck, Tom had expected to wind up spending the next few days in a tent. Instead, she drove him to a lodge perched on a mountainside. Well stocked, almost sybaritic in its comforts, clearly designed as a men's hunting hangout... He looked around, shaking his head.

"I don't usually hide out in five-star lodgings."

"You'll be safe here," Renate said. "It's not hunting season, so nobody should come by, and I told the time-share people that we wanted it for a honeymoon."

"Brilliant. Of course, it's a solo honeymoon. Who pays your expense account, anyway?" He could just imagine the Bureau's response if he wanted to stay in a place like this at their expense.

"It's off-season."

That appeared to be the only answer she was going to give him.

She gave him a Glock 9 mm, a stack of clips, a pair of binoculars with night vision capabilities, and a shotgun with a box of shells.

"I thought you said this place was safe."

She gave him a crooked smile. "It is. But if I don't come back in forty-eight hours, you may need to go it on your own. If I don't come back, call this number."

He looked at the card she gave him. "Henley Griswold Importers?"

"Friends. They'll get you out of here."

If he hadn't been so stiff and sore, he might have tried to argue with her. The thing was, he knew perfectly well that he wasn't in good enough shape to be anything but a hindrance.

She went back out to the pickup, then returned with a metal briefcase. She set it before him, worked the combination and opened it up. A metal-cased computer lay inside.

"Here," she said. "You can keep busy with this. You'll find you can access more from here than from your computer at the Bureau."

"Modem?" He looked around.

"Wireless satellite uplink, encrypted."

He looked at her, for the first time getting a serious inkling of this woman's capabilities. She wasn't simply some rogue agent doing her own thing. She had a lot of power behind her, and a lot of money.

She suddenly smiled, as if she had read something on his face. "Don't worry, Law. We're the good guys."

"Law?" Then he remembered his new name: Lawton Caine. "You could at least have let *me* choose."

She was still laughing when she left.

Tom Lawton, alias Lawton Caine, listened to the roar of the pickup's engine as it faded away, leaving him alone in snowbound silence.

His head still felt as if someone were working it over with a sixteen-pound hammer.

Guatemalan Highlands

Terry would be worried sick about her, Miriam knew. And the Bureau wouldn't be able to tell him a damn thing. Radio communications in these mountains were patchy at best, telephones nonexistent.

She lay on the priest's cot, at his insistence. He said

he would sleep in the other room. Probably on the floor, she thought. As rectories went, this hut offered almost nothing in the way of amenities. No running water, an outhouse. Of course, it boasted a second hut for cooking. And it had stucco on the walls, although the roof was thatched.

Toying with a leather pouch that hung around her neck, doubtless put there by the village shaman, she noticed that it was raining again. The rain actually made a nice sound on the thatch.

Restless, she eased herself into a sitting position, wincing as the wound in her side pulled. The *curandera* had given her a couple of coca leaves to chew— something the Bureau would probably fire her for if they knew—and proceeded to stitch up her side. The leg wound had been painful, but minor. Still, there was swelling above the knee, and she had to grit her teeth to bear weight on it.

The coca had long since worn off, and she refused to help herself to the additional leaves the *curandera* had left in a basket by the bed.

Moving gingerly, she attained her feet and limped out into the main room. To her surprise, Father Lorenzo was not asleep. He was sitting in a wooden chair beside a lantern, reading what appeared to be a Bible.

He looked up when he heard her and smiled. "You're feeling better."

"That's a matter of degree," she answered dryly, taking the wooden chair across from him.

"Can I get you something? Pulque? Water? I used those tablets in my drinking water, so it should be safe."

"Water, please."

It was tepid, in a clay mug, with a vague chemical taste to it, but she downed it in one draft. Immediately he brought her another. This one she sipped.

"I was able to get in touch with the Guatemalan police. A man named Pablo. He said to tell you they haven't forgotten you."

"Thank you. How about the others? How many were lost?"

"Two policemen were killed," Lorenzo said. He shook his head sadly. "And seven villagers."

"My God!"

"As for your prisoner..." He hesitated. "I guess he hasn't told them much...yet. From what I know of the *policía*, he will, sooner or later."

Miriam felt her heart lurch. "Father, I can't do anything about it. I'm merely an observer. Are you taking me back to Guatemala City tomorrow?"

"If we survive the night." He sighed and closed the Bible, which he had left lying open on the rickety table beside his chair.

"Ms. Anson, do you have any idea what life is like in most of these mountain villages? The poverty, the death rate, the disease? Most of us in the U.S. would feel hopeless if we lived this way, but these people cling to hope and find joys in the smallest of things. Or perhaps they are the biggest of things. For example, the birth of a healthy child. That's not as common as it should be."

She nodded, listening.

"They have next to nothing. Oh, there are programs to help them learn more effective ways to farm, and to help ensure healthier births, longer lives and less disease. Money funnels into this country. Unfortunately, little of it reaches those who need it most. And as for the programs…it takes a very long time for them to reach everyone."

Miriam nodded.

"Of course, we occasionally receive help from other religious missions. They come here and build churches from which to convert the indigenous population." He snorted. "It would be far more help if they brought food and clothing. Or if they got their hands dirty in the fields teaching better agricultural methods."

"Aren't you a missionary?"

He smiled. "Hardly. This parish dates back three hundred years. It's long past the mission stage. And still only half of these people are Catholic."

"You can live with that?"

"Of course. There are many paths to God, Ms. Anson, not just one. I have even been known to speak of Kulkulcan from my pulpit. He taught some of the same lessons that Christ did."

"You're a rather unusual man."

"I'm just a priest. But these people are in my charge. The curandera has chosen to give you sanctuary, but if the rebels hear of it..." He shook his head. "They are furious about the raid. They want revenge, and they'll get it somewhere. Whether it's here will depend on whether these rebels are prepared to take on Paloma."

"They believe she's powerful?"

"They *know* she's powerful. And she is, Ms. Anson. I suggest you keep that pouch around your neck until you get back to Guatemala City. She wasn't kidding. In these mountains, the jaguar is very powerful."

Miriam sat quietly for a few minutes, mug cradled between her hands. Her leg and side throbbed in time to her heartbeat, and periodically the throbbing rose to the level of pounding. Finally she said, "I feel as if I've stepped off the edge of reality."

The priest nodded. "I felt that way the first time I came here. It's very different from anything we Americans are accustomed to. But you haven't stepped off the edge of reality. What you've done is move into the reality of most of the world's populations."

He rose from his chair and walked over to the window. It was nothing but a rectangular hole in the wall, containing no glass at all, although battered shutters hung there, on the inside. Outside, all was dark, but the dripping of the rain was loud, almost symphonic as it hit various leaves and surfaces.

"You see, Ms. Anson—"

"Miriam, please."

He smiled over his shoulder. "Then call me Steve. The thing is, while the world's great religions claim to be the sole faiths of millions, when you get down to this level you find that much older religious beliefs survive to one extent or another. The world would call Guatemala a Catholic country. So would the Catholic Church. Certainly it would be called Christian, even by the protestant missionaries who come here to save souls from the Catholic Church. But in the villages—on the ground, as it were—other beliefs still hold sway."

"Like the belief in the jaguar."

"The jaguar god. Yes. Paloma comes to Mass every Sunday and every Holy Day. Sometimes she even comes to daily Mass. And while she believes in a single supreme being, that does not prevent her from believing in lesser deities and powers. Spirits, if you will."

He turned to face her. "The first time I was assigned to this village, I was here for eight years. During that time, I came to appreciate her beliefs."

"Doesn't your church believe in demons?"

"That's a matter of some theological dispute these days. Some in my church aren't even sure they believe in Satan."

"Do you?"

He smiled. "Oh, yes, I definitely believe in the Enemy. I have looked into the deadened eyes of a terrible killer and seen the cold emptiness of hell. So yes, I believe. And I believe that for the most part Satan works through us."

"I can accept that. I've certainly seen enough to make me think there might be some…evil influence greater than humanity's foibles."

He nodded. "My Church still performs exorcisms.

Not often, and not easily or quickly, but they still happen. Sometimes there is no other explanation, and no other hope. And sometimes the exorcism results in a cure." He shrugged. "If it works…"

"Yes, if it works, that's all the justification needed."

"Exactly. And I have seen things here…. Suffice it to say, keep wearing the jaguar protection. 'There are more things on heaven and earth…'"

He returned to his seat and regarded her steadily. "I don't know exactly what is happening, Miriam, but I can assure you that Paloma is right when she says you are being manipulated by powers you do not know. There are things happening in this country even now that I have only a vague idea about. But they are big things. Things that could change the course of world history."

Miriam resisted the idea. "Really, Steve, such a small country…"

"It is not the poverty or size of Guatemala that matters," he said. "It is something that is happening here. Something that is important far beyond these borders. A battle that has been going on for thousands of years. And right now, it is focused here."

Miriam returned to bed thinking that Steve Lorenzo had been alone in the jungle too long.

But even so, she had the worst feeling that he might be right.

God, she needed to get out of here and back to Guatemala City, back to the sanity of the twenty-first century.

Just as she was drifting off to sleep, however, a

thought snaked through her mind, cold and clear: The assassination of the ambassador and the shooting of Grant Lawrence had happened awfully close together.

Al Qutayfa, Syria
1123 A.D.

Hugues de Payen studied the dark-skinned man carefully. Hasan ibn al-Sabah was small and wiry, but there was no mistaking the lethal intensity of his gaze. Nor was there any doubt as to the effectiveness of his organization. For over three decades, Hasan's men had struck with impunity, killing and robbing at will. They came out of the night, and sometimes in broad daylight, falling upon their victims with a drug-induced fury that left terror in its wake.

"Salaam aleichem," Hasan said.

"And peace be with you," Hugues replied in flawless Arabic. After ten years, he had learned the language well; only the tiniest trace of his French roots remained in his voice. "So, shall we deal?"

Hugues had founded the Order of the Poor Knights of Christ and the Temple of Solomon—the Knights Templar—on the pretext of providing safety to Christian pilgrims to the Holy Land. The Hassasim, or hashish-eaters, had made that task all but impossible. If Hugues was to secure the financial backers he needed to continue his search, he had to cut a deal with Hasan's band of killers.

Of course, if word of this deal got out, Hugues's life would be forfeit. But he was ready to lay down his life if need be. His quest was that important, for within it lay nothing less than the future of the faith.

"What do you offer?" Hasan asked.

"I respect your zeal," Hugues said. "Our men have met several times. Your men fight well. So do mine. You know that."

Hasan nodded. "We both serve Allah, though you follow another prophet. Your men are indeed skilled. You have shed our blood, and we yours."

"Exactly," Hugues replied. The fact was, Hasan's lightly armed killers relied on stealth and surprise, and were no match for Hugues's knights. Were that not the case, Hasan would never have agreed to this meeting. However, appearances must be kept and respect paid. "And we could go on, year upon year, shedding blood to no purpose, when we both seek a higher goal. What I propose is simple. You will give safe passage to those who travel under the cross. In exchange, my knights will ignore your other operations."

Hasan closed his eyes for a moment, as if thinking, though Hugues knew that he would accept this part of the deal. It was the rest that could create problems, both for Hasan and for himself.

"What else?" Hasan asked.

"You are indeed a wise man," Hugues said. "There is more. I may upon occasion have need of your services. There are those who oppose my quest. Men who want me to fail, who will stop at nothing to protect their power and positions."

"I understand," Hasan said.

Hugues had been sure he would. Hasan, too, had acquired enemies. Even in the Islamic world, there were divisions. Some opposed Hasan's Shiite faith, while others opposed his methods. The Turks were seeking to expand their empire in the southern lands, and Hasan had refused to submit. But he could not risk an open confrontation.

"Of course, in return, my knights might be made available for selected operations," Hugues said. "I am sure you have those whose…end…would serve your needs, but against whom you cannot move directly."

Hasan's dark eyes glittered. "So my men could remove your infidels, and your men could remove mine."

"That would describe it well," Hugues said. "Of course, you would be compensated for any operation."

"And you, as well," Hasan said.

"Donations to my order would not be rejected," Hugues said. "We are, after all, poor and humble knights."

At this, Hasan laughed. "And I am a poor and humble goat herder."

"Precisely," Hugues said. "Have we a deal?"

After a long moment, Hasan nodded. "Yes, I think we can work together."

Hours later, as he lay in the arms of the Arab woman Hasan had provided, Hugues smiled in the darkness. A just God would recognize the sacrifices Hugues had made, including his obligation to accept the gift of the woman lest he offend his host. A just God would recognize that Hugues was serving a higher end, and that sometimes higher ends demanded messy means. A just God would know all of this and reserve for Hugues a special place in heaven.

For now, Hugues was free of the need to protect the pilgrim routes, and he could focus on his primary task, a task that lay buried beneath the ruins of Solomon's Temple. The truth was there. The old legends spoke of it. And he would find it. The true faith would be his legacy.

18

Kevin Willis had known Edward Morgan for a long time—since college, in fact—but he had mixed feelings about the relationship. Sometimes Edward was a great ally. At others he could be a good tool. Right now… Right now Kevin was having some serious problems as he looked over the information that his researcher had returned.

Tom had been right. A quarter million dollars had passed from Ed Morgan to Wes Dixon and disappeared from the face of the earth. But sums like that just didn't disappear.

The researcher, given free rein, had noted that upon his trip from New York to Idaho, Wes Dixon had detoured by way of Atlanta. That alone was unusual, since the ordinary connection would have been made in Chicago or Denver. Atlanta was well out of the way.

Even more interesting was that Wes Dixon had apparently spent the night in Atlanta before continuing to Denver the following afternoon, and thence to Boise.

The obvious conclusion was that Dixon had met someone in Atlanta, then someone else in Denver, but after eighteen months the trail was stone cold. It was unlikely they would find anyone at this late date who would recall Dixon or anyone he might have met.

Still, Kevin picked up the phone again and called Linda. "See if you can find the names of any associates of Wes Dixon who might be living in the Atlanta area."

Then he waited, drumming his fingers on the desktop.

Watermill, Long Island

Feeling entirely too pleased with himself, Ed Morgan made the call to his boss. "Bookworm is dead. I checked it out with the hospital."

"Excellent," said the familiar voice. "We don't want her interfering again."

Her? Suddenly Edward's heart was in his throat. He couldn't possibly tell this man that he had misinterpreted his order. That would be a fatal mistake. After a moment, he cleared his throat. "Uh, yes. Auto accident, head injury. Bookworm died in the emergency room."

"Excellent," the voice said again. "We're all very pleased with you, Morgan. Keep up the good work."

"Thank you." Morgan's hand was trembling as he returned the phone to the cradle. A cold sweat had broken out on his skin. For the first time in his life, he knew unmitigated terror.

Damn it! Bookworm. How the hell was he going to find her now?

Still shaking, he reached for the phone again, this time calling Dixon. "Get everyone out of there," he said, without any hint of greeting. "Now. Your man hit the wrong target."

Dixon Ranch, Idaho

Perched in a tree that gave her a view of the training facility, Renate watched through binoculars as men moved pallets of weapons into an underground bunker. They moved with speed and purpose. These men were well trained and self-disciplined. Not at all the ragged rabble that Tom's FBI file had suggested. A bus marked with the logo of a tour line stood at one end of the training camp, door open.

They were on their way out.

Renate watched for a few more minutes, realizing that the men were almost done with their cleanup and would soon be boarding the bus.

Yes, there. Two men were beginning to load backpacks and rifles into the bus's luggage compartments. The packs didn't worry her nearly as much as the rifles. Where were they going with them?

She had to get out of the tree and back to her vehicle, then around to the ranch's gate so she could follow them and find out where they were going. She tucked the binoculars back into the case and began to work her way down the tree, gloves protecting her hands from the sap.

She had just reached the foot of the tree when a voice said, "Halt!"

She turned slowly, raising her hands, and found herself face-to-face with a man in fatigues. He was pointing a rifle directly at her.

"What are you doing?" he demanded.

At least he wasn't Guatemalan, she thought. Which meant he was someone appointed by Dixon to cover the retreat that was under way. "I'm a bird-watcher," she answered. "For goodness sake, do you have to point that at me?"

The rifle never wavered. "Why were you in the tree?"

"I thought I saw a nest of red-winged bobbinmars. Do you have any idea how rare they are? It would have been the first sighting in this area in over thirty years. Unfortunately, it was only a sparrow's nest."

She pointed upward, as if to show him the nest. He glanced up, and in that split second she was able to step in close, too close for his rifle to be a useful weapon. He started to voice an objection, but never had the chance. She flattened her hand and drove the tips of her fingers into his Adam's apple, turning her hips and shoulders to add the full force of her body to the strike.

His cry died in a gurgle, and he dropped the rifle to grab his throat. That exposed his entire body, and she took immediate and deadly advantage. She continued to move in on him, slamming her knee into his crotch and tipping her head forward. As expected, he began to double over, and his face smashed into her hairline with a crunch of cartilage and bone.

He fell to the ground, writhing in pain, rolling onto his side and curling into a fetal ball. She delivered the coup de grace, a savage kick to the base of his skull. He twitched twice and went limp as his medulla ruptured.

The entire confrontation had lasted less than ten seconds, and he had barely uttered a sound after his first challenge. Still, she knew she had to hurry. Dixon was too organized to let his people wander on their own without checking in. The body would be discovered soon, and once it was, all hell would break loose.

As she made her way back to her pickup, she realized that her situation had become tenuous. So far, she'd been invisible, nonexistent. As far as anyone knew, Tom had been working alone. They would know differently now.

She circled around the Dixon ranch and made her way to a gas station at the intersection of State Roads 52 and 55, in a town called Horseshoe Bend. It was a calculated risk. If the tour bus headed west, she would miss it. But she suspected Dixon would head south to Boise, then take Interstate 84 down through Utah and on toward the Mexican border. It would be his easiest escape route.

She sipped from a bottle of water and fought the

nausea that kept rising within her. She'd been trained to defend herself and to use deadly force if need be. But never before had she killed someone.

The worst part was, it had been sickeningly easy. During her training, she'd always imagined that she would hesitate at the thought of taking a life. But she hadn't. Her training had taken over, and she had moved with swift, ruthless efficiency. *Strike, knee, head butt, kick. Larynx, crotch, bridge of the nose, base of the skull.* In little more than the time it took her to say those words, she had ended a man's life.

Her melancholy reverie was interrupted when the tour bus approached on Route 52. She doubted if anyone would notice a woman sitting in a pickup truck at a gas station. Still, she slid down a bit in her seat. To her surprise, the bus did not turn right and head south toward Boise. Instead, it headed north.

Momentarily confused, Renate asked herself why Dixon would head that way. Then the answer hit her, obvious and simple. Dixon was headed for the border, yes. But not the Mexican border. He was headed for Canada.

19

Guatemalan Highlands

Miriam awoke to the sound of gunfire. As she rolled off of her cot and scrambled for her boots, Steve Lorenzo appeared in the doorway.

"The rebels are here. We must go. Now." To her surprise, he pushed an AK-47 into her hands. "I'm a man of the cloth. But you're not. Let's go. *Now.*"

The ancient church had a back door, past the sacristy, and Miriam followed at a painful jog, still trying to wrap her mind around what was happening. When they emerged, she saw a cluster of women and children, including Paloma, obviously waiting for Lorenzo.

"*Vámonos,*" he told them. He turned to Miriam. "We must go up into the hills. Can you cover our retreat?"

She nodded. "I'll do my best."

Lorenzo led the others up a trail that wound into the rain forest. Miriam stayed behind for a few minutes, found cover and watched the village. Dark-clad men walked from house to house, firing into every room. A young woman emerged from one of the houses, clutching a nursing infant to her breast. The rebels cut her down without hesitation. This was no military attack. This was a massacre.

Every fiber in Miriam's being screamed for her to intervene, to do something to protect those who had been left behind in the village. But she knew it was pointless. She could do nothing for them. She could, however, help save those who had escaped.

Mouthing a silent curse, she turned and headed into the stifling jungle. She caught up with the others within five minutes and took up her place at the rear of the ragged column. From time to time she would halt and let them move on, waiting for the sounds of their passage to be lost in the night, and listen for pursuers. Twice she thought she heard sounds behind them, but she could not be sure if they were human or animal. Only when the sounds did not seem to be approaching did she turn and catch up to the group.

After an hour of steady walking, the group stopped alongside a stream. Miriam accepted the water that was passed around, and sat on a rock, wiping perspiration from her face, the AK-47 between her legs.

Steve approached and sat at her side, shaking his head. "We'll have to do this for days."

Miriam turned to him. "Why? What do they want?"

Steve nodded toward a young man with an assault rifle at his side. "They want him."

Miriam glanced over quickly and saw the man helping a woman feed three young children. "Who is he?"

"Unless I'm wrong," Steve said, "he was involved in the assassination. That's his sister next to him. I gave both of them First Holy Communion, years ago, when I was posted here. I officiated at her Confirmation. Now I fear I will perform their funerals."

"The rebels are cleaning up loose ends," Miriam said.

"Exactly." Tears welled in his eyes. "She told me her village would die."

"This is all so…so…"

Miriam didn't need to finish the sentence.

"Yes," Steve said. "When I was a new priest in Savannah, before I came here, I worried about preparing my homilies for daily Mass. I visited the sick. I fretted over parish budgets and staff squabbles. And I rarely thought about what life is like for much of the rest of the world. Now I ask myself—what is the real atrocity? Is it what just happened in that village, what's happening now? Or is it that I spent years living in the luxury of peace and stability, ignoring the pain and fear and death that stalks so much of the world?"

"And what could you have done?" Miriam asked. "I don't mean to be harsh, but there it is. Yes, you could have fretted about this hour upon hour. You could have filled every homily with mention of the suffering of the poor in war-torn lands. But would that have helped the people of your parish? Would it have helped the people here?"

"So we should just let them murder each other?" he asked. "These people's lives have been ripped apart by Western greed. First the Spanish. Then us. We take what we want and leave them to pick up the pieces. I'm sorry, Miriam, but I can't just shrug that off."

"You heard Paloma, Steve. This is a war that began long before the Spanish arrived. Yes, others have taken advantage of that war. Perhaps even nurtured it for their own interests. But you didn't pull the triggers in that village, Father. Those rebels did that. They chose to do that. And I hate them for it."

Lorenzo reached over and put his hand on her arm. "That is the one thing we can't do. We can't give in to the hate. If we do, everyone loses. And we lose far more than our sensitivities. We lose our souls."

She met his eyes. "Father, forgive my saying so, but let's worry about saving souls later. Right now we're trying to save lives."

Steve simply smiled. "Life is fleeting. The soul is eternal."

"Well," Miriam said, rising to her feet, "if it's all the same to you, I'd rather my life and your life and their lives weren't quite so fleeting. So let's get moving."

He nodded. "Yes. We can discuss this more?"

Her answer died on her lips as she heard the distinctive, rhythmic sound of marching feet.

"Tell the others to find cover," she said, readying her rifle. "And keep them silent."

Steve spoke to Paloma, who began to issue quiet orders. In twos and threes, the villagers disappeared—all except for the young man Father Steve had pointed out to her. He stayed to help sweep away the signs of their passing, and he did it with a professionalism that spoke of a great deal of training.

When she melted back into the jungle, he melted with her and stood at her side.

Right now she couldn't afford to think of him as the murderer she had come looking for. She had instead to think of him as a victim of the rebels. She couldn't allow her task to be clouded by anything.

"You go hide, *gringa*. These are my people. I brought this on them. If anyone should die, it should be me."

She glanced up at him. "You should have thought of that before you killed the ambassador."

In the near-darkness of the rainy jungle, she could barely read his face. But she could make out his tension.

She continued speaking. "People have already died. One of them a woman with a baby. I don't want to see any more die, except these bastard rebels."

The footsteps were drawing nearer, and the two of them quieted as if on signal. Together they crouched in the undergrowth, ignoring rain and insects. Miriam hoped the antimalaria drug she had been taking was still working, although she hadn't had any since yesterday morning.

But the thought was nothing but a slight distraction from the approaching threat. The dampness of the jungle floor muffled the thud of the marching feet. She couldn't tell how many were approaching.

Suddenly she turned toward the youth and signaled for him to backtrack and count how many were coming.

He nodded and slipped away into the undergrowth.

Now all she could do was wait.

Boise National Park, Idaho

Renate wasted no time gathering up Tom—or Law, as she now insisted on calling him—repeating the name with a frequency that left no doubt she was trying to drum it into his head.

"They're headed toward the Canadian border," she told him. "We've got to get going."

The hammer working on his head was hitting with less frequency now, and the throb in his leg was nothing but a miserable nuisance. "That's clever," he said, helping her to collect the guns she had left with him.

"Yes. I expected them to go south."

"Are you sure they didn't see you following them?"

She looked at him, freezing as she did so. "They didn't see me. But they probably know someone saw them departing."

Her eyes looked hollow, he realized. Impulsively, he reached out and clasped her arm. "What happened?"

She shrugged. "I had to kill a sentry."

But her face and, even more so, her eyes belied that shrug. It was tearing her up inside, and she didn't have time to deal with it right now. He knew the feelings so well that his next act was one of pure impulse.

He pulled her to him, heedless of the weapons she held, ignoring the way they pressed into his gut. He hugged her tightly and pressed her face to his shoulder. "I'm sorry," he said. "I'm so sorry."

For a couple of seconds she leaned against him, then she pulled away and resumed packing.

"We need to hurry," she said quietly. "We must catch up before they slip too far away."

Need had clashed with need, and her emotional needs had lost. Such things always had to be dealt with later. Tom wasn't sure that was healthy at all.

He gathered the rest of their gear and followed her out to the truck. Once everything was stowed in the bed under a tarp, they climbed in and headed for the highway.

"They're on a tour bus," she told him as they covered the five miles of dirt road toward the highway. "Headed north. They packed weapons as well as other supplies."

"They won't be able to cross the border with that stuff. Hell, the Guatemalans might not be allowed across the border no matter what, even if they have passports."

"I don't think they're planning to go through a border crossing station."

Tom turned to look at her. "You think they're crossing through the mountains?"

"Probably, if they cross at all. They may just be going into hiding."

"Jeez. It's still winter up north in the mountains. Deep snow, closed roads…"

"I know."

"We aren't outfitted to follow them on foot."

"We will be if we need to be."

Her chin had set; her eyes were locked to the darkening road. Clouds and the mountains dimmed the world early.

"Jesus," he said, thinking of it. He hoped those men didn't try a run through the mountains. He doubted any of them, Guatemalans, Renate or himself, were truly prepared for that.

They came to an abrupt stop at the highway; then, after checking that all was clear, Renate hit the pavement and the accelerator. Much to his surprise, the rattletrap old truck seemed to have a Ferrari engine under the hood. Renate drove as if she were on the autobahn.

Tom decided it might be a good time to have a conversation. He started, of course, by annoying her. At least she wouldn't be thinking about the sentry she'd had to kill.

"Where the hell do you get off giving me a name?"

"You needed to be someone different."

"And where do you get off killing me?"

She barely spared him a glance. Her attention was riveted to the road. "You needed to be dead."

"You don't think it's remotely possible that I could have drawn on my own resources? That I could have called my boss and told him that someone was trying to kill me?"

"You were unconscious, and I had to get you out of that hospital before someone came to finish the job on you."

"Yeah, right."

"I also don't want your FBI involved. It has too many leaks."

Now *this* he really did take exception to. "You don't know what you're talking about!"

"No? Then how did I know your boss was about to put you back on suspension?"

He had no answer for that, and he shifted grumpily in his seat. "Do you realize what I'm doing?"

"Riding in a truck."

"I'm doing a hell of a lot more than riding in a truck. I'm riding in a truck with an admitted killer who has arranged my fake death and turned me into some person I don't know and never wanted to be. I should have you arrested next time we stop."

"Just give it a rest and let your head stop aching."

"My head wouldn't be aching at all if I hadn't fallen in with you. I think you owe me some explanations, or I'm going to blow the lid off whatever it is you're doing. Faking the death of an FBI agent is no joke, either. I could probably see you locked up in a federal prison for a very long time."

"You could. Perhaps."

"Then start talking." Because now, as he thought over this entire thing, he was getting very angry. Mad enough to spit, come to that. Although the facts were different, he was beginning to feel that he was being used in the same way he had been used in L.A. And his aching head and throbbing leg weren't making him any less irritable, especially when she drove as if they were in the Grand Prix and was jolting him around on the truck's tight suspension. "You've got until the next town to convince me I should continue being an accessory after the fact."

She sighed, and her foot pressed down even harder on the accelerator as they raced through a curve. He leaned and nearly groaned out loud as his leg shrieked at him.

"All right," she said finally. "You want to know? I'll tell you, but if you try to tell anyone else, you'll wind up as dead as that sentry. If I don't do it, someone else will."

"How scary," he said sarcastically. "In case you've forgotten, I'm already dead."

"So am I."

Those simple words caused him to stare at her. "Why?"

She was silent for a few moments, as if considering where to begin. "I wasn't always Renate Bächle," she said. "I was born Gretchen Ziegtenbach, in Mannheim. I majored in computer science and accounting at the University of Heidelberg, then became an agent with the Bundeskriminalamt, the BKA. The German equivalent of your FBI."

"I know who they are." His voice had grown quiet, as had his anger. With that one statement from her, things had grown immeasurably clearer.

"Yes. Well." She steered them expertly through another curve. "I was in a task force working on some suspected illegalities in the German banking community. The more I looked, the deeper I got. I stumbled across a group that called itself the Frankfurt Brotherhood."

"Ya gotta worry when they give themselves a name."

She glanced at him. "Yes. You do."

Twilight was beginning to settle, but she left her headlights off. He almost mentioned it, then realized he didn't want to interrupt her story.

"By then we'd wrapped up the initial elements of the investigation. A couple of minor indictments. The task force was disbanded, and I was sent to Köln to begin another assignment. But I was stubborn. I didn't want to let it go. So I continued to look around on my own time. I got into their computer files. I kept digging. The Frankfurt Brotherhood was more than a group of German bankers. Their scope and influence was worldwide. I had gone beyond my official mandate, and my superiors wanted no part of what I had found. After all, these were close associates of the Six Wise Men."

"Who?" Tom asked.

She laughed. "The committee of economic advisors to the German government. We call them the Six Wise Men."

"Important guys," Tom said.

"Very. Their associates are not the sort of people the BKA wants to go after. Especially not on the basis of illegal computer searches. I was told to leave it alone."

"But you didn't."

"No, I didn't," she said, a brief smile flickering over her features. "I started to leak information about them to the media. Things they would not wish to have known. I was hoping I could force them out into the open, or at least clip their wings. Instead, they killed me."

Her eyes grew distant for a moment. "The Schwarzwald is such a lovely place, Law. The Black Forest. The Alps. The headwaters of the Rhine. My family moved there when I was ten, and I went there often on weekends to visit them and play poker. My father was a dealer, and later a floor manager, at a casino. My media contact liked baccarat. We exchanged information in the bar."

"And these Frankfurt Brotherhood guys found out?"

She nodded. "They ran my car off the road as I was driving back to Köln. It was a twisting mountain road, with a steep gorge off to the side. I jumped free as my car began to tumble, and landed in a thicket of trees. My car tumbled on into the gorge and exploded."

"Cars don't do that except in movies," Tom said.

"You're right," she replied. "Unless someone has rigged the gas tank. Which they had."

Tom put up a hand. "But there was no body in the car. The killers would have known."

"Yes." Her eyes misted for a moment. "If there had been no body in the car, they would have known."

Suddenly it became clear. "Your contact."

She nodded. "She had been my best friend all

through high school. She was afraid, so she'd left her car in Stuttgart. She didn't…we didn't think they would kill a BKA agent. So she hid in the back seat. I was going to drop her off on my way back."

"I'm sorry."

"Yes."

She drove on in silence for a few minutes. He tried to think of something to say, and realized any comfort he attempted would be rejected. He settled on prompting her to continue the story.

"So you became someone else?"

"Yes. As it turned out, I had gained the attention of another organization, as well. They gave me a new identity. And a new life." She hesitated and looked at him. "We are called Office 119."

"And who's this 'we'?" he asked.

"After the September 11 attack," she said, "the world was focused on terrorism. Many countries had far more experience in dealing with it than the U.S. Some of them didn't think the U.S. would handle it well, so words were whispered in the United Nations. Arrangements were made. Money was found. Office 119 was established. All of this was very quiet. Invisible. We don't officially exist.

"The founders had contacts in the world's major law enforcement agencies. They began to identify and track people who seemed capable. People who had operated on their own initiative in researching or investigating these kinds of criminal conspiracies. They had found me. They heard about the accident, and found an anonymous woman in a German hospital. Me. They recruited me."

"Like you've recruited me," Tom said, realization hitting him like a punch to the stomach. "None of this was accidental. If Wes Dixon hadn't accommodated you by trying to kill me, you'd have found another way."

"Yes," she said. "I would have. Every Office 119 agent is officially dead. We don't exist. We have no families. No home country. No politically motivated superiors. No nationalist agendas. Our sole allegiance is to the United Nations. To the people of the world."

Suddenly she jammed on the brakes, bringing them down to a more reasonable speed. "There they are."

Tom looked ahead and saw the bus ahead of them, traveling briskly toward the edge of what appeared to be a small town.

"There's a map in the glove compartment," Renate said. "Get it out. We can't lose them. And we can't get lost."

Tom found the road atlas and opened it to the map of Idaho. "I saw a sign for Grangeville a few miles back. This must be it ahead."

"So," Renate said, slowing as they neared a roadside diner, "do I let you out here? Do you want to return to your old life and try to dance in the straitjacket of the FBI? Or do we keep driving?"

Tom had no doubt that everything she had said was

true. Including the part about dancing in a straitjacket if he returned to Washington. He'd pressed on with a case he'd been told to drop, and he could give no explanation that would not compromise Renate. At best he would be sent to some backwater field office. More likely, he would be out of a job, and if Wes Dixon and Ed Morgan found out he was alive, he would spend the rest of his life looking over his shoulder, waiting for them to clean up a very loose end.

He looked into her eyes and for the first time saw beneath the predatory glint to the pain she had endured, the sacrifices she had made. A lifelong friend had died in her place. She had left behind a family she could never again visit. Now he understood why she had buried her emotions. Thinking about her past would do nothing except lead to a mistake, and in her profession, mistakes could be fatal. So she lived in the moment, focused on her mission, ignoring the self-desiccated desert of her heart.

Was that how he wanted to live?

But there was something else in her face, he saw. A sense of purpose. A clarity. A freedom. An anger that he recognized all too well, mated with a mission and the means to achieve it.

He remembered his mother wasting away with cancer, his father's death in jail. He remembered the screams of a twelve-year-old girl, betrayed on a beach in California. He remembered the shock he'd felt when Grant Lawrence was shot, and the pain he'd seen etched on Miriam's face as she listened to the description of his wounds in the briefing.

Suddenly, irrationally, Tom assigned the blame for all those memories to Wes Dixon and his financial backers. Too many good people had suffered because of their machinations and secret cabals. Too many lives had been ruined.

He looked at Renate again.

"Keep driving."

20

Guatemalan Highlands

Miriam felt more than heard the young man's return. He moved with the silence of a jungle cat, and once again she had to admit a grudging admiration for his training.

"Twelve men," he said almost soundlessly. "They have split into two columns. They know these mountains and this stream. I think they expected that we might stop, and have split up to surround us."

"They're good," she said.

"*Sí, gringa.* They are very good. If they were coming in one column, we might ambush them. But like this…"

He didn't have to finish the thought. Any plan of an ambush was now gone. They had to get the villagers out of the trap before the rebels closed in.

"Tell the others," she said. "Get them across the stream and farther into the jungle. Just a couple hundred meters will do. Let the rebel jaws close on empty space. Then we have a chance."

His smile sent chills down her spine. *"Sí. Está correcto. Voy ahora."*

Even Miriam's rudimentary Spanish, gleaned over the past weeks, allowed her to understand clearly. *Yes. That is correct. I go now.* He had been testing her, seeing if she was fit for the task the priest had assigned her. She had passed.

He melted into the jungle, and she heard quiet rustling as the others moved away behind her. Blinking her eyes against the rivulets of sweat, she waited until their rustling had died and she judged that they were safely across the stream and out of the trap. Then she belly crawled backward, listening for sounds of the rebels' approach, until she felt a hand on her back.

"They are close," the young man whispered. "Come. This way."

She followed him, silently cursing her relative clumsiness. He was accustomed to this terrain and could slip through it as easily as a mountain breeze. She seemed to catch every thorn, get tangled in every patch of brush.

After what seemed like an eternity, she leaned back against cool, damp stone at the site he had selected. It was a good spot, on a knoll overlooking the clearing where the path intersected the stream. They had both concealment and surprise in their favor. The rebels had numbers. She wondered how the competing advantages would weigh against each other, but only for a moment.

The young man touched her arm and nodded toward the far side of the clearing. A branch stirred, and then another. Slowly, patiently, she scanned the thick undergrowth for signs of movement. Three. Four. Five. And, yes, there was the sixth.

She glanced over for a moment and saw that he was tracking the approach of the other group. Identifying his targets. Waiting for the right moment.

"I have them all," she whispered.

"I do, too," he said. "Let them reach the clearing. They will stop to discuss what to do next."

"Yes," she said.

"You know what to do then," he said. "Don't hesitate. They are paper targets, moving in the breeze."

She had heard the same words at Quantico, during her training. Dehumanizing words. She had hoped she would never have to act on those words. And while she'd shot a man once before, that man had been firing at Grant Lawrence, whose kidnapped children she had just rescued. This was different. These men weren't shooting at anyone. She forced herself to remember the woman clutching the baby to her chest as bullets shredded them.

Paper targets, moving in the breeze.

The rebels had reached the clearing, querulous looks on their faces. One spoke. Another answered. They moved closer. Closer.

Now.

She squeezed the trigger and felt the kick of the stock against her shoulder as she focused on paper targets moving in the breeze. Watched, as if from high above, as they spun and tumbled, mouths flying open, arms flailing. The scent of cordite biting her nostrils. The clatter of the young man's rifle mixing with her own, ringing in her ears. The ping of brass shells ejected onto rock. The brief cries as the paper targets fluttered to the ground and lay still.

"Está terminado," he said, placing his hand atop her rifle.

Her hand still clenched the grip, her finger tensed on the trigger. Paper targets littered the ground. She pulled her eyes away and met his.

"Está terminado," he repeated. *"Vamos."*

Yes, she thought, unable to look back at the clearing. *It is finished. Let's go.*

Grangeville, Idaho

It had been chilly in Boise, given that it was only April, but neither Renate nor Tom was prepared for the arctic cold that had apparently pushed its way into the northern part of Idaho. To step out of the truck was to step into a meat locker. At once noses and fingers began to tingle, and within moments earlobes were aching.

That didn't keep them from creeping alongside the deserted campground road to find out what Wes Dixon's group was doing. At this time of year the rangers weren't even out to collect fees. The gate was open, and a sign announced lack of facilities until the campground officially opened in May.

They left the truck at the gate and walked into the

campground, following bus tracks carved into several inches of otherwise unmarked snow. They walked well off to one side, so their passing wouldn't be noticed by anyone on the bus when Dixon moved on. It wasn't long before they heard sounds, and a few minutes after that, through the thick trees, they could see that tents were being erected.

Worse, they could see that all of the men were dressed for the weather in camouflage parkas and gloves.

Rachel tapped Tom's shoulder and indicated with a jerk of her head that they should go back to the truck. Tom was glad to oblige. The wound in his leg was blessedly numb from the cold, but the other parts that were growing numb concerned him.

They crept back the way they had come, even stepping in their own footprints. Not that so much care was probably necessary, Tom thought when they reached the truck. It had begun to snow heavily.

"Okay," Renate said. "We're going to need some serious cold-weather gear."

"You get that feeling, too?"

She flashed him a glittery smile. "I just hope they're planning to stay at this campground all night. I've never used snowshoes, but I'm fairly good at Nordic skiing."

By that he presumed she meant cross-country skiing, not downhill. He was fairly good at that, too, from his youth in Michigan. But in mountains like the Rockies...well, it was probably a very different kettle of fish. It might be smarter to learn how to use snowshoes.

Renate backed slowly out to the highway, then headed away from the park. Before long they were back in Grangeville, where they found an outfitter's store.

She pulled into a spot in front of the store and they went inside, to find the owner alone, sitting at his cash register in the back, reading a book on conspiracy theories. He looked up and greeted them with a big "Howdy," though he didn't smile.

Tom recognized the look immediately: small-town suspicion of outsiders. He also knew how to deal with it. Affecting a mild Southern accent, he extended a hand and said, "Howdy, I'm Lawton Caine. Brrr. Do y'all grow this cold yourselves, or import it from Canada?"

The man chuckled and took his hand. "Burt Reynolds. No, no relation. My mother was a starstruck fan. Nah, this here is homegrown cold. When it comes in from Canada, you have to thaw out your bladder to pee. So what can I do for you?"

Tom had glanced at his wares on the way in and held slim hope that they would find what they needed. The store was stocked for the summer activities that were right around the corner.

"We're looking for some winter gear," he said. "My wife and I are visiting up here and thought we might do a little hiking. Don't see this kind of weather in Georgia."

"I've got that stuff in the storeroom," the owner told them genially. "Holding on to it for next fall. Come on back with me and we'll get you outfitted. I've got the best of everything for winter hiking and skiing."

He leaned toward them a bit as he opened the door to the back. "A lot of survivalists in the mountains around here. When they buy, they want the best."

"If it comes to that," Tom said, "we're all going to need the best."

"You got that right," the man replied.

Before long, Tom was holding winter camouflage parkas and snow pants, boots with replaceable felt liners, and a box of replacement liners.

"Here," Reynolds said, relieving Tom of the heap. "Let me go put this on the counter out front. You two just keep looking. Don't miss those survival blankets. And those tents in the corner? They fold up to nothing, weigh only a couple of pounds and give the best wind protection you can get. Come in one- and two-man sizes."

Renate nodded and started building yet another stack. Backpacks, canteens, one two-man tent, Mylar survival blankets, some flares, dried food, and two pairs of cross-country skis with boots, binders and poles.

"What happened to traveling light?" Tom asked a little while later as they loaded the truck.

Renate looked at him. "This *is* light if we're going to be out in the woods. I know this kind of weather. It will kill you if you're not prepared."

Half an hour later, Renate was booking them into as sleazy a motel as he had ever stayed in.

"You just stretch out on the bed and save that leg," she told him. "I'll bring everything in."

"No, I'll help."

She turned to him, her gaze as hard as twin chips of blue flint. "No, you will not. I'm not letting your masculine ego get in the way of finishing this job. You need to save that leg in case you have to spend all day tomorrow walking on it."

He gave up. The German duchess had spoken.

He had to admit, though, that it felt good to stretch his leg out on a level surface. The throbbing eased almost at once. And the pillow beneath his head was so soft....

He drifted off to sleep without realizing it.

He awoke an hour or so later to see Renate packing the knapsacks on the other double bed. She certainly seemed to know what she was doing.

She apparently noticed he was awake, because she began to talk. "I used to spend a lot of time hiking in the Schwarzwald and the Alps. I learned how to pack one of these things the hard way."

"Blisters?"

"Mostly a shrieking back. Balance is important."

"Yes, it is."

"Do you hike?"

"Sometimes. The Appalachian Trail."

She smiled. "Good. You know how."

"I don't generally do it in snow."

At that she laughed. "Do you know how to ski?"

"Some. I did it as a kid, in Michigan."

"You'll remember quickly," she said. "Dixon needs to get out of the country with his men. I doubt the Guatemalans will know how to ski, so they'll probably be moving slowly once they have to abandon their bus. We'll have the advantage there, provided we're not seen. We need to keep tabs on them and pick a good spot for the FBI to take them down."

"We're taking them down?" he asked.

"No. That would be pointless. Office 119 has no legal jurisdiction. We rely on local authorities to make arrests. But I want to pick the place. A place where our well-armed friends will be least likely and least able to resist. Once we've done that, we'll have to get the information to your old colleagues, without them knowing where it came from."

"I think I can do that," he said. "I know what words and phrases to use to catch their attention. Even with an anonymous tip."

He watched her continue to organize the backpacks and realized that she hadn't bought as much as he had thought at the store. Everything was fitting snugly away, leaving ample room for more, even as the stacks on the bed diminished. She was very good at this. Even had room for changes of underwear and the thick white socks that had been one of her purchases.

She glanced at her watch and said, "Oh!"

"What?"

"I need to go get us some dinner before it is too late. I'll be back shortly."

Grabbing her new parka, she disappeared through the door. A moment later he heard the truck engine turn over. Yes, it *did* purr like a Ferrari. This woman was full of endless surprises.

Putting his hands behind his head, he stared up at the water-stained ceiling and thought about what he'd seen so far. She seemed to have a free hand in what she did, and a boundless budget. It was very different from what he'd dealt with.

Not that he wanted to go outside the law, but being part of a huge governmental bureaucracy caused a lot of problems. Layers upon layers of command combined to bollix up too many operations. Then there were the budgetary restrictions, sometimes to the point that agents paid for some items themselves rather than wait for the Bureau to put through a voucher.

On the other hand, staying with Renate would mean leaving behind everyone he knew. Thinking of Miriam and Terry, he felt a deep pang. They had been good friends, and had gone above and beyond the call in caring for him since L.A. Allowing them to think he was dead seemed like a betrayal.

He sighed and continued to stare at the ceiling as if the water stains might rearrange themselves and spell out some kind of cosmic answer. He would have to ask Renate about these things. Surely she had had friends whom she'd left behind, as well as her family in Freiburg.

How did she deal with their grief? And her own guilt?

Bottling his feelings and freezing them in a glacier was not an option. Somehow, he would have to make peace with the decisions he was making. Otherwise he would eat himself alive. He'd done it before. He didn't want to do it again.

If he was going forward with her, he needed to be clear and sharp. Of that much he was certain. If only the water stains on the ceiling could talk.

Watermill, Long Island

Edward Morgan didn't at all like the tone of voice he was hearing from his contact on the other end of the line.

"His shield and personal effects are being shipped back to me," the voice said. "You didn't have anything to do with that, did you, Edward?"

"What are you talking about?"

"You've been asking about him for weeks. Now he's dead. Are you going to tell me you don't know anything about it?"

Righteous anger rose in Edward Morgan, as it always did when he was questioned. It didn't matter whether he was in the right—right and wrong had ceased to matter to him so long ago that righteousness was his response any time he was angered. "Don't you dare talk to me in that tone."

"What?" The voice on the other end was quiet for a moment, then a chuckle filled the line. "My old friend, have you forgotten you're merely mortal like the rest of us?"

"What do you mean? Are you threatening me?"

"I don't need to threaten you. But if you think our current relationship has given you any importance beyond what you had when we first met one another, you're sadly mistaken. And I'd better not find out that you had anything to do with the death of Tom Lawton."

"Of course I didn't!"

"Hmm. We'll see, won't we?"

Morgan hung up, shaking again. He'd been shaking entirely too much lately. Instead of pouring his usual drink, he went to the liquor cabinet and got out the Irish Cream, filling a tumbler with it.

Things were beginning to feel very much out of his control, and he needed to figure out how to get them back within his grasp before everything he had worked for exploded in his face.

Kevin Willis would have to be sacrificed.

21

Dos Pilas, Guatemala

Miriam followed the column almost woodenly, putting one foot in front of the other, listening to the jungle behind them for sounds of pursuit. The constant climbing had aggravated the severely bruised muscles around her knee, and her side was aching, as well. But she had to press on. She had no doubt there were other rebel forces looking for them. To stop meant to invite the rebels to overtake them. And that would mean more killing.

For the past five hours, she'd fought a battle with her conscience. The young man, whom she now knew as Miguel, had offered a couple of comforting looks at rest breaks, but she found little comfort in his eyes. He was, after all, the man who had cold-bloodedly murdered the U.S. ambassador. He had too much blood on his own hands to wipe the blood from hers.

They had branched off the trail twenty minutes earlier, and now they waded through chest-deep undergrowth. Miriam tried not to think about what might be concealed in the deep tropical forest. Instead, she focused on lifting one foot and then the other, repeating the process into what had come to seem like infinity.

The woman in front of her turned and put a finger to her lips. The column went silent as they skirted around a clearing and edged their way toward what looked to be the ruins of an ancient city. After another half hour, they had wound around to the far side of the ruins and settled into a sheltered clearing two hundred meters into the jungle.

Miguel joined her for a moment. "You are a good soldier," he said.

"Thanks, I guess," she said.

"No." He put his hand on her arm. "You did what any soldier is trained to do. You are a good soldier."

"Where did you train?" she asked. What she had seen was no haphazard assortment of farmers who had taken up arms. "Where did the rest of the rebels train? In the Guatemalan Army?"

"In your country," he said in heavily accented English.

She gripped his arm in turn. "Tell me where. You know you can't return to the rebels. God knows how you're going to survive if they keep looking for you. But you can help keep others from stepping into your shoes."

His dark eyes burned. "They will keep stepping in my shoes because of the way we are treated. And I will be arrested by you, and my village will be safe again. So I have nothing to say."

"You have plenty to say," she told him, her jaw tight.

"Listen, Miguel. You tell me who trained you, and I'll go back to Guatemala City and tell them you died out here."

His head jerked back. "Why?"

"Because you're being used, Miguel. You and all your fellow rebels. I want the people who are using you."

"We would fight anyway," he argued.

"Perhaps so. But at least you'd be fighting for your *own* purposes rather than for someone else's. Think about it, Miguel. Why are they running a training camp for you? Don't you ever wonder?"

He was silent for a long, long time. Miriam bit her lip, and forced herself to let go of him and wait.

After what seemed like an eternity, he lifted his eyes. "I trained in Idaho," he said. "One of your former army men has a big ranch there. He gives us weapons and trains us. I do not know his name."

Miriam sagged back against a rock, still looking at Miguel. By damn, Tom had been on to something. Miguel might not know Wes Dixon's name, but she did. Suddenly she was desperate to get back to Washington.

"I'll tell them all you're dead, Miguel. So change your name, and look after your sister and her family."

He nodded, his chin setting. "I will look after all my people. I brought this on them, now I owe them."

Paloma approached her as she sat on a log and tried to massage the pain from her knee.

"*Caliente, sí?*"

"Yes," Miriam said, nodding. "It's very hot."

The woman nodded and placed her hands on Miriam's knee, feeling around the tissue, pressing. Miriam stifled a cry as her fingertips prodded the bruised area. The Mayan smiled and dug into a pouch at her belt, then held out a small clutch of dried leaves on her palm.

"She's offering you medicine for the swelling," Steve Lorenzo said, joining them. "It's quite harmless. It's an herbal analgesic."

Miriam nodded and took the leaves, unsure of what to do next. "Do I eat them?"

Paloma laughed quietly, and Steve shook his head. "Soak them in water first, then hold them in your cheek," he said. "It will feel a bit strange at first, but it's good medicine. Just don't swallow the leaves. They wouldn't harm you, but they would upset your stomach."

"*Gracias,*" Miriam said, smiling at Paloma.

The old woman looked around, as if feeling the vibrations of the jungle. She spoke in Spanish, and Steve translated.

"The end started here," he said. "The end of a great people."

"Where are we?" Miriam asked.

"Dos Pilas," Steve said. "It was once a small but prosperous trading city. She says this was over a thousand…fifteen hundred years ago. Two great kingdoms were to the north—Mutul and Calakmul. They were…

I guess the closest word would be *superpowers*. They were at war, and this city was important to both of them, because it was the gateway to the wealthier cities in the south."

"A pawn," Miriam said.

"Exactly." Steve listened as the woman continued, then picked up the translation. "The trade moved along the Pasión River, she says. Jade and obsidian, quetzal feathers and shells. The Pasión is the river we have been traveling near all day, where you fought the battle earlier."

Miriam nodded, not wanting to think of what had happened as a battle. It had been an ambush, then a massacre. She fought down the images and listened.

"The king of Mutul sent his young brother, only four years old, to be the ruler here. Balaj Chan K'awaii was the boy's name. He remained loyal to his brother until the armies of Calakmul captured this city. Then he served that king, fighting under his banner, and waged war upon his older brother at Mutul. The war lasted for ten years, and finally K'awaii won and destroyed Mutul. He brought his brother and the other members of the royal court back here, and slaughtered them all. Their skulls were piled up, and he danced in a pool of their blood."

Miriam shuddered. "This is legend, right? Oral history?"

Steve translated the question, and a smile broke out on Paloma's face. The woman dug into a bag and pulled out a tattered copy of *National Geographic*. Steve laughed and translated.

"Not legend. She learned it from our books. Her people simply speak of this as the place of betrayal. The place where the beginning ended and the end began. It was those wars that destroyed the great Mayan cities. People fled for their lives, into the jungles. When brother kills brother, only the blood of the dead remains."

Miriam nodded. "She's right, unfortunately."

Paloma spoke again, and Steve translated. "She asks when are you going to take the medicine. She says your knee will swell up more the longer you wait."

Miriam smiled and poured a bit of water into her hand, working the leaves until they became damp, then tucked them into her mouth. The taste almost made her gag, and the old woman laughed.

"She says this is the way it must be," Steve says. "It's only good for you if it tastes bad."

"Tell her she sounds like my mother," Miriam said.

He translated, and Paloma let out a cackle that echoed through the trees. She patted Miriam on the head and left to join the rest of the group.

"So this stuff really works?" Miriam asked.

He nodded. "Yes, it does. You'd be surprised how many of our 'modern' medicines are derived from ancient tropical remedies. Those leaves have a chemical compound that's very similar to aspirin. And aspirin itself was first derived from birch bark. The native peoples used to chew it to relieve pain. The *curanderas* are not witch doctors, Miriam. They simply know the medicines in their environment."

"Well, it tastes bad enough to be medicine," she said.

He looked at her. "That's not the only bad taste in your mouth, though, is it?"

"You mean what happened earlier," she said. "Is it that obvious?"

"Miguel told me about it. He said you fought well."

"Coming from him…" she said, not needing to finish the sentence.

"We may disapprove of his past actions," Steve said, "but he knows a good soldier when he sees one. From what he told me, I agree with his assessment. But that doesn't make it any easier on the soul, does it?"

"He said something I hadn't heard since Quantico. 'Think of them as paper targets moving in the breeze.' And that's what I did. But they weren't paper targets. They were human beings." She looked down for a moment. "I guess this is where I'm supposed to say 'Forgive me, Father, for I have sinned'?"

"If you like. Are you Catholic?"

She shook her head. "My parents were Episcopalian. Now I go to a Baptist church. With Terry."

"Terry?"

She smiled wistfully. "Terry Tyson. My I-wish-he'd-go-ahead-and-propose-already partner. He's a homicide cop in D.C. We're going on two years now, but he's still dealing with the death of his wife."

"You're impatient with him?" he asked.

"I don't know if that's the right word," she replied. "I understand his grief. They were married for twenty-seven years. That's not a switch you can flick off. He needs time."

"And still you stay with him."

She nodded. "I love him. I know I'll never replace her. I don't want to replace her. I just want to be with him. He makes me smile. He makes me laugh. And he makes me feel beautiful. What more can a girl ask for?"

"A clean slate?" he suggested.

"Are you saying…?"

He put up a hand. "Not at all. The two of you seem to be well-matched. But we all want to look forward, not back. He looks back to his wife. You look back to this afternoon. If the two of you keep looking backwards, you will never see the future together."

"So I should just forget about it?" she asked. "I'm sorry, Father. I can't do that."

"No, you can't. And you shouldn't. But you need to understand it, Miriam. What you did, you did to protect these people. Women and children. Innocents. I'm not saying it was right. And I won't say it was wrong. It was *necessary*. Blood was going to be shed, no matter what you did. These people's blood. Your blood. My blood. Or the rebels' blood. I don't think a loving God can condemn you for that."

"He might not have to, Father. What if I condemn myself?"

"Then," he said, "you have committed the worst sin of all. You have put yourself above God. Let God be God, Miriam. You're not qualified for the position, and even if you were, it's not available."

She nodded. She hadn't thought about it that way, but what he said made sense. It didn't ease the ache in her heart, but it filled a void in her mind. Finally she looked at him and spoke. "Forgive me, Father, for I have sinned."

He moved closer and placed his hands on her head, speaking in a voice of solemn conviction. "God, in his infinite mercy, has granted unto us the gift of his forgiveness, purchased by the sacrifice of his own son. By the power vested in me through the sacrament of Ordination, and with the promise of God's eternal love and mercy, I absolve you in the name of the Father, the Son and the Holy Spirit. Go and sin no more."

Miriam felt the tears sting her cheeks. She scrubbed them away with the heel of her hand. Nearly a minute passed before she trusted herself to speak. "Thank you, Father."

"It is my honor and my duty," he said. Then he cracked a quick smile. "Or, to put it in common language, just doing my job, ma'am."

Which raised an interesting question, and one she had never stopped to ask. "So, Father, what exactly are you doing here?"

"Ah." He looked away from her into the depths of the darkening jungle. "I suppose, being non-Catholic, you wouldn't be aware that we priests, particularly ordinal priests, go where we're told."

"I'm aware of that. I'm also aware when someone is evading a question."

His gaze met hers. "FBI training?"

"That or women's intuition."

He sighed and sat on the boulder beside her, watching the others gather their children close and feed them what little they'd been able to take away with them, along with wild bananas and other fruits they had collected en route.

"I'm not supposed to discuss it," he said.

"Don't you think we've had a few too many secrets lately? Look at Miguel. What secrets drove him to kill a man he'd never met?"

"His father was hanged by the army. The army was supported by the U.S. There's a trail of logic in there."

Miriam sighed. "So what's the logic of you being here? You said something about working here years ago and then going to Savannah."

"Well, actually, I went to Rome between here and Savannah." He looked thoughtful. "Rome was where my life took a turn, I guess you could say."

"What kind of turn?"

"I used to think I knew. Now I'm not as certain."

Miriam waited patiently. The distasteful wad was still stuck in her cheek, but the throbbing in her leg was easing. As night began to settle over them, a night that would be without fire or protection from rain, it felt as if she had all the time in the world to wait for the priest to speak.

"In Rome I was persuaded by a friend to join a group dedicated to preserving the true faith. They are called the Stewards of the Faith. It all seemed quite innocent at the time, to devote oneself to defending the Church from lies and half-truths, to dedicate oneself to living the gospels."

"But it's not innocent?"

"I don't know. At times I'm not so certain anymore. You see, Miriam, I have an extraordinary curiosity. It's not unheard of in a Jesuit, but it often gets us into trouble. When I left Rome, renewed and fervent in my faith, and returned to my home in Savannah, I began to do some deep study. Have you heard of the Nag Hammadi gospels? The Gnostic Gospels?"

Miriam nodded. "Vaguely. Aren't they supposed to have been written by other Christian groups?"

"It gets a little more complex than that. The early days of the church were a time of great argumentation among apostles and the sees they founded. The bishops were often at odds." He smiled crookedly. "Even the apostles themselves couldn't quite seem to agree on what Jesus had taught. In the end, the Church decided to acknowledge only four Gospels. Three, those of Matthew, Mark and Luke, are considered to be synoptic, in that they give a synopsis of the life of Christ, and all three seem to derive from a common source, referred to as Q. It's pretty clear they were written by the last quarter of the first century, so they weren't too far removed from Christ's time."

Miriam nodded. This was something she'd never heard before, and it was fascinating.

"And then there was John, quite unique and, unlike the others, slanted against the claim that Peter was appointed to head the church. But that's a minor detail right now. It was accepted. It fit well enough. But a bunch of other gospels and writings, called 'apocryphal,' were discarded and basically lost until first century copies of them were discovered at Nag Hammadi."

"Okay, I follow."

"Tell me if I bore you." He smiled. "Suddenly we had fragments of other gospels again. A gospel of Mary Magdalene, of Thomas, of Philip... I read all of these, Miriam. They were quite clearly influenced by eastern religions. Some of them I felt were so far out of line with anything Jesus could have said that I wondered at their authors. But the contents don't matter. The study simply led me to start wondering a bit about what I'd always held to be the true faith. Mistakes may have been made. Politics were certainly involved. But they didn't strike at the core of my belief in Jesus, the crucifixion or the resurrection."

She nodded. "I'm sure they wouldn't strike at mine."

He looked at her. "But there's this one little detail that kept coming through."

"Which is?"

"That Jesus was married to the Magdalene, and that they had a child."

Miriam drew a sharp breath. "Um…"

"I know. I felt quite the same way. But there are Mayan legends that…seem to corroborate it."

"So that's why you're here? To find and demonstrate proof that Christ was married?" She was stunned.

"No, my dear. Others are seeking to do that. I was sent here to find it first. And destroy it. The Church has many enemies, Miriam. Some have been around nearly since its inception, and they continue to this day. Living in the shadows. Waiting for the moment to strike. And when they do…"

"Religious chaos," Miriam said, clearly seeing the implications. "It might start a war."

He shook his head. "Not just *a* war. The *last* war. Armageddon."

22

Dos Pilas, Guatemala

It had begun to rain again, a soft rain that pattered on the leaves over their heads. In the growing darkness, families settled down to sleep, wrapped in colorful blankets that doubled as part of their clothing. Little children fussed for a while, then fell silent.

Steve and Miriam were still sitting on the boulder, an ominous silence enveloping them as she struggled with what he had earlier said. For nearly half an hour now, Steve had sat with his head bowed in silent prayer. Sometimes his lips barely moved; other times he was as still as a saint gripped in ecstasy. She envied him a depth of faith that could bring him to this place to minister to these people under such trying circumstances. She was here by accident, and steadily growing more aware of her need for a hot shower and a hot meal. She could never do what Steve Lorenzo was doing.

Finally he lifted his head and crossed himself. His

prayer was done. He looked at her. "I'm sorry, I forgot to grab blankets for us."

"Frankly, I'd suffocate under a blanket. I'm not used to this heat and humidity. It's actually nice to feel my clothes starting to get wet. In fact, if we get a downpour, I'll be wishing for a bar of soap."

He smiled, his teeth gleaming in the little bit of light that still managed to penetrate the jungle canopy. "The higher we go, the cooler it will get. We may yet regret our lack of blankets."

"I'll take my chances. Listen, Steve…what you said about Armageddon… Isn't that rather extreme? I mean, I've been sitting here thinking that it wouldn't affect my faith at all to know that Jesus had married. That he had a child. Why not? It's what everybody did in those times."

"True. Some scholars argue that he would not have been granted the title of rabbi if he hadn't wed. That only married men could be teachers of the faith."

"So then…"

"But the problems continue from that, Miriam." He sighed quietly. "Where to begin? It is all so complex."

"Pick a spot. I'll follow you in circles if necessary."

He gave a quiet laugh. "All right. Let us start with the Middle East. We are already at war there, and many Muslims regard that as a Fourth Crusade, an attempt to exterminate Islam."

"Extreme."

"Maybe not so extreme. Put yourself in their shoes. The U.S. has supported Israel since the beginning, at great cost to surrounding Arab nations in terms of land and the Palestinians. We also need their oil. Perhaps we think it would be easier to get it if we just simply removed all opposition in the form of Islam."

"What a horrible thought."

"I quite agree with you. To make matters worse, there are some in our country who *do* want a Fourth Crusade. They follow the doctrine of Dominionism."

"I don't follow you," Miriam said.

"These people believe that the United States has been anointed by God to establish a new Christian dominion in this world, to prepare the way for the Second Coming. It's a Calvinist philosophy that has gained a great deal of strength with the rise of the radical religious right. In fact, many scholars, especially abroad, consider the United States to be a radical fundamentalist nation, little different from the Islamic nations we are fighting. And they have strong evidence to support their views."

She nodded. "I've heard some of the talk since the 9/11 attacks, but I've always thought it was extremists."

He shrugged. "Extremists sometimes gain power, either visibly or invisibly. It's happened somewhat in Israel, as well, with the rise of their ultraright factions. They worked to free Jewish terrorists who tried to blow up the Dome of the Rock, on the Temple Mount. They believed that the terrorists were serving the will of God, because the Islamic shrine must be destroyed so the

Temple can be rebuilt to usher in their Messiah. And most of those prisoners—terrorists, as judged by the Israeli courts—have indeed been freed."

He paused and stirred the ground with his foot. "So we have three strains of fundamentalism fighting for religious and economic dominance. Suffice it to say the Middle East is extremely unstable and a hotbed of anger."

"I'll agree with that."

"It wouldn't take much of a spark to set it all into a conflagration."

"But how does Jesus's marriage come into this?"

"Let me take a step back and talk a bit about the Koran. Muslims believe that the Koran was given to Muhammad in its entirety. They also believe that Jesus was a great prophet, who spoke the word of Allah, as did earlier prophets. Muhammad spoke of Christians, Jews and Muslims as people of the book. In short, the old revelations were not cast aside. You might think that this would be a great point for understanding."

"Well, yes." Miriam shifted as her leg began to throb again. Since the mash in her mouth didn't seem to be working any longer, she averted her face and pulled it out, tossing it into the jungle. Then she took a deep drink from her canteen.

"Actually, this becomes a source of great dissension," Steve continued. "By the time Muhammad came along, certain beliefs among Christians had been set in concrete—the Trinity, crucifixion and resurrection. On these three points, Islam disagrees."

Miriam stared at him, trying to absorb what he was saying.

He continued. "Islam teaches that Christ was never crucified, nor was he resurrected. Nor did Allah ever have a son. Their reasoning is simple. The entire world we know is profane. Allah would never enter into human form, thus sullying his divinity with the satanic. Nor had he any need of a son."

Miriam nodded. "Okay. I can see that."

"So Islam believes that Christianity has perverted the word of Allah as passed to us through Jesus, first by claiming he was crucified and rose from the dead, and secondly by creating a Trinity, when for Islam there is no god but the one God, Allah. That makes Christianity a perversion of the true faith and a tool of Satan."

"Big bones of contention."

"Exactly. Insurmountable, really. But many early Christian sects didn't believe in the crucifixion or resurrection, either. That sort of heresy was stamped out in the first millennium."

"So back to Jesus's marriage. How could that result in Armageddon?"

"What happens if you can prove that Christianity lied? That the basic foundations of the Christian faith were shaped by jealous men who wanted to guard their power base against Mary Magdalene, a woman whose presence they resented? What happens if you can prove that Christianity was founded on a huge lie?"

"Ouch!"

"Exactly. If Jesus was married, and we've been told for two thousand years that he was not, how much authority does the Church really have? How much can we truly trust? If all of Christianity is based on lies, what happens to the New World, which was apportioned out according to papal decree? Does that become invalid? Plenty of native movements would use that.

"In short, Miriam, the Catholic Church would lose its moral authority, and while it seems like a rather outdated thing in the U.S., around the world it is still a strong moderating force against radical fundamentalism. If you shatter that, what are the others going to do about it?"

"Move in."

"Frankly, I can't even begin to imagine the amount of bloodshed."

"But what can you possibly think you would find here? This is so far from the seat of Christianity."

He hesitated, then decided to get the rest of it off his chest. "There are those who believe that Christ's grandson sailed for the New World to spread the gospel. And that here he was known as Kulkulcan, or Quetzalcoatl. The Maya were rich with Christian imagery when the Spanish arrived. Red crosses set in temple frescoes and carved in rock. Legends of a white, bearded man— Quetzalcoatl—who came from the sea to teach a doctrine of love and peace, and whose arrival sparked the ascent of the Mayan people. If there's any proof of that, it has to be destroyed."

Miriam fell silent and stared off into the night, seeing in her mind's eye what could very well happen if Steve was right. On the other hand...

"Steve?"

"Yes?"

"Does it bother you that you might have to destroy the truth?"

"It bothers me, Miriam. It plagues my soul night and day. But if one long-forgotten truth must be sacrificed to save millions of lives, what can I do? I pray about it constantly. All I can do is trust that God will lead me to do his will. Otherwise, I'm lost. Religion can be a great tool for good, Miriam. But when turned, it can be a terrible force for evil."

As Miriam stretched out on the cool ground, she thought about all that Steve had told her. The pieces were there, and yet there was more. She didn't think he had held back. The pain in his face had been too real. But there were pieces missing. Forces he had not mentioned. Forces for whom murder, even wholesale religious slaughter, was no deterrent. For whom such a tragedy might even be profitable.

She wondered about the kind of heart that could believe so strongly in its own rightness that it would sacrifice millions of lives to pursue its ends. And what she could do to stop it.

23

Dos Pilas, Guatemala

Steve Lorenzo watched the activity a mile away on the far side of the ruins and knew what he would have to do. She would hate him. But that, too, was part of the price.

Miriam had heard what he'd said in terms of ideas and abstractions. But for Steve, no such gloss existed. He had spent years of his life in these jungles, watching blood spill and flow and ruin families. She'd had a taste of it yesterday, at the stream, but that was only a sampler of what he'd witnessed in his time here. Death stalked these mountains with the implacable silence of the jaguar, and it struck with equally cruel indifference.

The realization had hit him after she'd fallen asleep. Their conversation had set his mind adrift over memories he wished God could somehow wipe from his mind, and he saw with utter clarity what the future of these people would be if the Kulkulcan Codex existed, and if it were revealed to the world.

These people were safe only in their relative anonymity—such safety as they knew, anyway. Reveal to the world that their Kulkulcan had sprung from the same Biblical background as Christ and Muhammad, reveal that their prophet might not have been a myth or simply an out-of step Mayan, but truly the grandson of the Christ, and it would not be tolerated. It would create too much guilt, and such guilt would be transformed into deep hatred.

Armageddon might reach its ugly adulthood in the sands of the Holy Land, but its birth would be here, among these people. Long before all the religious posturing began over there, the blood would flow here. And like the ancient king, the enemies of these people would dance knee-deep in that blood, exulting in joy at the first threat removed, even as they knew the mortal danger had not passed.

Memories of a future yet unborn flitted around him like stubborn moths. Paloma, her throat slit, left in a jungle to be eaten by the carrion crawlers. Miguel, any hope of a wife and family splattered over the rocks as bullets tore through his body. Rita and her children, eviscerated like their distant Mayan ancestors to appease new gods of vengeance and power.

As the moths battered against his soul, a white-hot anger grew within him. Anger at a God who could permit such atrocities to be committed in his name. Anger at his believers, whose belief could not reach beyond their own earthly positions. Anger at himself, for the pride that made him think he was any different than the worst of the worst. He was just another white man bearing the white man's burden, clumsily gouging at sawdust in others' eyes because he could not see beyond the beams in his own.

That ended right here, right now.

But even as the angry thoughts filled him, he knew they were only cover for the real feelings that lay deeper. He had been betrayed. He had given his life to a church that had preached life but practiced death. The Church hadn't begun the wars here. Paloma was right about that. But it had fed those wars, flowered in them, here and elsewhere, for century upon century, blood upon blood.

And now it was going to happen again. He hadn't been sent here to preserve a true faith. He'd been sent here to protect a power base. And in the machinations of religion and power, the lives of these people were a widow's mite to be collected and banked with interest.

He'd been sent here because these people trusted him. He'd been sent here to betray that trust. And he'd gone willingly, almost eagerly, believing in the rightness of his faith and mission. Looking around at the faces of the people he'd come to betray, he realized how wrong he had been for so much of his life. They deserved better than to join their forebears in a river of death.

Miriam Anson was a beautiful dove of a soul, committed by nature and training and experience to the pursuit of truth and justice. But truth and justice would be ugly ideals in these mountains. Truth would kill these people, and others would call that justice.

In the end, what mattered was not truth, or justice,

but life. The lives that could be saved. The lives that would be lost.

As he watched the fresh-faced people begin to set up their camp on the far side of the ruins, salvation reached down in the form of cold betrayal.

He would loathe himself for what was coming next, but it had to be done.

He returned to the village campsite and circulated among the others, quietly stirring them awake, shushing their questioning sounds, explaining what had to be done in whispered tones that drew shaking heads at first, then gave way to grudging nods. They could see it was the only way.

Perhaps Miriam would see that someday, also.

As he wrote the note and placed it on the ground beside her, he looked at her clear, quiet features. God had created beauty in her, and that beauty was owed more than this. But this was the best he could give her.

Silently, he and his people began their bitter exodus, a journey to hide forever a truth that might kill them.

Miriam awoke to the screams of macaws and the silence of an empty campsite. Her breath caught in her throat as she sat up and looked around. Even before she rose to search the area, she knew the truth. She had been abandoned.

As a curse rose within her, she looked down at the paper lying on the ground, then picked it up and unfolded it.

Miriam: I'm terribly sorry, but our paths must diverge here. On the far side of the ruins, you will find archeologists arriving to resume their work. There are Americans among them. I am sure they can get you back to safety. I wish we could walk together farther, but it cannot be. You want a justice that will never happen in this land, and the price of seeking that justice would be more than these people can bear. I know you are angry with me, but we must each follow our own journeys. I wish you peace. Steve.

She savagely crushed the note in her hands. Then she rose and made her way into the ruins of a bloodstained city in a bloodstained land.

Washington, D.C.

Kevin Willis tossed back a Scotch and soda, and looked at the others around him in the bar. It was a government bar. Lawyers. Lobbyists. Legislative aides. Networks. Contacts. Connections. The lifeblood of democracy and government. Get along and go along.

It had seemed so easy in the beginning. It was the way things were done. You need a source. Your source needs a source. You scratch. You get scratched. And you call it justice. It had been the same story on the streets of Chicago, when he'd needed informants to make cases. But here, in the shadows of marble monuments and the seat of weighty pronouncements, the stakes got higher.

And the price got uglier.

Tom Lawton was dead. He'd died because Kevin had decided to protect an informant. Oh, he could tell himself it was because Tom had gone off half-cocked on a case he'd been told to leave alone. But Kevin knew that was self-absolving bullshit. He'd known Tom Lawton. The man was a brilliant investigator. And stubborn. And feeling way too betrayed to trust in authority and follow orders.

At some level, Kevin had known Tom wouldn't let it go. And he'd turned Tom Lawton loose among the wolves, alone, without any backup or official authority, without the protective mantle that sheltered every FBI field agent on assignment.

The memorial service had been that afternoon in a small chapel often used by FBI agents for weddings— and funerals. It had been mercifully brief. Terry Tyson had flown up from Florida to attend, asking questions Kevin could not answer. Questions about Tom. Questions about Miriam. Questions about the investigation and the lack of notable progress. The accusation in Terry's eyes had been unveiled—raw and direct and on target.

Terry's friend Grant Lawrence lay in a hospital bed, slipping in and out of a coma. The brilliant mind, the charismatic smile, the visionary who saw an America more beautiful than the one around him, all erased in the seconds it had taken a gunman to pull a trigger. A great man stilled. Perhaps forever.

Terry's lover, Miriam Anson, was lost in the jungles of Guatemala, captured by rebel forces during what ought to have been a simple arrest. She was a hero, according to the Guatemalan police. She had saved several lives by her quick thinking, training, leadership and courage. But she was gone, and Terry's anger had burned hot every time he'd glanced at Kevin.

And Tom Lawton, killed in an auto accident that had not been an accident. Forensics had confirmed that his brake line had been cleverly severed. The Boise police were on the case, but Kevin knew they would find nothing. No witnesses had seen the crash or the saboteur at work. It was another professional killing, the culprit as ephemeral as the cigarette smoke that hung in the bar. Seeing it was easy. Grasping it was impossible.

Kevin knew Ed Morgan was involved. The coincidences were too great to ignore.

Harrison Rice, the now certain Democratic nominee, was leading his opponent by a twelve-point margin, and that margin increased with every new body shipped back from the quagmire in the desert. Rice and Morgan were old friends. College roommates and fraternity brothers. Rice had been in Long Island, a guest at Morgan's home, the day after Grant Lawrence was shot. The meeting hadn't been covert; the wedding of a Morgan daughter had been a social splash, complete with paparazzi. If asked, Rice would simply say he'd been sharing his old friend's joy. And there would be no way to prove otherwise.

Morgan's wife was married to Wes Dixon, the Idaho sheep rancher Tom had gone off to chase on his own. And Tom had been murdered—after Morgan had asked about him. Coincidence? Of course not. But with no witnesses and no leads, there was no trail to follow. Kevin had ordered surveillance on the Dixon ranch, but that had come to naught. Apparently the ranch had shut down, Wes Dixon and wife having left for a long-planned vacation in the Mediterranean.

A trail of blood and money stretched from New York to Idaho to Florida, and Kevin knew he could no more take hold of it and shake the truth from it than he could shake the toxins out of the smoky barroom atmosphere.

The worst of it was, he'd been used. He'd made the mistake of trusting a friend of a friend, a man who from time to time fed him information about the money networks behind Al Qaeda and other terrorist cells in the U.S. Those tips had been very good for Kevin Willis's career. He'd risen through the ranks on the basis of his uncanny ability to track down sleepers in the most unlikely places, thanks to the help of West Point buddy Wes Dixon's brother-in-law and his connections in the arcane and mysterious world of international banking.

When Tom Lawton had tripped over the Idaho Freedom Militia in the FBI database, Kevin Willis had done what he thought was the sensible thing. He'd called his friend and informer, Ed Morgan, and asked him about it. He'd laughed along with Morgan at the patent absurdity of it. Morgan had given him a heads-up about a lead in Atlanta, a lead that had run dry, as leads sometimes do. In the meantime, Kevin had taken Tom off the case and sent Miriam to keep tabs on the investigation unfolding in Guatemala.

In that act he'd sentenced Tom Lawton to death, and very possibly Miriam Anson, as well.

When Terry Tyson had looked into his eyes at the memorial service, Kevin had had to look away. The accusation was clear. And he could do nothing but silently admit his guilt.

He'd tried to catch up with Tyson after the service, as they filed out, but the huge black man wouldn't speak with him. He'd walked out, stiff and silent and full of righteous anger, and Kevin had known there wasn't a damn thing he could say to change any of it.

Three shots of Scotch hadn't dimmed the pain. They hadn't even taken the edge off. The more he pondered the world he had let himself walk into, the more he felt tempted to drive off to Rock Creek Park and eat his service weapon.

But a part of him rebelled at that notion, and he clung to that painful part with the desperation of a man on the edge of a cliff. One more death wouldn't wipe the slate clean.

He would have to do, and be, what he should have done and been from the beginning. It was time to take his own blinders off and recognize his responsibilities.

Old friendships and profitable connections be damned. Because after the networks and contacts and whispered words were swept away, there was still a man lying in a hospital bed in Tampa, a woman lost in Guatemala, and a man dead in Idaho.

Those were not vague or ephemeral things. They were human beings whose lives he had darkened by his own ambition. And they were crimes he could avenge.

It took a long moment for him to notice the cell phone purring at his belt. He pushed the button and held the phone to his ear, pressing his finger in his other ear to hear above the dim but insistent babble of deals being made and promises broken.

"Willis."

"Kevin, it's me. Miriam. I'm in Guatemala City, at the airport, waiting for a flight. We need to talk. And not at the office."

Sometimes, Kevin thought, a providence divine or otherwise reached down into the darkness of the human soul and lit a single candle.

"Yes," he said. "I'll pick you up at Dulles. A lot has happened."

"Tell me," she said.

"Tom…" His voice caught, and for the first time all day, tears fell on his cheeks.

"Oh, God, no," Miriam said.

"I'm sorry."

"They killed him." It wasn't a question.

"Yes," he said. "They did."

"I'll be there in six hours," she said, a hardness in her voice that he had never heard before. "I'm going to get them, Kevin. However I can. Whatever it takes. You can say no all you want, but I'm going to do it."

Kevin looked at his fourth drink and pushed it aside. "I'm not going to say no."

24

Grangeville, Idaho

The sun hadn't even risen when Renate took the pickup truck out behind the motel and gave it a good splotchy spray down with Rust-Oleum. Tom had to admit that only the license plate would give it away as the same pickup that had pulled in here yesterday.

By six, with night still heavy on the world, they were sitting at the crossroads sipping hot coffee, and eating some egg and biscuit concoction that passed for food and was at least warm.

The clerk at the diner had been kind enough to fill two steel thermos bottles with hot coffee for them and charge them for only two large coffees. They were going to need it. This truck might run like a Ferrari, but if it had a working heater, he couldn't feel it this morning. Both he and Renate had decided to don their snow pants and insulated vests.

The truck was parked to one side of a run-down gas station and probably looked like a part of the local scenery. Just as the first light began to appear, the tour bus came rumbling up the highway and turned right onto U.S. 12.

"I guess we're going to Missoula," Tom remarked.

"It looks that way." Renate gave the terrorists just enough time to disappear around a bend in the road, then took off after them.

Yesterday's meltwater had left the highway treacherous in places, coated with a thin sheath of ice, and they tended to fishtail.

"They're going to leave us in their dust," Tom remarked.

"I won't let them."

That was what he'd been afraid she would say. However, since she'd apparently cut her teeth driving in the Bavarian Alps, he wasn't going to get into an argument with her about it. Instead, he put away another biscuit and sipped more hot coffee. "Continued misdirection," he remarked. "Do you think our happy campers are purposefully headed the wrong way?"

"Happy campers?" She laughed. "I like that. We'll call them that from now on. But yes, I think this is purposeful. I wouldn't be surprised if the Guatemalans initially entered the country through Canada. U.S. Immigration, especially at the Mexican border, has become a serious hindrance for even the most casual tourist. Fingerprinting and all that."

Tom said nothing. He was aware of the tightening of immigration policies, and given the terrorist threat, he wasn't necessarily opposed to it, even if it could be annoying for innocent people.

"So," she continued, as if his lack of response had gone unnoted, "these Guatemalans probably found it a great deal easier to come in by way of Canada."

"With the same problems at the border crossing."

She looked at him.

He chuckled. "I guess I need more coffee. Yes, you're right. The border is a sieve. Especially up there."

"Exactly. But this time I suspect they will choose a more difficult way to make their crossing."

"Why?"

"Because their sentry was killed. They know someone is looking for them."

He couldn't argue with that, not by any stretch of the imagination. Glancing through the windshield, he saw the bus taking a curve well ahead of them. So far, nobody was going terribly fast. He was glad of that, because he could distinctly sense that they were rising in altitude.

A sign advised them that they were entering the Clearwater National Forest; then another sign announced the distance to Missoula: 172 miles.

Steadily the road became more crowded. Not crowded as in D.C. or L.A. crowded, but there was an increasing number of vehicles, including some big semis. The one that unnerved Tom the most was a postal service truck, a tandem rig whose last trailer seemed to want to fishtail a lot as it overtook and passed them. "Damn things ought to be illegal," he muttered.

The bus was still in sight, however, staying below the speed limit as if determined not to draw attention. The other traffic was continually trying to pass, not the safest operation on this road. It was going to be a long day.

"So," he said, looking at Renate, "tell me more about this organization of yours. Are you after Al Qaeda?"

She shook her head. "Not me personally. We have a group on them. I'm looking for backers. The people who are pulling their strings, and the strings of other groups like them around the world."

He stared at her, wondering if it would be wise to go down this rabbit hole after her. Paranoia was sometimes justified, but what he was hearing between the lines made him uneasy. Curiosity caused his jaws to flap, anyway.

"Are you suggesting…?" He paused, uncertain how to phrase such a thing.

"Yes," she answered. "I am. There's a lot of money in the hands of a very few families. It's to their advantage to influence world events in ways that make them more money. And there's a *lot* of money to be made off war. In your country alone there are PMCs—private military corporations—that have taken over many of the duties of your military."

"I've heard a little about that."

"But you haven't heard the extent of it. In theory they

provide logistical and support services. In fact they also have private security forces—mercenaries—who can be sent in with the support teams. And sometimes, if your government doesn't want to take an official stand, these PMCs send in their mercenaries, so the government can deny all knowledge. Your Pentagon even has a catchy acronym for it. Military Operations Other Than War, or MOOT-W. It's part of a slow but steady push to entirely privatize your military—and your government."

"I find that hard to believe."

She shrugged. "That's fine by me. Believe what you want. I'm simply telling the truth. Not surprisingly, the push for privatization is coming from the contractors themselves, because they stand to make huge profits. But they don't get paid just for sitting around. If they're not performing, they can't bill the government. And considering that some of these corporations derive the majority of their income from PMC contracts—we're talking tens or even hundreds of billions of dollars—they gain nothing from peace. Nothing at all."

She turned her head, giving him a steady look from glacial eyes. "Al Qaeda is the least of the world's problems. They're funded by the people who stand to gain through their actions. And while they may believe they're involved in Jihad, the simple fact is they're pawns on a chessboard bigger than they can imagine, constructed and funded for the simple purpose of stirring up war. It's no accident that Osama bin Laden comes from one of the wealthiest families in Saudi Arabia, a family that has forty-year-old ties in the Texas business and political community."

"The road," he said, pointing forward.

"I see it," she replied, already slowing to avoid the remains of an overnight avalanche that had left a three-foot drift halfway into their lane. "This reminds me of home."

"I knew that Osama bin Laden came from a wealthy family," Tom said. "I didn't know about their connections in the U.S., though. It wasn't my area of expertise."

"Then you probably didn't know that, when Al Qaeda bombed a U.S. air base in Riyadh, Osama bin Laden's brother got the contract to rebuild it. Or that, in the days after 9/11, dozens of bin Ladens and other wealthy Saudis were allowed to leave the U.S. on private jets, at a time when other air travel was still grounded. All of this despite the fact that almost all the 9/11 hijackers were Saudi citizens."

"So you're saying the Saudis are behind everything?"

"Hardly," she said, shaking her head. "I'm saying my organization was formed because, unlike your government, we have no ties to these people. Maybe all these facts are innocent. Maybe Osama really is the black sheep of the bin Laden family, and the others are decent, innocent people who shouldn't be tarred with their brother's brush. Maybe all of those

Saudis who fled your country after 9/11 were in fear for their lives. Anti-Arab violence did rise over the following months, after all. Maybe, maybe, maybe. But when the financial and institutional entanglements are that knotty, do you really think your government is in the best position to spearhead the global war on terrorism?"

"Jesus." He didn't like what he was hearing, wanted to reject it all, telling himself it had the seduction of all conspiracy theories. But deep within he knew he was going to have to check out what she was saying, regardless. The intelligence failures before September 11 stood out starkly against the background she was describing.

"Just one more thing," she said, as she downshifted for a steep grade. "The deeper I've investigated the Frankfurt Brotherhood, the more I've come to realize that even they aren't the top of the pyramid. There's someone behind them, too."

"Okay," he said. "That's enough for now. I'm going to need some proof."

"That's fair," she said. "I want proof, too. That's why I'm here. In the meantime, we need to take down Wes Dixon and his private army, nail them for the assassination in Guatemala and the shooting of Grant Lawrence."

Tom fell silent, pondering all she had just told him, wondering how it could be true, and fearing that it was.

Dulles International Airport, Virginia

Miriam came out of the security area and ran into Terry's arms.

"Oh, God, I've missed you," she said, sinking into his tight embrace, enjoying his strong arms around her body. It had been way too long since she'd felt this. For an endless moment, neither of them spoke. Finally she stretched up and kissed him. "Now I'm home."

"For a little while," Terry said, angling his chin over his shoulder toward Kevin Willis. "Why do I think you won't be staying long?"

She averted her eyes. "Honey…"

He nodded. "I know. You have to."

They broke the embrace, and she shook Kevin's extended hand. "Kevin."

"Miriam."

She'd called Kevin from Guatemala, then Terry. Terry had filled her in on a lot of the details that Kevin had left out in their brief conversation. Terry had also shared many of his suspicions. Now she regarded her boss with colder eyes than she would have liked, despite their long friendship.

"I'm sorry," he said, as if reading her thoughts. "I screwed up. I shouldn't have put Tom back on suspension. I knew he'd…"

She nodded. "Let's get out of here."

They piled her suitcase alongside Terry's in the trunk of Kevin's car. She considered joining Terry in the back seat, if for no other reason than to enjoy the comfort of holding his hand. But she wanted to be able to see Kevin's face as he talked.

"I think an old friend of mine is involved in this," he said, as they made their way onto I-66 and east toward the city. "Wes Dixon and I went to West Point together. I don't know if you knew that."

"I didn't," she said. "It wasn't in the file. And it should have been."

"Maybe so," he said. "We served in the first Gulf War together, though in different units. I saw him maybe twice the entire time I was there. And only once or twice since, years ago. But he introduced me to Ed Morgan, and Morgan's been a good source on some money laundering cases. He seemed like an upstanding guy. Old money, but he didn't act like it. So when you came to me with the file about Dixon's militia group, I was shocked. Wes didn't seem like the type to go rogue. I thought it was absurd. I called Ed Morgan and asked him about it. He said that yeah, Wes had some group of guys out there who liked to run around in the woods and play soldier. Ed called it a paintball game with ranks, a bunch of paunchy, middle-aged guys who wanted a military experience without any risk. And that pretty much lined up with what we had in Dixon's file."

"And that's when you pulled Tom and me off the case," she said.

He nodded. "I was wrong."

"What if I told you that the man who killed Ambassador Kilhenny was trained at Wes Dixon's ranch?" Miriam asked.

Kevin's face froze. "You have a source for this?"

"The horse's mouth," she said. "The shooter's name was Miguel Ortiz. I met him."

She described what had happened after the raid in Dos Ojos. She kept Steve Lorenzo's name out of it, not wanting to disclose what seemed like paranoid conspiracy theories. When she got to the firefight in the jungle, she tried to keep her voice even, but Terry's steadying hand on her shoulder let her know that she hadn't.

"Damn," Kevin said. "What a mess."

"It's a lousy way to live," Miriam said. "And a worse reason to die. And apparently your friends are in this up to their old-moneyed necks."

"So it would seem," Kevin said. "But suspecting it and proving it are very different things. It's going to be tough to follow the money trail on a man who's spent his life in international banking. Hell, I needed his help to do it against people with less expertise than he had."

"Fringes," Terry said from the back seat.

"Excuse me?" Kevin asked.

"Pick at the fringes. Sooner or later, the shroud always unravels."

"Idaho," Miriam said. "That's where the trail is."

Kevin shook his head. "Dixon's flown the coop. He's supposedly on vacation in the Mediterranean. The ranch is shut down."

"They must have left evidence behind," she said. "With what Miguel Ortiz told me, we can get a warrant and turn the place inside out. We'll find something. Nobody is that good."

"Maybe so," Kevin said. "But what then? Dixon will fight extradition, if we even find him. Morgan has ties all over the world. Dixon can disappear into that network, and it'll be years before we track him down. If ever."

"You sound like you've given up," Terry said, disgust thick in his voice.

"Not at all," Kevin said. "I just want us to know what we're looking at. This won't be easy."

Miriam's face hardened. "They killed Tom Lawton. I don't give a damn how hard it is."

"Neither do I," Terry added.

"Whoa," Kevin said. "This is an FBI case, Terry."

"Bullshit," Terry replied. "Grant Lawrence, my partner's lover and a man who tried to stand up to these people, is lying in a hospital bed with a machine helping him breathe. Miriam's friend, a man who was staying in our home, is dead. If you think I'm not in on this, you're dumber than I think you are."

"Terry—" Miriam began.

"Don't even start with that tone of voice," he said. "I'm in. Period."

"From what Miriam tells me, you're good," Kevin said. "You'd better be."

"Yeah," Terry said, pulling out his cell phone. "Likewise. So where do we start? Idaho? The warrant?"

"We start at home," Miriam said. "I need a shower and a meal. Then Idaho."

"That works," Terry said, dialing the phone. "Hi, Grace. How are ya? Great. Listen, the reason I'm calling, I need you to hook me up for three tickets from Dulles to Boise. First available. Tonight, if possible. Call me with the confirmation? Thanks, Grace."

"Does he always work this fast?" Kevin asked, a faint smile on his face.

Miriam turned and winked at Terry. "Almost always."

25

Missoula, Montana

The descent into the valley had been hair-raising. The weather had turned ugly, a late-spring snow coupled with ever-building winds over the mountains to create a driving nightmare. Renate had handled it as skillfully as Tom had ever seen it done, but he still felt a welcome sense of relief as they pulled into the parking lot of a small, rustic motel.

"That was…hairy," he said.

"Excuse me? Hairy?"

"Aah," he said, smiling at her querulous look. "Your English is so flawless, I forget that you aren't a native speaker. It's a colloquialism. Frightening."

"Well, yes," she said. "It was hairy."

They checked in and carried their bags through deepening snow to their room.

"This is like Lincoln's house," Renate said, looking at the log construction. "We learn about Abraham Lincoln even in German schools."

"Color me impressed," Tom said, dusting the snow from his jacket and hanging it in the closet. "You probably know a lot more American history than I do German history."

"Probably so," she said. "Americans tend to look in the mirror a lot."

"We're not all bad," Tom said, beginning to resent her repeated comments about his homeland. "We did, after all, rebuild your country after you destroyed Europe."

"I'm sorry," she said, looking away. "You have to understand that, outside your borders, you are often seen as, well, an arrogant bully. And I know you aren't like that, and your country has done many wonderful things in the world. I sometimes—"

He held up a hand. "No worries. Just don't keep beating me up over it. I'm not always proud of America, but it's still my home. It always will be. Like Germany will always be your home."

She sat on the bed, shrugging out of her coat and the sweater she'd worn beneath it. "I guess. I haven't been there in two years."

"That must be hard."

"I deal with it," she replied. "Driving through the mountains today, with the snow and the trees, well, I felt homesick."

"Your parents don't even know you're alive?" he asked.

Her face was impassive. "Office 119 policy forbids contact with family or past acquaintances. For our safety *and* theirs."

"That's not what I asked," he said.

"I know it isn't." She paused and took a breath, then rose and began searching through her backpack for a change of clothes. Finally she stopped and looked at him. "Yes, Law. They know I'm alive. I fought. I argued. I should have listened to my boss, because, believe it or not, it's worse that they know I'm alive. When I knew they thought I was dead, at least it was final. There was no hope of ever seeing them again, for me or for them. Now…"

"Now you sometimes wish you could pick up the phone and call home," Tom said.

"Yes. And I know they wish I would. And that hurts even worse. I know they worry. And if I die, they will never know where or when or what happened."

"Ouch," Tom said.

"Please, let's change the subject?" she asked.

"Good idea." He unpacked his shaving gear and headed for the bathroom. As the frigid water from the faucet warmed, he called out to her. "I think Dixon and his band are holed up for the night in that campground we passed a few miles back. I can't see them driving any farther in this mess."

"I agree," she said. "Dixon's too careful a planner to head out in this weather. If anything goes wrong, he can't call for help."

The water was now steaming, and Tom soaked a washcloth and held it to his face. Then he smeared shaving cream over the moistened skin and began working the razor in slow, even motions. The repetitive, mindless task relaxed him, as it always had. With that relaxation came the accumulated fatigue of two days on the run with too little rest and too much stress. By the time he finished, his body felt leaden.

He emerged to find her already working on her computer. "How do you do it?"

"What?" she asked.

"I'm ready to fall into bed and sleep through the night. And you're hard at work."

She shrugged. "I wasn't in a car accident a few days ago. Besides, needs must, as the English say."

"American translation, you do what you have to do?"

"Yes," she said. "I have to check in with my superiors and find out what, if anything, they have learned about Wes Dixon's contacts in Canada. He must have some. If we can find out where he's going, we can look for a good intercept point."

Tom nodded, stretching out on the bed and watching the back of her head. She'd let down her hair, and it seemed to flow in a golden river. Whatever he'd thought of her at first, she wasn't the human iceberg he had believed. He found himself trying to imagine her life and how she must feel about it. What came to mind was emptiness. She had surrendered everything to devote herself to a mission.

He'd done much the same thing in working undercover. He'd given up the few friends he'd had, living in a shadow world where every thought, every feeling, was a lie. In the end, he'd fallen so deeply into the shadows that returning to the real world had left him wondering who he really was. For the first week he'd stayed at Miriam's, he'd reached for his gun every time the doorbell rang.

That was the life Renate was asking him to return to, and this time it would be permanent. It wasn't hard to see how she had come to be so detached. Detachment was the only way to get through each day. *Needs must.* It was a mantra she lived by. The mantra she was asking *him* to live by.

"*Scheiße,*" she said, snapping him out of his reverie.

"What?"

She turned in her chair and looked at him. "Have you contacted anyone at the FBI?"

"No, why?"

"Kevin Willis, Miriam Anson and Terry Tyson boarded a flight for Boise an hour ago."

"They don't think my death was an accident," Tom said. "If my brake line was cut, they'll have found out."

"Why not turn it over to the Boise field office?"

"Miriam was my friend. This is personal."

"But Kevin Willis is Wes Dixon's friend," Renate said. "That's why I've had him under surveillance."

"Now wait a minute," Tom said, sitting up. "Kevin's a good agent. He may have known Wes Dixon years ago, but that doesn't prove he's connected to what's going on."

"He pulled you off the case," Renate said. "And sent Miriam Anson to Guatemala to make sure she was out of the way. That smells connected to me."

Tom shook his head. "I lived with Miriam and Terry after I came back from L.A. I know them. I'd trust them with my life. If they thought Kevin was dirty, he wouldn't be with them."

"And maybe they simply have no reason to suspect him."

"Maybe," Tom said. "And maybe there's a monster under this bed. But maybe this is a good thing. Now we have a way to get the Bureau to take Dixon down. And if I know Kevin and Terry, they'll find a way to turn the Dixon ranch upside down when they get there. But we need to give Miriam all we know, Renate. We can't leave her working blind."

"You say you trust Miriam with your life," Renate said, looking at him. "Do you trust her with mine?"

"Yes," Tom said. "Look, you contacted your parents because you didn't want them to grieve a dead daughter who wasn't really dead. I don't have any family. But Miriam and Terry are as close as I've got. I honestly don't want her to go on thinking I'm dead."

"I told you what happened when I contacted my parents," she said. "It's not going to make your life better."

"Maybe not," he said. "But if it'll help us get Dixon, it's worth it. Who else do we have to turn to?"

She studied him for a moment, as if measuring his soul. Finally she nodded. "Okay. Let's contact her. But I want to see every word before you send anything."

"Fair enough," Tom said. "How do we do it?

Boise, Idaho

Miriam, Terry and Kevin entered the Boise FBI field office together and soon were in a private meeting with Fred Milgram in the conference room. Kevin took the lead, trying to wend his way through a potential minefield of politics. Fred, after all, was the SAC of this office, and he might well perceive Kevin as stepping on his toes if this weren't handled carefully.

So he started out the safest way possible. "I need your help, Fred."

Fred nodded slowly, an acknowledgment of the request, but not an answer.

"A case we were working on has mushroomed," Kevin continued. "Special Agent Anson just returned from Guatemala, where she learned that one of your local ranchers has been training and outfitting Guatemalan rebels on his land. I also have reason to believe that Agent Lawton discovered the training camp and was killed because of it."

Fred Milgram's whole demeanor changed. "Are you saying this was going on under my nose and I had no hint of it?"

Kevin realized toes had been stepped on, anyway. Sighing inwardly, he pushed on. "Put it this way, Fred. One of our agents had to go to Guatemala to find this out. This guy is apparently very smart and very careful. *None* of us had any idea that he was up to anything."

"What about Lawton? Why was he working here without informing me?"

Miriam spoke. "Agent Lawton was on suspension. He told everyone he was going fishing."

"Damn." Fred rubbed his chin. He was a good agent, a good man, but Boise was a bit of a backwater as field offices went. Consequently, even he knew he was protective of his turf. However, this time he pushed aside his feelings.

"Who is it?" he asked.

"Wesley Dixon."

Both of Fred's brows rose. "Wes Dixon? The guy's got a five-man militia group that likes to play army on weekends. You're telling me that's a cover?"

"Apparently so. We need a warrant to go out to his ranch and find his training facility."

"I'll take care of it," Fred said. "And my guys are in on it."

"This whole office is in on it," Kevin said. "If anything is found, it will be found by you. We just need to know."

Just then there was a knock on the door and an agent stuck his head in. "I have a message for SA Anson. It came by e-mail."

Fred nodded and motioned him to give the message to Miriam. She accepted it with thanks and began reading.

Then she folded the paper and looked up. "Is there somewhere I can make a phone call? Personal business."

"Sure," said Fred. "Use my office, two doors to the right."

"Thanks. I'll use my cell." She rose and left. The others resumed their discussion of what they would need to do at the Dixon ranch.

In Milgram's office, Miriam took a chair near the window, away from his desk. Then she opened the cryptic e-mail again, her heart pounding. All it said was, "Check your voice mail," followed by a phone number with a Washington area code. Anyone would have supposed that the number was hers. What was going on?

Deciding to follow the instructions, she punched up her own voice mail and listened. Sometime while they had been en route to Boise, a message had been left for her. Tom's voice was as clear as a bell.

"I'm in Missoula. We need to talk, but no one else can know. Get here as fast as you can. There isn't much time."

She immediately deleted the message, then sat for a few minutes with her phone to her ear, listening to the mindless repetition of the voice mail menu, while trying to absorb her second major shock in two days.

Yesterday she had been told Tom was dead. Now she had heard him on her voice mail, clearly time-stamped today, while she was flying to Boise.

He was alive and apparently in hiding. There was no question about how to handle it. Slapping her phone closed, she rose and returned to the conference room. Everyone stopped speaking as she entered.

"I have a personal emergency. How fast can I get to Missoula?"

"They're having some bad weather heading that way," Fred Milgram answered. "Traffic's barely moving, if it's moving at all. Heavy snow."

"Can I fly in?"

Milgram thought for a moment, then leaned forward. "Let's find out. Are you all going?"

"No," said Miriam. "Kevin and Terry need to stay here and see what can be found at the Dixon ranch. I have a sister up there. She's in a bad way."

She knew Kevin wouldn't know much about her family, but Terry did. The look that passed between them was brief and invisible to anyone else, a look between soul mates that communicated everything that needed to be said. He would cover for her if things got squirrelly here. Thank God for that, she thought. She had to get to Tom and find out what was going on.

As it turned out, getting a flight to Missoula proved relatively easy. A commuter run was scheduled, and the forecast was for clearing conditions. At her own insistence, Miriam took a shuttle to the airport and boarded the puddle jumper, a plane that could carry no more than twelve passengers.

The ride over the mountains was rough enough to be extremely uncomfortable and at times terrifying, but the pilot persisted in making jokes about it, including one to the effect that they had nothing to worry about until they hit the ground.

As luck would have it, they didn't hit the ground until

they landed in Missoula. The runway had been cleared, but the heaps of snow on either side told the story. And now, as they slowed, she could see that flurries were falling again.

She passed through the charter arrivals terminal and was reaching for her phone when a woman appeared at her side and spoke quietly.

"Special Agent Miriam Anson? Don't look. Just keep walking and nod."

Miriam nodded and continued toward the glass doors.

"The picture doesn't do you justice," the woman said. "Get a cab at the curb and ask to go to the Lonely Cowboy Lounge. Ask the bartender where the rest rooms are. They are in the back of the lounge, on either side of a hallway. You'll find a service entrance at the end of the hallway. Go out that door, and I'll be waiting in a pickup truck to take you to Tom."

"Why all the—"

"I knew you were arriving, didn't I? Our enemies have their own contacts. I'd bet your life that you're being watched right now. Would you?"

Miriam stepped aside as a crowd of college students came in through the glass doors, all wearing maroon and gray, many with their faces painted, as well. They were doubtless on their way to an athletic event of some kind. She turned to look at the woman who had been speaking to her, but she'd melted into the crowd.

Deciding she had no choice but to follow the mysterious directions, Miriam waded through the press of students and made her way to the curb, where she flagged down a cab.

A little while later, the driver deposited her in front of the Lonely Cowboy Lounge, and she stepped inside. The bar was everything and nothing she'd expected. Yes, there was the obligatory mechanical bull in the center of the room, but it was a surprisingly upscale establishment and seemed to cater more to wanna-bes than to cowboys themselves. As instructed, Miriam asked the bartender for directions to the rest rooms, then made her way back through the crowd in the direction he had pointed. A commotion began behind her as a man in khaki slacks and Top-Siders took his turn on the mechanical bull, but she left the noise behind as she stepped out into the alley.

26

Missoula, Montana

Renate prided herself on having a cold detachment that allowed her to keep a clear head in a deadly environment. But she wasn't feeling detached now, and she had to fight to contain her emotions. As soon as Miriam was in the truck, Renate jammed her foot down on the accelerator, causing them to fishtail as they started down the alley.

Allowing Tom to call this woman and bring her here had been a dangerous mistake. The woman's beauty also made her uneasy in ways that were utterly absurd, yet which she found herself utterly unable to dismiss.

She slammed on the brakes and skidded up to the stop sign at the end of the alley. They were clear to the left, and she jammed down on the accelerator again, turning right onto the street.

"I'm Miriam Anson," the agent said. "And you're…?"

"Renate."

"A friend of Tom's?"

"No. Colleague."

"Ah."

Renate kept her eyes on the road but noticed as Miriam looked her over, noticed as she took in the maroon and gray that Renate wore, which had allowed her to vanish into the crowd of college students.

"So what is it with mechanical bulls?" Miriam asked. "Why send me to an *Urban Cowboy* bar?"

"We had to shake the tail," Renate said.

"What tail?"

Renate glanced over at her. "The tail you picked up the instant you made flight arrangements to come here. I wasn't the only one to meet you at the airport. I paid the guy who climbed on that stupid bull a hundred bucks. The commotion gave you time to slip out the back before your followers could catch up to you."

"Would it offend you if I told you that sounds paranoid?" Miriam asked.

Renate forced herself not to flinch, blink or even shrug. "Think whatever you want. I'm trying to stay alive and keep Tom alive. And now I have to keep *you* alive, too."

"I think I can handle myself," Miriam said.

"You did well in Guatemala," Renate said. "But this is a different kind of jungle. And more dangerous."

"How do you know about Guatemala?" Miriam asked. She was obviously taken aback by the statement, which was exactly what Renate had intended. She had the advantage now, and she had no intention of giving that up.

"I have sources," Renate said, making her voice as cold and flat as she could. "Tom and I are involved in an investigation that reaches farther than you can imagine. It's also more deadly than you can imagine."

"I know that Wes Dixon is training guerillas at his ranch," Miriam said. "I know Tom suspected something was wrong there. And I know damn well it was dangerous enough for him to almost get killed, then fake his own death."

"I faked his death," Renate said. "To save his life."

"Then I must thank you."

"You know," Renate said, keeping her voice cool, "once your friends in Boise go out to the Dixon ranch, Dixon will hear about it. He'll put two and two together, and my job will get a lot more dangerous."

"Your job?"

"Yes," Renate said.

"And just what *is* your job?" Miriam asked. "Who do you work for?"

"Not yet," Renate said, glancing in her rearview mirror as she made another turn, finally convinced that anyone following them had long since been shaken. "I don't know whether to trust you yet. And until I do, we play by my rules."

Minutes later, they emerged onto a main road and soon parked at a rustic motel. Miriam had kept her silence for the remainder of the drive, weighing what Renate had said, drawing tentative conclusions. The woman was obviously in the intelligence community. Her actions were clearly the product of training and experience. But that didn't make Miriam any more comfortable. Quite the contrary. Her experience of the intelligence community had been that they manipulated those around them to their own ends, and those ends were often morally ambiguous, to say the least. This woman had a lot of questions to answer before Miriam would let Tom stay with her.

When Tom opened the door to the room, Miriam's heart both warmed and sank. His face and arms were bruised, and he moved with a pained stiffness.

"You look like hell," she said, hugging him.

"I feel like hell," he replied, ushering her in and taking her coat. "Still nice to see you, though."

Miriam sat in one of the two faded armchairs and watched as Renate headed into the bathroom to change. She left the bathroom door open, so Miriam spoke softly.

"I take it the car accident wasn't faked?"

"Unfortunately not," Tom said. "The only thing fake about it was that I didn't die."

He briefly recounted all he said he remembered of the accident and the days since. There were gaps, Miriam noted, but she wasn't sure what to make of them. He'd undoubtedly gotten at least a minor concussion in the accident, so memory gaps were to be expected. Or he could be holding back. With Tom, it was always difficult to know.

"So what happened to you?" he asked. "I hear you had some problems in Guatemala."

"You might say that," Miriam said. "There's a civil war going on, and I got caught in the middle of it. I guess you know I was wounded."

He nodded. "And that the Bureau doctors say you're healing well. That's good to hear, at least."

"I'm glad they think so," she said. "This cold is making things hurt like hell."

"Tell me about it," Tom said, half smiling. "Riding in that truck when your body feels like you've been a tackling dummy for the Vikings' defensive line is no fun."

"So what's going on?" Miriam asked. "Why fake your death?"

Tom glanced over her shoulder, and Miriam turned to see Renate emerge from the bathroom in jeans and a sweater. She sat on the edge of the bed and met Tom's eyes for just an instant, but Miriam could see that the glance both spoke and concealed volumes.

"What do you know?" Renate asked.

Her face and voice gave no offer of quid pro quo, and Miriam considered whether to answer at all. She wasn't going to jeopardize an FBI operation to sate the curiosity of someone whose agenda and reliability she did not know. Nor did she think she had to prove herself to Tom. So she turned to him.

"What do *you* know?" she asked.

He glanced at Renate again, then shook his head. "It

can't work that way, Miriam. I'm sorry. Trust me when I say the Bureau is out of its depth on this one. I'll need you, yes. And you'll get the credit. But this isn't going to be a two-way street."

She could hardly believe what she had just heard. This was her protégé, an agent she'd shepherded through the difficult early years of his career, befriended, taken in when his life had gone to hell. And now he didn't trust her? This woman had gotten to him somehow.

"This is absurd," Miriam said, turning to Renate. "We can sit here and play verbal games all day, but it won't get us any closer to what we want. If you want to play it that close to the vest, I'll call a cab and go back to Boise. At least there people trust me."

"But do you trust them?" Renate asked. "That's the real question. And if so, you don't know as much as you think you do."

"You mean Kevin Willis," Miriam said. She looked over at Tom, who nodded almost imperceptibly. "When did you find out?"

"Before I left to come out here," Tom said. "In fact, that's *why* I came out here. He's a mole for some dangerous people. People who tried to kill me."

"That's not true," Miriam said. "Look, Terry and I talked with Kevin about this. Yes, he screwed up. He said so. He knew Wes Dixon in the army, and Dixon introduced him to Ed Morgan. Morgan was a source on some key cases Kevin worked. When all of this came up, Kevin thought it was absurd. So he called Morgan to ask him about it."

"Christ," Tom said. "He set me up."

"No," Miriam said. "He didn't. Not intentionally."

"Even if what you say is true," Renate said, "intentions are irrelevant. He leaked key facts in an investigation to the very people you were investigating. He took you off of the investigation, sent you to Guatemala, and cut Tom loose for the wolves. This isn't a man I trust."

Miriam realized that, from their perspective, Kevin Willis *was* a mole. But they hadn't seen his face as the truth came out. Still, she knew there was no way she could convince them. Tom was never going to trust Kevin again. And Renate didn't seem inclined to give second chances.

"Kevin doesn't know why I'm here," Miriam said. "I told him I'm up here visiting a sick sister."

"He'll figure out that's bullshit," Tom said. "He's not stupid."

Miriam shook her head. "No, he's not. So you'll have to give me something I can spin. A way to work things so I don't have to tell him you're alive."

"You think you can lie to him?" Tom asked.

"I think you're not giving me any choice," Miriam replied. "And I don't think you contacted me and brought me up here just to let me know you're okay. So like I said, we can play games until I get bored and fly back to Boise, or you can tell me what's going on."

Renate nodded. "You're right. So we share notes. What do you know?"

Boise, Idaho

With Kevin at the wheel of a Bureau car, he and Terry left the office building and drove toward a motel that Fred Milgram had recommended.

"Fred's a good man," Kevin said.

Terry nodded. "Seems to be."

"He'll have the warrant by tomorrow morning, as promised."

Terry nodded again, saying nothing.

"Are you going to tell me what's going on with Miriam?"

Terry looked at him. "She told you."

"Come off it, Terry. We came here because Tom was killed and she learned that Wes Dixon was running a guerilla training camp. I know Miriam. She wouldn't leave an investigation like this to look after a sick sister, especially a sister she's never mentioned."

Terry turned in the seat to confront Kevin directly. "You're her boss. You have a professional relationship. There's no reason for her to talk to you about her family members."

"But you know for a fact she has a sister in Missoula?"

Terry gave him a cold stare. "You heard what she said. If you don't believe her, why are you going to believe me?"

"I believed Tom Lawton when he said he was going fishing. Instead…"

"Maybe he meant a different kind of fishing."

"Obviously."

Kevin was silent for the next couple of blocks, then finally turned into the lot of the recommended motel. He pulled into a parking space, turned off the ignition and sat there for a minute.

Then he turned toward Terry and said, "You two better not be up to something behind my back."

"You know as much as I do. You were there."

After a beat, Kevin nodded. "You have any objections to sharing a room? The Bureau will cover me, and I don't see any reason you should have to pay out of your own pocket."

"Fine by me," Terry said, reaching for the door handle. Then he paused and looked at Kevin. "Listen, man, we're all on the same side here, right?"

"That's the idea."

"Then I'm cool. But I want you to know one thing."

"What's that?"

Terry shook his head. "I don't like the way you treated Tom Lawton. The man's head was pretty messed up by what went down in L. A. He needed support. Instead, you cut him loose. And don't give me any bullshit about procedure. If we don't stand by our own, what have we got?"

It was a moment before Kevin climbed out of the car. When he did, he faced Terry over the hood. "He was unstable."

"My ass," said Terry. "He was pissed. Can you stand there and tell me you wouldn't have been pissed if you were in his shoes?"

Kevin didn't answer for a long moment, then just said, "Let's get that room and find a meal."

"Fine," Terry said. "But know this. If you get Miriam hurt in this, there is no hole deep enough for you to hide in, no contacts powerful enough to protect you. I'm going to marry that woman. I've let that slide for too long, and I realized it when I thought she might be dead in Guatemala. When she came back, it was like God gave me a second chance. Don't you dare fuck that up."

"I've lost one agent because I made a dumb mistake," Kevin said quietly. "I won't lose another."

27

Missoula, Montana

"Wes Dixon trained the team that killed Ambassador Kilhenny," Miriam said. "I know that for a fact."

Renate nodded and pulled two photos from a file folder. "We suspected, but we hadn't confirmed it. How did you?"

"I met the assassin," Miriam said, taking the photos as Renate passed them to her. She closed her eyes for a moment after looking at the shot of the assassination. "Yes, this man. His name is Miguel Ortiz. Where did you get these?"

"One of our operatives has a contact who happens to work in an office overlooking that intersection," Renate said. "Pure luck that his contact had a camera at work that day, heard the initial rattle of gunfire and got to his window in time to snap that picture."

"You keep ducking around the part where you tell me who you work for," Miriam said.

"You're right," Renate replied. "Perhaps later. I took

the other photo, the one at the Dixon ranch, last fall. We've been looking at Dixon for some time."

"I guess so," Miriam said. "So do you know why he's doing this? Who he's working for?"

"Dixon works for Ed Morgan," Tom said. "Between the fishy loans I found, and the other connections, and what we've seen since…his operation must be getting outside funding. It makes sense that Morgan is the source."

"And if money flows down," Miriam said, "authority flows up. No way Morgan funds something he can't control for his own purposes."

"Exactly," Tom agreed.

"But how do we prove it?" she asked. "And even if we do, Dixon has disappeared. Somewhere in the Med, we're thinking now. But with Morgan's contacts in international banking, Dixon could go anywhere."

Tom chuckled and shook his head. "He's not in the Med. He's at a campground five miles from here."

"You've been following him?" Miriam asked.

He nodded. "That's why we're here."

"So we take him down," she stated.

"It won't be that easy," Renate replied. "He has a busload of armed men with him. Guatemalans he's been training. We think they're headed for the Canadian border, getting out of the country. If you send a team into that campground, it's going to be war."

Miriam considered what she'd seen at Dos Ojos and nodded in agreement. "So what's the plan?"

"We need to find out exactly where they're going,"

Tom said. "Then we need to pick a place where we can take them down with maximum surprise and minimum risk. We need Dixon alive. He's our only link to Morgan."

"And what do I do?" Miriam asked. "What do I tell Kevin that he'll believe?"

"We're going to continue shadowing Dixon," Renate said. "His intentions will become clear in the next day or two. You need to get the media on this. Get his face on television—suspected assassin, training terrorists, whatever you want to say. Set up a tip line. Once we know where he's going to be, we'll pick an ambush site and call in. The tip will include the word *aluminum*. That way you can arrest him, with no direct contact to us. You get all the credit. We stay invisible."

"You're big on invisible," Miriam said.

"It's how I stay alive," Renate said. "And it's how Tom will stay alive if he stays with us."

"Which brings us back to who you work for," Miriam said. "And why you're doing this."

Renate leaned forward. "All I can tell you, and all you need to know, is that we're a group of people working to stop terrorism and assassination as political tools. You won't find me, or any of the rest of us, in your databases. Or anyone else's. We don't exist. And that's key to our operations."

"Thus Tom's death," Miriam said, putting the pieces together. "You're dead, too, am I right?"

Renate nodded. "All of us are."

"And it has to stay that way," Tom said. "I'm sorry, Miriam, but I'm not coming back to the Bureau. I've got nothing left there. Not now. So I'm dead. You didn't get a call from me. You didn't meet me. You can't even tell Terry. And you damn sure can't tell Willis."

She could see why he didn't trust Willis, and she would have to respect his wishes on that. As for Terry, keeping secrets from him was not something she wanted to do.

"I trust Terry," she said. "He wouldn't say a word."

"You can't tell him," Tom said, looking into her eyes. "Not yet. Not for a long, long time. If you go through with this, you're burning a tiger's tail. They're going to be watching you. Listening to your most intimate moments. Wanting to know where you got your information. And they aren't going to quit."

"So I spend the rest of my life being paranoid," Miriam said. It wasn't a prospect she relished. "That's the price, isn't it?"

"Yes," Renate said. "That's the price."

"We can't let them win," Miriam said. "I'll get back to Boise and get the media angle going. Let's do it."

Then she turned to Tom and took his hand. "But you've got to promise me one thing."

"What's that?"

"That every year or so you'll let me know you're still alive. Send me a flower. Just one. And that if you need my help on anything…well, you can count on me."

He reached out and hugged her. "I know I can. And

I'll send you a white rose every year. If anything changes, well, you won't get a rose."

"She'll get a rose," Renate said, seeming to have relaxed somewhat. "A red one. If it's ever necessary."

Boise, Idaho

Ever since Miriam's return, Terry had been looking at her as if he felt slightly betrayed. She did her best to act as if nothing had happened, however, explaining to both him and Kevin that her sister's emergency had been overrated.

Neither of them looked as if they believed her and Terry knew she had no sister, but on this one, too bad. She'd made a promise, and she didn't break her promises, even if keeping them made her heart ache. She'd explain it to Terry later. Maybe he would forgive her.

They reached the Dixon ranch just after dawn the next morning. With them came every available agent and vehicle that Fred could rustle up on short notice, which was most of his field office. Behind them, at Miriam's insistence, trundled the local TV and newspaper people.

Kevin had argued with her last night about the media, but Miriam remained insistent that they needed whatever local information was available. Fred Milgram had backed her up and even agreed to set up the tip line. It was the kind of story that would make him look good as long as they found something, and since Miriam had talked to a Guatemalan rebel who had named Wes

Dixon, he was sure they were going to find *something*. God willing, it would be something great for the TV cameras.

A few hundred yards from the house, they fanned out in their vehicles, surrounding the buildings. Agents in body armor made a slow, steady approach, keeping low. Miriam watched tensely from the lead SUV, praying that there would be no gunfire. She kept seeing all that had happened in Guatemala, fearing she might have led these agents into an ambush.

But not a shot was fired, and finally the team was at the house, battering on the door, calling out, "FBI. Open up!"

No one answered. Nothing in or near the house seemed to stir. Finally one of the agents used a stapler to pin the warrant to the door. Then they battered their way in.

Five minutes later, an agent stepped out to give the all-clear.

Fred drove them up to the door, and the four of them climbed out.

The air was frigid, cutting knifelike through layers of clothing that had been meant for a milder climate. Miriam shivered and felt Terry touch her arm. She glanced at him and saw that his gaze was concerned. She forced a smile. "I'm fine," she said, though she was far from it. Guatemala was looming on the edge of her memory, threatening to strike at any moment.

"He lives well," Miriam remarked as they stepped into the foyer. "Better than you'd expect on his reported income."

"Wealthy wife," someone said.

Kevin looked at Miriam and shook his head, as if warning her not to mention their suspicions. She almost sighed, thinking Kevin ought to know her a whole lot better than that.

"Okay," Kevin said to Fred, "how about we leave a couple, three agents here to check everything out and box up any papers? Letters, financial records, anything of the sort. And maybe you have someone who could track down Dixon's wife? Given what we learned, she may be on Long Island with her brother, Edward Morgan. Or do you want me to handle that?"

Fred shook his head. "I'll handle it." Leaving them, he went to give orders to a few of his agents.

Terry leaned toward Miriam and murmured, "Wouldn't that be a nice shoe in the door, finding the wife with Morgan?"

Miriam gave him a faint smile, but she wasn't counting on luck. "We should also check State and see if she really *is* on a Mediterranean cruise."

Fred came back in time to hear her and nodded. "We're on it."

"I guess now we wait for the chopper," Kevin said.

The helicopter, with its bird's-eye view, was being used to spot the training camp that otherwise might be a needle in a haystack on a ranch this size. It was already out there flying a grid pattern, seeking anything unusual.

Miriam opted to wait indoors, out of the wind, while

Fred went and spoke to the reporters. She couldn't hear what he was saying, but she was sure it would make him look good. Terry joined the others in hunting through the house, and Miriam found herself missing him. When this was all over, she wanted them to take a vacation, somewhere far away. She wondered if he would agree.

The cold had once again made her aware of her wounds, and surreptitiously, she slipped a hand inside her coat and up under her sweater. Dampness. Reluctantly, she pulled out her hand and saw that the wound in her side was oozing again. Nothing major, she assured herself. She would get it looked at later.

It took another half hour, but the chopper found the camp and came back to lead the way. By that time boxes full of papers were being stacked at the door.

They climbed into the line of black SUVs and followed the chopper over rugged terrain for nearly five miles. With each jolt, Miriam had to suppress a wince.

At first glance the camp appeared to be nothing but some run-down old buildings, but it was obvious people had been there recently.

"It's too cleaned up," Miriam said as she scanned the site. "Like they expected us to find it."

"I agree," Kevin said. "Everybody! Maximum precautions. If it's a training area, there may be mines or trip wires. And they may not have removed them all."

Miriam, still aching from her wounds, the pain much worse in the cold, remained in one of the SUVs with

Terry and watched her fellow agents move from building to building. It looked like a training exercise, she thought. It didn't look real at all. Real had been what she had experienced in Guatemala only four days ago. God, she hoped *this* didn't turn real.

Ten minutes later, the first arm shot up. Everyone froze in their tracks, and Miriam's heart caught in her throat as the bomb squad crept in to check the scene. After a long, tense examination, one of them triggered the device, and a geyser of fluorescent green paint erupted.

"Practice booby traps," Terry said, squeezing her hand. "Let's hope there are no live ones. You feeling okay? You keep wincing."

She nodded. "I think a stitch pulled out. With the cold and the walking around, it's hurting. But I'm fine."

"We can get you back to a doctor," Terry said. "You don't have to be out here."

"Yes, I do."

"You're a stubborn lady, you know that?" His smile said more than the words.

"Yeah, I am," she said. "But that's why you love me."

They watched as, over the next four hours, the search team went from building to building, alley to alley, field range to field range. There were over two dozen booby traps, but, like the first, all were compressed gas paint packs. The agents recovered hundreds of shell casings in various calibers, from 5.56 mm M-16 rounds to .50-caliber heavy machine gun rounds.

"We've got him on firearms violations, at least," Kevin said as they drove back to the office. "There was a lot of ordnance out there that civilians aren't allowed to have. If we can find anything at all in the files we seized…"

"Just don't give me another Ruby Ridge," Fred Milgram said. "Folks up here have long memories, and they don't give much of a damn about firearms violations. If you're going to go after this guy up here, you need more than a few shell casings. I have to live here after you guys go back to Washington."

"We understand that," Miriam said. "Nobody wants to crap in your backyard. But the thing is, Fred, this is different. Majorly different. We have an eyewitness who says Dixon was training Guatemalan guerrillas."

"An eyewitness who's dead," Fred reminded her.

"I'd be willing to bet there's an underground arsenal. He couldn't have carried *everything* away with him."

Fred nodded again. "We'll look into that tomorrow."

"For tonight," Kevin said, "the news has enough to get the tipsters rolling."

Terry leaned forward and tapped Fred's shoulder as they hit the outskirts of town. "Can you get us to an emergency room? Miriam's wound opened up."

"Jesus." Kevin turned in his seat until he could see her. "I thought you looked like hell."

"Everyone's telling me that," Miriam said, smiling weakly. "Maybe it's my hair."

"Just keep trying to be tough, baby," Terry said, squeezing her hand. "We'll get you fixed up."

Kevin turned to Fred and whispered, "She's looking pretty pale."

"I'm going as fast as I can," Fred answered.

28

The flurries had not abated, and Renate grew worried as they climbed higher into the Rocky Mountains. Dixon and his private army had headed north out of Missoula, following Highway 93 past the shores of Flathead Lake, then into more rugged terrain. The deeper they drove into the mountains, the more the area reminded Renate of home. And she was well familiar with the dangers of Alpine driving.

"I think I know where they're going," Tom said, wrapping his hands around a mug of hot coffee they'd picked up at a convenience store three blocks past where the bus had stopped for fuel. "Glacier National Park is another thirty miles up the road. It's basically empty at this time of year, and it extends across the border as Waterton Lakes National Park in Canada. I'm guessing there are lots of trails they could take through the mountain passes and up into Canada. Trails that wouldn't be watched on either side of the border right now."

"That makes sense," Renate said. "Have you been there before?"

"Once," he said. "A long time ago. I was ten years old. I guess it was the last vacation we ever took."

"What happened?" she asked.

"On the vacation? Nothing special that I remember. We drove the Going to the Sun Road, which was beautiful. A couple of months after we got back, Mom was diagnosed with ovarian cancer. She died the next winter, and that was the end of my childhood."

"I'm sorry," Renate said. She'd read the basic facts in his file, but she hadn't asked about any of the details. Now that they were going to be working together, perhaps it was time to ask. "What happened, exactly?"

He looked out at the snowy peaks for a while before answering. "The medical bills cleaned Dad out. He was spending so much time at the hospital with her. Used up all his sick days and more besides. The foreman had to let him go. The union fought it, but by the time they were done arguing, she was dead and he'd mortgaged the house to pay for the doctors and the hospital and the funeral."

"That wouldn't happen in Germany," she said. "But I don't suppose that makes any difference to you."

"Not a bit," he said. "The union finally got Dad his job back, but he wasn't much for it by then, and he lost it again. He'd taken to drinking. The doctor had prescribed something to help him sleep, but he didn't want pills. He said the booze did the same thing."

"Grieving people often self-medicate," she said.

"Well, he did," Tom said. "Big-time. I tried to keep him going, keep him looking for work. It wasn't like it is now. The auto plants hadn't closed and gone to Mexico. He could have found a job. He did find a couple, but with the drinking, he didn't stay around long. The mortgage company had long since run out of patience, and he wanted to keep the house. His father had built that house, after all, and he'd grown up there. So he fell in with the wrong people."

"Drug dealers," Renate said.

"Yeah." Tom paused to sip his coffee. "It was easy money, he thought. He started at the bottom, selling dime bags of pot to the locals. A lot of them were ex-hippies from the sixties, so it was popular. Then he started muling. They flew the stuff into Canada, where customs inspections were weaker at the time. He'd drive across the border, load up the trunk and deliver it to the players in Detroit and Pontiac. That's when the trouble really started."

"Why?" she asked.

"One player wanted another's turf. Dad got caught in the middle. Somebody didn't like who Dad was dealing with, so they drove into town one night and took a couple of shots at him through our living room window."

Tom laughed bitterly. "The neighbors might have been ex-hippies who wanted their pot for a weekend buzz, but now they had jobs and kids. They didn't want *crime* in their town. Dad went from the poor guy who lost his wife and job to the bastard who was putting their little angels at risk. Somebody tipped off the cops, and he ended up in jail. The same pricks who'd been buying from him when he started, turned around and testified at his trial."

"And you went to live with your aunt?"

He nodded. "I was fifteen by the time the trial was over. My aunt lived a couple of towns away. Everyone in school knew who I was, of course. The dope dealer's kid. Half the kids wanted to buy from me. The other half treated me like a pariah. I graduated a year early, applied to Georgetown because I liked Patrick Ewing and it was far away, and I got the hell out of Michigan as fast as I could."

"Patrick Ewing?" she asked.

"The center for the Georgetown basketball team. They were a national powerhouse back then."

More of the pieces had fit into place. The bare facts she'd read lacked the grim reality of hearing him tell it. Betrayal had been his constant companion in childhood, and that explained a lot about his reactions to what had happened in Los Angeles. And about why he had needed to contact Miriam Anson.

"You did well at Georgetown," she said, smiling.

He looked over. "Thanks. I guess you've read my transcripts, huh?"

She laughed. "Of course. Very impressive."

"Well," he said, "I felt like I finally had a chance. Nobody knew who I was. Or who my dad was. I didn't talk about my past. I didn't get homesick. I just focused on my courses. I tumbled into a communications law class because I was studying journalism and discovered I was good at law. So I applied for their law school. I guess I thought I'd fix the system that had screwed my dad. Turned out one of my professors was an FBI agent, and he told a lot of stories in class. So instead of trying to fix the system, I became part of it."

"And then the system betrayed you again?" she asked.

"Maybe," he said. "I still haven't worked that out yet. I screwed up. I know that. Breaking my SAC's nose was definitely a stupid thing to do. I'd made the classic undercover mistake. I'd gotten emotionally attached."

"Which means you're human," she said.

"I don't know what to make of that, coming from you."

"You think I'm not human?"

"You try not to be."

That was true, she realized. She told herself it was essential to her work. She had to be invisible, and people who made emotional connections didn't stay invisible for long. They talked about old subjects that had to remain buried. They exposed themselves. And yet, she couldn't deny an emotional connection with Tom. They'd been working together twenty-four hours a day for long enough that she'd begun to find him comfortable.

"I guess I do," she said.

"Part of the job?" he asked.

"Yeah."

She drove in silence for a while, keeping an eye on the tour bus, which was little more than a glint on the horizon, disappearing and reappearing as they crested hills. Signs on the side of the road announced the main entrance to Glacier National Park, but the bus continued north.

"Maybe they're not going into the park," she said.

"Have to be," Tom said, digging through a road atlas. "It's the only thing that makes sense. Dixon must be planning to use another entrance, closer to the back trails. But there aren't many, and he's going to have to cross the Continental Divide to get into Canada through the parks."

"Hannibal through the Alps," she said. "Look for passes."

"There are only two I can see," Tom said, studying the map. "And eventually they'll have to go through Brown Pass. It's on a park trail. Elevation 6800 feet or so, in the midst of several glaciers. That ought to be a lot of fun at this time of year."

"It's also a good place to take them down," Renate said. "They'll have to be on foot, and there shouldn't be any civilians around. It's about as isolated as we can hope to get them."

"Should I call Miriam?" Tom asked.

She shook her head. "Wait until they turn into the park. We'll only get one chance to call that tip line, so we have to be right. If we have to call twice, it's going to sound very suspicious."

He looked at the map again. "Once they get up to those lakes, they'll have to hike the rest of the way. They'll have twenty-four hours at most to get the intercept team organized and transported up there. That's an awfully thin margin."

"Life," she said, "is an awfully thin margin."

Watermill, Long Island

Edward Morgan was feeling frantic. Kevin Willis was out of town, according to the FBI, and they refused to do anything except take a message. Wes had phoned and said that one of his comrades in the militia, a former military associate, now insurance agent, had been killed while on sentry duty at the ranch. Someone was watching them. They had taken off for the border, and more than that he would not tell Edward.

And somewhere out there, Bookworm was still alive, doing whatever mischief she could. He knew her as a computer nerd, but suddenly he was wondering if she was capable of killing. And whether she was working for herself for some strange reason, or if there was something else important he didn't know.

And now his sister, who had just backed out of a cruise in the Mediterranean—a cruise she had summarily refused to take without Wes—was walking into his study looking like an avenging Valkyrie.

"Where is Wes?" she demanded. "I've been trying to reach him."

"How would I know?"

She put her hands on her hips. "Edward Morgan, you're a lousy liar. What did you get him into? I've wondered for years what was going on between the two of you."

"Katherine, nothing is going on, I assure you." Which, of course, was why he could feel his collar growing damp.

"Don't lie to me, Edward. Not any longer. Wes has been getting increasingly…nervous. For months now. And every time he talks to you it gets worse."

Edward forced a sigh and spread his hands. "Kathy…"

"Don't you Kathy me." Her eyes were sparking, and the anger she radiated was an almost physical force pressing him back in his chair. "When he quit the military, I knew it had something to do with you. He had such a bright future before him. My God, he could have been chief of staff by now. And he left all that behind because of you."

"I swear—"

"Bullshit," she said succinctly, the first time he had ever heard such an unladylike word pass her lips. "I've spent too many years confined to a half-assed sheep ranch in Idaho to believe you any longer. That man didn't just up and decide to raise sheep. The sheep raise themselves while he's off doing something else. And it's consuming him, Edward. It's eating him alive. And all those military friends of his moving out to join him… What kind of fool do you take me for?"

"I've never thought you were a fool."

"Really? I suppose you think I believed that you and Wes thought a cruise alone would be good for my health. There's nothing wrong with my health. All that's wrong with my life is too many secrets and the way they're consuming the man I love."

A tear trickled down her cheek all of a sudden, making him feel lower than a worm. "I want my husband back, Edward. I want the man I married back, not this hush-hush, always-looking-over-his-shoulder, secretive... I don't know what he's become. But I don't like it, and I blame you."

"Wes hasn't done anything he hasn't wanted to."

"No?" She dashed away the tear and glared at him again. "My Wes is a proud man. I'm sure you used that against him, reminding him of the style of life I'm supposedly accustomed to and how he couldn't provide it. I'm sure you made him feel just awful, then sank your hooks into him somehow, just the way you do with everyone else you want to use."

Shock struck Edward out of the blue. Had he been that transparent? Or was it just that Kathy knew him so well? Even so, the description of himself struck some long-forgotten ethical chord, and he squirmed just a bit.

She pointed her finger at him. "You get my husband back to me, Edward Morgan. And then set him free to be the man he was meant to be."

Edward waited a moment, then shook his head. "My dear, I'm afraid that Wes *is* the man he was meant to be."

With a gasp that sounded like a sob, Katherine turned and hurried from the room. The slamming of the door behind her reverberated even in the carpeted, book-lined room.

For a moment, only a moment, Edward hated himself. Then he shoved the useless emotion aside and went back to trying to figure out a way to save his own life.

A man had to have his priorities straight.

Columbia Falls, Montana

At Columbia Falls, well before reaching the main west entrance to the park, the bus turned off on a county road headed north. Driving conditions immediately deteriorated, but as Tom studied the map, he felt his spirits rise.

"This is the only road they can take. It runs along the western side of the park as far as Polebridge. Conditions are questionable."

"At least we won't have to follow so close now," Renate answered. She slowed down and let the bus take a huge lead. "What's at Polebridge?"

"I don't know if it's a small town or what. Must be, since it's outside the park. But from there you can enter Glacier by way of the Polebridge Ranger Station, and there's a trail there. It goes over the Continental Divide, then turns north toward Canada."

"Sounds like exactly what they'd be looking for."

He nodded, feeling as if things were really starting to go their way. "Have you ever been up here before?"

"No."

"When I was a kid, after we left the park, we drove west toward Libby. It was a lumber town then. Maybe still is. But what I remember most was passing through this tiny spot on the road, a tavern on one side, a couple of mobile homes on the other. And a sign that said "Happy's Inn, Population 8."

Renate smiled, then laughed. "I can see why you'd remember it."

"That was back when the wide-open spaces were still really wide-open. When wilderness wasn't just a name but a reality. Maybe, after we're done with this job, we can look around a bit."

"Maybe." The word was indifferent, but her smile said otherwise. "As a European, I'm still frequently stunned by the sheer size of your country."

"I can imagine. I ran into some Swedes once at a campground in Colorado. They needed some help because their car was mired, and then they confessed that they hadn't realized it was going to take more than two weeks to see everything they wanted to see. They were feeling a bit disappointed."

"I can imagine." She slowed down again as the road grew a little more slippery and the tail of the bus came into view in the far distance. Just then the flurries stopped, and a few minutes later, like a blessing from above, the sun came out, bouncing brightly off the new-fallen snow. Renate reached for her sunglasses.

Tom was looking out the side window. "You know, it looks like most of the winter snow already melted. So all we're dealing with is the fresh stuff."

"That'll change when we climb some more."

"I know. But before we do, I suspect we may be dealing with a lot of mud."

"Better than ice." She took a curve carefully. With the clearing, they could now see the peaks within the park, and Tom began to wonder if he was in good enough shape to be a mountain goat. God, it looked forbidding in there.

Renate glanced at her watch. "They'll leave the bus at the entrance and push into the park for a while. And we'll be right behind them."

Given the woman he was with, Tom had little doubt of that. He hoped the return of the sun was a good omen.

29

Boise, Idaho

The tip Tom had promised came in that evening. The stitch replaced at the E.R., Miriam had insisted on remaining at the office with Fred and Terry, and dining on some takeout of indeterminate origin. She nearly leaped up off the sofa when a female agent appeared with a sheet of paper.

"I think I saw that man from the television—Wes Dixon—in a bus with an aluminum trailer," the tip said. "Headed north of Bowman Lake to Brown Pass."

At once Miriam asked for a map of Glacier Park. A scramble ensued throughout the office until finally Terry said, "How about looking on the Web?"

Fred immediately turned to his computer, and in less than two minutes had a map of Glacier Park on his screen.

"There it is," Miriam said, pointing. "Bowman Lake Trail. And Brown Pass. Then the trail turns north into Canada."

"We're going to need to get Missoula in on this,"

Fred said. He sounded as if something great had just slipped from his grasp. He looked at Miriam. "That's what you went to Missoula about, wasn't it."

She looked at him. "I don't know what you mean."

"You're too sure of this for it to be just another anonymous tip."

She hesitated. "Listen, Fred, like you said, we're going to need help from Missoula. I'm sure you have contacts there. Can you help us out?"

He nodded. "Sure. I'll set it up. And I'm coming with you."

"Of course." She pretended surprise that he might consider doing anything else. "I'm sure your team here will find the weapons caches out at the ranch. You don't need to be there."

Instantly he was torn; she could see it on his face. And she hated doing it to him. But now he was weighing whether he wanted to be here, so he could announce the discovery of arms caches on the news, or there, so he could be in on the kill.

But he didn't say anything. Instead he just turned toward the phone and said, "I'll set Missoula up for you."

She was pretty sure he had decided to stay here.

Bowman Lake, Montana

Tom felt beads of sweat trickle down his spine, and hoped he and Renate were as invisible as she had promised. But it didn't much matter. As she had said, this was their one chance to get ahead of Dixon and his men. So he pressed on, trying to lose himself in the rhythm and quiet shushing of cross-country skiing, yet always tempted to glance back over his left shoulder, toward the far bank of the lake.

Bowman Lake was a narrow sliver of water high in the foothills, carved by glacial advance and withdrawal, and eons-old floods of meltwater running off the mountains. In moonlight those mountains ahead loomed huge, menacing and achingly beautiful. They seemed to lean out over the landscape, their steep, jagged faces a deadly dare to adventurous souls. Renate knew better than to take that dare, and knew Dixon would, as well.

"I grew up in country like this," she had said that afternoon. "You have heard of the Matterhorn and the Eiger. I've skied in their shadows. We can't fight the mountains, and Dixon won't, either. So if we're going to beat him to the pass, we'll have to do it here, on the lake. And we'll have to do it at night."

Tom hadn't argued, except to toss her a look. He knew he needed sleep, but this wasn't the time. He had driven himself harder for longer at Quantico, during his training. He had pulled countless all-nighters in L.A. But back then he hadn't been recovering from a concussion and nursing an aching thigh bruise. A bruise that seemed to scream louder as the temperature dropped lower with each passing hour.

The daytime temperatures had neared fifty down in Polebridge, but when the sun slipped over the horizon the thin mountain air chilled almost immediately and kept on getting colder. Renate's alpine experience seemed to include skiing on frozen lakes, because she had absolutely no doubt that, despite the warming springtime temperatures, the lake would still be frozen solid enough to support them.

Her plan was simple and direct. Dixon and his men had been forced to abandon their bus outside the park, and they had trudged uphill on foot all day. They'd reached the shores of Bowman Lake in the late afternoon, and by early evening they'd decided to set up camp rather than press on. Once they passed the lake, the land would begin to rise, and whatever advantage Tom and Renate had on skis would steadily vanish in a battle against gravity. But the lake, like all bodies of frozen water, offered level, smooth going. Seven miles of it. So they'd set out for the south bank and hugged it as closely as they dared, pushing into the night.

Still, the lake was less than a mile wide, and the same level, smooth going that he and Renate enjoyed also yielded wide-open sightlines. Even from the far bank, Tom wondered if they could be seen by alert eyes in Dixon's camp, if there were any turned their way. By moonlight, even in their winter camouflage, they might be visible because of their movement. And if any of Dixon's men had night vision equipment, Renate's and his heat signatures would probably glow, plainly visible. All the more reason to press on, yet Tom couldn't resist glancing over his shoulder for signs of activity.

After an hour, though, he began to relax. When he lifted his gaze from the terrain just ahead of him, he never failed to catch his breath at the sight of the jagged mountains looming all around them. It was clear that their bases continued down into the lake, that the ice he skied over now was nothing but a filler between rocky upthrusts. But what lay beneath him held no candle to what towered over him. The moonlight carved the craggy peaks in brilliant relief six thousand feet above him. In some places, mostly the bowl-like cirques carved so long ago by glaciers, snow clung and reflected the moonlight with eerie brilliance. In others the sides of the mountains were too steep to collect anything, and gray rock frowned down from nearly vertical walls.

Those mountains were not only beautiful, they were terrifying in their challenge, and it seemed to Tom that they must somehow be alive themselves. A brooding moodiness, a kind of watchfulness, seemed to emanate from them.

He shook his head, dismissing fancy, forcing himself to once again look directly ahead.

He couldn't yet see the far end of the lake, but the mountains there seemed to be almost on top of them now. He guessed they'd covered five of the seven miles, and there was little chance, if any, of their being spotted at this point. He closed in on Renate and tried to fall into the easy, effortless rhythm that he had once known, and that she was obviously adept at. Instead, he found himself gasping for breath in the thin air, making it difficult to talk. The sound of his breath was nearly lost in the quiet, rhythmic shushing of their skis over the loose, fresh power from the day's snowfall. Only occasionally did they hit wind-bared ice that scraped and crunched.

Under any other circumstances, Tom would have found this to be one of the most beautiful experiences of his life. He'd never skied in moonlight before, and reality took on a soft, otherworldly feeling. The steady sliding of their skis felt hypnotic. Gradually, even though he was panting from exertion, altitude and weakness brought on by his recent injuries, he almost felt as if he were in a dream, a lovely dream. He was even able to forget for a little while that they were carrying rifles on their backs and that some of the heaviest stuff in his pack was ammo.

Then his ski skidded on some unexpected ice, jolting him and jerking his injured leg. A grunt of pained surprise escaped him. Though it was soft, in the night's stillness it seemed ominously loud.

"Almost there," she said quietly.

"Then we grab a few hours sleep?" He knew it was a stupid question, but he was getting woozy enough to be stupid and not care.

"Hardly," she said. "We push on up the trail. I want to stay a few hours ahead, and we're going to lose time on the steepest slopes."

"I don't know how long my leg is going to hold up."

Renate looked over at him. "It will be worse if we

stop to sleep for a couple of hours. Right now you're moving, so the blood is flowing and it's warm."

He didn't need to hear the rest. The bottom line was that they needed to keep moving so Dixon couldn't close the gap too much. Once they reached the head of the lake, they would be on the same trail Dixon would follow, and only time and the stiff mountain winds could hope to hide the tracks of their passage. Renate had estimated that Dixon and his men would need twenty hours to cover the fourteen miles from their campsite to the pass.

Tom glanced at his watch and saw that it was nearing midnight. Dixon was probably an early riser, and he would push his men hard. But would he try to negotiate the pass at night? Probably. He wanted to cross the border into Canada at night, and that would be an all-day hike from the pass. Stopping for the night before the pass would add two days to Dixon's journey. He would push on.

Tom tried to work the numbers and finally shook his head.

"What's wrong?" Renate asked.

"I can't do simple math," he said. "It's just after midnight, and I figure Dixon will probably have them up and moving by six at the latest. You said twenty hours. What does that add up to?"

"Two tomorrow morning. But that's a rough estimate."

"Why couldn't I figure that out?" Tom murmured.

"We need a rest break," Renate said, a look of concern on her face. "Between the concussion and the altitude, you're starting to get fuzzy. I need you sharp."

"Let's get off this ice first," he said.

"The lake head isn't far. Another half mile or so, I'd guess. Then we'll get up into the trees a bit and let you get some fluids into your system. That will help with the altitude."

"And then we figure out what we're going to do when the cavalry arrives," Tom said.

"The cavalry?"

"The FBI. They'll send in a SWAT team. And that leaves us in a delicate situation. I assume you want to stay invisible. So what are we going to do?"

When they at last reached the trees, Renate shrugged off her pack and began to pull things from it. Bending with difficulty, Tom released his own skis and realized that walking felt awkward now that he was no longer gliding forward. Worse, even inside the snow pants and parka, he sensed he was growing chilled, at least at the surface.

Renate pulled out a small campstove of the kind hikers preferred, and in moments she had the single burner glowing.

"They'll be able to see that," he remarked.

"No, we're far enough into the trees, and the moon is bright. But if you notice, there's a fallen log there, and snow over it, blocking any direct view."

The flame didn't create a whole lot of light, anyway,

he realized. It burned a pure blue, blending with the moonlight.

On it, she began to heat a pot of snow. "Soup," she said. "We both need it."

She helped him out of his pack and told him to sit on it. Then she pulled out a survival blanket and wrapped it around him. She sat on one herself, protecting herself from the damp cold ground as she pawed through her bag, passing him jerky and candy bars. Instant calories.

They munched while the snow melted and began to steam.

"Where will your cavalry arrive?" she asked him.

He pulled the well-folded map out of his jacket pocket and used a hooded penlight to scan it.

"If it were me, I'd bring the team in at the Goat Haunt Ranger Station, then backtrack to Brown Pass for the ambush."

She nodded, looking at the route with him.

"It wouldn't make sense to try to follow them in. They couldn't catch up."

"No," she agreed. She continued to study the map. "We need to block their retreat."

"Yes." He poured over the trails and contours for a few minutes longer. "At some point we need to get behind these guys. An avalanche would be great."

She looked at him, an odd smile on her lips. "What, you will just clap your hands?"

In that moment she sounded foreign, a fact he'd

nearly forgotten. Foreign and exotic. Something within him stirred in a way he didn't need right now, most especially not with this woman.

"We have the rifles. Look, I don't claim to know a whole lot about how to cause an avalanche, but it seems to me that if we see a snow overhang that looks likely, maybe we should try to set it off."

"If we shoot our guns, they'll know they're not alone."

"I'm not saying we should shoot before they reach the others. Maybe we won't even try this. I'm just saying, if the opportunity arises, we *might* try it. Mainly I'm thinking we have to be a rearguard, so that if anyone tries to run back down the trail we can pin them down."

"So we find a good blind to shoot from." She nodded again. "Good plan. We'll see what it's like as we get closer to the pass. You think your team will attack there?"

"That would be the likeliest place to keep them from scattering every which way."

"Right." She leaned back and emptied packets of dried soup mix into the pot of now boiling water. Instantly a rich aroma filled the air around them.

"I'm glad," he remarked, "that the grizzlies are hibernating. Otherwise they might join us for a midnight snack."

A little chuckle escaped her. "I've heard about grizzly bears."

"So have I. And I'd rather not meet one."

The candy replaced lost calories quickly, but the soup made him start to feel warm again. She had made generous servings to drink out of aluminum mugs, and while they enjoyed the warmth, she melted more snow for drinking. Overhead, the wind tossed the treetops, sounding cold and lonely. At ground level, however, bodies were warming up again and feeling stoked for the next leg of the journey.

"Let's go," Renate said finally when she judged they had drunk enough warm water to replace what they were losing to the dry air as they breathed.

Tom rose and found he was stiffening up. He hobbled around the area, loosening his leg as Renate repacked her knapsack.

"Ready?" she asked finally. He nodded and let her help him into his backpack again. Apparently, when he'd hit his head, he'd also done a little something to his neck. It wasn't cooperating with some of his movements too well.

Then he slipped back into his skis and picked up his poles from where they leaned against a tree.

"This is going to be rougher," Renate said when she, too, was ready to move. "Feel up to it?"

"Actually, I do now." In fact, he felt revitalized.

She passed him a few more candy bars. "Keep these in your pocket."

As soon as they stepped out of the woods and back onto the trail, the wind hit them in the face, blowing down from the heights ahead of them. Tom was glad to see, however, that it was sifting the dry snow around. Behind them, their trail had already vanished.

He tightened up his snorkel hood, then skied after Renate on a slight upward slope that he didn't doubt was going to become extremely difficult before long.

But she was right. As long as the moon gave them light, they had to keep going. He just hoped his leg was up to doing a herringbone, or they were going to lose a lot of the advantage they'd gained. Perish the thought.

Moonlight silvered the trail, and the wind snatched away any sound they made.

It was as if they were wraiths, lost, alone and unseen.

30

Watermill, Long Island

*F*ishing, Edward Morgan thought with disgust. His operation was in a critical phase, and he needed to be here, in his command center, to monitor events in Montana and offer guidance if Dixon contacted him by the encrypted satellite link Morgan had provided. He'd finally caught up with Kevin Willis, through another contact at the Bureau, and knew Willis would be meeting a SWAT team in Goat Haunt. Apparently the bastard had betrayed him. Well, so much the better. Morgan had him marked for death regardless.

Once Dixon checked in, Morgan would tell him about the impending ambush, and Dixon would take steps of his own. His well-trained Guatemalan soldiers, with state-of-the-art equipment, would be an easy match for the FBI's SWAT team. He would instruct Dixon to make sure Willis died in the firefight, along with Miriam Anson, who was also on the scene. Dixon himself was expendable, and after the firefight, he would have outlived his usefulness. Katherine would blame him—she always did—but she wouldn't be able to prove a damn thing, and neither would the FBI.

The official story would be that Grant Lawrence had been the target of a crazed, right-wing militia group. Harrison Rice would win the election. And the Frankfurt Brotherhood would have a malleable pawn in the White House, ready and eager to continue a very open and profitable war on terrorism. Any connection between Dixon and the civil war in Guatemala would be lost on the margins of the public outcry for justice in the Lawrence shooting, an outcry that Morgan's allies were already stirring to a near frenzy.

The operation could still work, despite the setbacks. Despite Bookworm. Every operation had its share of twists and surprises. That was what management was for. And on this day of all days, Ed Morgan needed to be here to manage the situation through its endgame.

Instead, his father had called and summoned him for an early spring fishing trip. Just a day, out on Long Island Sound. Fresh air. Sunshine. Relaxation. Dad was tired of being cooped up in his Manhattan penthouse, as if that were a trial rather than a life of utter luxury in which his every need was cared for by the simple expedient of lifting his diamond-laden pinky finger.

But Dad was Dad, and he still had heavy pull at the bank, despite his public retirement. There were only a few ironclad rules in Ed Morgan's life. "Don't cross Dad" was one of them, and indulging the old coot had served him well over the years. Dixon wouldn't be anywhere near the ambush site until the wee hours of tomorrow morning, and by then Ed would long since be back ashore and safely ensconced in his command center. So, okay, he would take a day with Dad and even pretend to enjoy himself while listening to the same old stories his father told every time they were together.

With a silent groan at the mere thought, Ed finished the brief message and hit the transmit button. Dixon would get it when he logged in, and by the time it mattered, Ed would be back in contact. In the meantime, he would drink his fill of fine German beer and work on his tan.

Everything would be fine.

Goat Haunt, Montana

"To the best of our knowledge," Kevin Willis said, standing before a computer-projected photo, "we can expect to encounter at least a dozen well-armed and well-trained men. This man is the principal target. Wes Dixon. He's a West Point graduate and a former classmate, so believe me when I tell you he knows what he's doing and can adapt to changes in the tactical situation quickly. The men with him are all Guatemalan rebels, all of them with years of irregular combat experience, and all of them fresh out of Dixon's training program in Idaho. Do not take Dixon, or them, lightly. They won't go down easily."

After some discussion, Miriam had agreed that Kevin should do most of the mission briefing and retain nominal tactical command. But she wasn't about to let another Dos Ojos happen. She would be in the loop—and stay in the loop—all the way to the finish. She watched as Kevin tapped a remote control, and the photo of Dixon was replaced by a magnified section from a United States Geological Survey topographic map.

"Our intercept point is here," Kevin said, pointing at the screen, "on the east side of Brown Pass. It's isolated and open, and the terrain will canalize and contain Dixon's men for us."

The park ranger stationed there, Adam Peltrowski, spoke. "That's very steep terrain there, a quick descent of about a thousand feet from the pass to here. It'll be very difficult getting down it through the snow, and impossible to get back up it with any speed at all."

"Exactly. The important thing is that we let them herd themselves through the pass and start the descent. Then we're all over them."

"What are the rules of engagement?" the SWAT team leader asked.

"We'll move in searchlights this afternoon," Kevin said. "Once Dixon and his men have walked into position, we'll light them up and bullhorn them once. I've spoken with the director of Homeland Security, who has spoken with the president. We are to consider them domestic terrorists and enemy combatants. If they don't surrender after one warning, we're to treat it as a combat situation."

"Collateral targets?" the team leader asked.

"There shouldn't be any," Peltrowski said. "The park is closed, and that pass isn't considered navigable until July."

"So it's a free-fire zone," Kevin concluded.

Miriam squirmed in her seat. She knew Tom and Renate would be up on that mountain, but she couldn't say a word about it. She would have to trust that they, too, would know the Bureau would treat it as a free-fire zone, and that they would stay out of the way.

Still, hearing phrases like "enemy combatants" and "free-fire zones" applied within American borders made her uneasy. It seemed more like a display of post-9/11 institutional gunslinging than law enforcement. This was the brave new world of the United States of America, and in this instance she understood the necessity. But she didn't have to like it.

"What should we expect from the Guatemalans?" a SWAT team member asked. "How good are they?"

"I'll turn that part over to Special Agent Anson," Kevin said.

Miriam rose and stepped to the podium. "First, never forget that these are a people who have been in a civil war for most of the last fifty years. Over a quarter million have died. Every one of those men up there has seen death, up close and personal. Friends. Parents. Brothers. Wives. Even children. The threat of violent death is an ever-present companion in their lives. They're not going to cower."

"Neither are we," the SWAT team leader said.

"Fine," she said, "but don't underestimate them. Any one of them probably has more actual combat experience than all of you together. The one difference, though, is that unlike you, they're going to adapt individually to whatever happens. Dixon's going to lose command and control from the moment the first shot is fired. But don't read too much into that. They'll adapt individually, but they're used to fighting together. Command and control is nearly intuitive for them. They've fought their way out of government ambushes before. Unless you take them down immediately, expect them to find cover and use it well.

"And," she added, "they'll be used to mountain air. The cold may bother them, but the altitude won't."

"Thank you, Special Agent Anson," Kevin said, rising. "Okay, we'll insert by helicopter, as near the pass as winds and weather will permit. We go in at fourteen hundred hours. That will give us about five hours of daylight to prepare our positions. At nightfall, we'll rotate out of the line for rest and hot chow. Then we settle in and wait."

"Depending on their physical condition," Peltrowski said, "they could reach the pass as early as midnight. But that would be exceptional. More likely it will be sometime after 2:00 a.m. It's going to get awfully cold up there, so be prepared."

"We'll be passing out thermoses of hot soup and coffee with your evening meals," Kevin added. "Keep them tucked inside your vests, and don't be afraid to consume them. The park rangers will be brewing up more at the command post, and we'll be sending runners out through the night. You won't be good to anyone if you're half-asleep with hypothermia and dizzy with altitude sickness. Stay warm and stay sharp."

They made it sound so clinical, Miriam thought. And it never, ever was.

Brown Pass, Montana

Three miles past the head of Bowman Lake, the night had turned harrowing. Renate and Tom had found themselves following a nearly invisible trail through the snow and trees across the side of Thunderbird Mountain. It climbed precipitously, and there were places where one false step would have sent them tumbling over the edge. Nor had Tom been able to forget the constant threat of avalanche. As near as he could tell, no human being had been here since last autumn's first snowfall. In more than one place a wind-carved cornice hung out, ready to slide its way to extinction if jarred even a little bit.

The cold of the night seemed to help them, however. Everything stayed frozen.

It was afternoon by the time they emerged into a meadow just shy of the pass. The wind blew stiffly here, and snow snakes wound their way across the surface with a ceaseless hiss. The air was thinner, too. The genuine breathlessness that had begun during their climb lingered even when they held still. Tom had a serious headache again, and felt sick to his stomach.

When he looked at Renate's face in its frame of fur, he thought she looked ill, too.

"Water," she said. "We need lots of water."

"But we're almost to the pass."

She shook her head. "Now."

"They'll be able to tell someone was here."

She shook her head again and pointed to some bushes thrusting up out of the snow. Or maybe they were trees. He had no idea what the snow depth here was. A hundred inches? Two hundred?

He skied after her to the designated place and realized he was beginning to lose his coordination. Too tired. Too much effort expended in that nerve-racking climb. Despite frequent rest stops on their way up, he had the feeling he was teetering on the brink of total exhaustion.

Renate seemed to feel little better. She needed his help shrugging off her pack. Together they sat on survival blankets and worked to heat some dried stew mixed with snow. While they waited for it, they munched candy bars, lots of them.

When he was feeling a little better, Tom pulled out the map again and studied it. "If Kevin has any sense, he'll go for them on the other side of the pass."

"Why?"

"Dixon and his men will have to funnel through the pass, limiting their scope of maneuver. And the trail makes a steep descent there. Not easy to get back up."

"Right. So we should find a hiding place in the pass,

no? And follow them down, so if anyone does try to come back up, we can block their way."

"Something like that. I'll feel better when I actually see the terrain. There's only so much you can tell from a topographic map."

He tucked the map in his pocket and pointed north. "That's where the pass begins. Then it heads directly south."

All around them, mountains still loomed high, a reminder that treachery lay everywhere on this terrain. If anything could be said for the snow, it at least evened out the landscape a bit. Tom imagined that on foot all of this would have been a lot more rugged.

Within a half hour, they had eaten and packed and were skiing upward toward the pass. Behind them, the wind whipped away their tracks.

At the pass itself, they entered a forest of subalpine firs. The trail was easy to see again, an open passage through the trees. However, it also acted like a funnel, sucking the wind directly at them with enough force to make it feel as if they were gaining no ground at all.

But the distance was a short one to a lookout that gave them a breathtaking view of all the mountains around.

"My God," breathed Renate in awe.

Tom, too, was struck by the beauty of this spot, a place that felt so close to heaven he almost believed he could reach out and touch the wispy clouds above. Yet the mountains rose higher still, another four thousand or more feet above them, forbidding crags that told a tale of the incredible forces that had carved them.

Then, amazingly, his eyes fell on a sign barely poking out of the snow: Goat Haunt. An arrow pointed the way.

He pointed it out to Renate. "I think we should stay here. The trees will give us cover. And if they try to come back this way…"

She nodded. "Here it is."

Fifteen Miles South of Long Island

The day was dying, and the Morgans, father and son, were still bobbing in the waves well beyond sight of land. All day they had fished the warmer Gulf Stream currents while his father's pilot, a guy named Mac, had steered the boat for them.

It always made Edward nervous to be out this far on a boat with his father, and more so when the daylight was fading. Even though he knew Theodore Morgan could captain this vessel to Bermuda and back, Edward still wasn't inclined to trust GPS and charts, or, even worse, his father's dead reckoning.

"About time to go back in, Dad," he said, trying to sound relaxed. They'd each managed to catch a couple of nice-sized bluefish, so his dad could go home, like the caveman that had always been part of his personality, with fresh kill for dinner. Edward didn't see the point and never had. He preferred his fish already filleted and cooked by a superior chef.

"Not yet, Son," said Theodore, even though he was putting away his fishing gear. "Our friends in Frankfurt are a little concerned."

Morgan sat upright, his heart slamming. "Uh... couldn't we have discussed this over drinks?"

"No. I wanted this time with you."

"Oh." Edward found that strange. It was rare that his father wanted time with him. "I've enjoyed it."

"So have I. I understand Bookworm is still alive."

"I find that hard to believe. I saw her die...."

"And that you arranged the killing of an FBI agent."

"It was necessary!"

"Perhaps so. But it was handled poorly, and as a result the FBI is now after Wes Dixon. You may think Dixon is expendable, but his wife does not. And she's my only daughter."

"But—"

"You fucked up, Son. In fact, I've learned that your prime contact at the Bureau is the man who has gone after Dixon. So something must have tipped him off."

"It wasn't me! I closed that door when I killed that agent."

"Apparently someone else knew what he knew. That someone else being Kevin Willis, who apparently was not the good friend you judged him to be. We've survived and thrived on invisibility, Son. You've made us visible."

"Dad..."

Theodore shook his head. "I'm sorry, boy, but you're a weak link we can't afford."

"But…" Edward could hardly believe his ears. Blood rushed in them, and his heart pounded until he felt it would leap from his chest. Surely his dad couldn't be saying…

At once he leaped from the bench seat and looked around, trying to find some way to defend himself. A boat hook would work…but the boat hooks were gone. Where were they? A piece of rope?

He swung around, trying to find something, and froze as he looked straight down the barrel of a pistol. It was held in the hand of the man who had been helping them fish all day.

"I'm sorry," said the old man.

"Dad, please!"

But his father just turned and descended the ladder to the cabins, leaving him alone on deck with the man and the gun.

"Look, whatever they're paying you, I'll double it. Triple it! I swear!"

The man simply shook his head.

Thirty seconds later, Edward Morgan's corpse was being tossed over the side into the dark blue water of the Gulf Stream. He might wash ashore someday. In Nova Scotia. Greenland. England.

Or he might not.

31

Thunderbird Mountain, Montana

Even these Guatemalan mountain goats he'd been training were finding the trail difficult, Wes Dixon thought as he called another rest halt. It was the snowshoes that were giving them trouble, he decided. Given the dirt floor of a jungle, they would probably have leaped along this trail like deer.

But they were cold, too. Colder than they'd ever been. Even the time at his ranch hadn't adequately prepared them, and he really hadn't put a lot of expense into winter clothes, because, in theory, they wouldn't have been needed when they finished their training.

They were paying for that now. Damn Edward and his penny-pinching, anyway.

Speaking of Edward… Wes signed to one of the men to take out the satellite phone and get him uplinked. Even though he didn't want to admit it, he needed this rest as much as the youngsters. This trail rated only moderate difficulty in the summer, but right now it was hell.

First he called his home phone to see if there were any messages. There were three from Katherine who was worried sick about him and told him to call her at Edward's house. Wes's heart squeezed as he heard her voice, squeezed with all the love he felt for her. All the love that had dragged him into this cesspool with her brother.

Oh, to be fair, he had to admit there had been a time when he had believed in what Edward had asked of him. Now he wasn't so sure; he hadn't been since the assassination of the U.S. ambassador. Now all he wanted was to get back to his wife and a normal life.

Then a rapid squawk told him Ed had sent an encrypted message. Dixon punched in the encryption key, then watched as the text scrolled across the digital display: BUREAU AMBUSH BROWN PASS

Gritting his teeth against cold and fatigue, Wes dialed the Morgan household number and in a few moments was put through to Katherine.

"Wes, I've been so worried!"

"I'm all right, darlin'. I just had to go out of town on business."

"When will you be back?"

"A couple of days. Then I'm going to fly out there and sweep you away to a second honeymoon."

She caught her breath, then laughed. "Honest?"

"Honest. I miss you, darlin'. I miss you like hell."

"I miss you, too. I just…I just want to say one thing."

"What's that?"

"Whatever my brother asked you to do…if it puts

you in any danger, don't do it. I'm sick of him and his conniving, and I'm sick of him using you."

It was something they had never discussed before, something that had, however, lain between them like a silent elephant ever since he'd left the army. His heart swelled, even as he realized that he had to go on lying to her. If Ed's message was accurate, he probably would not get out of this alive. But she didn't have to know that.

"Honey, I'm getting myself out of it right now. When I come back to you, I'll be a free man."

Her sob of joy was all he could hope for. He smiled into the teeth of the frigid wind. "A couple of days, darlin'. Then I'm all yours."

He disconnected and signed to the man to put the satphone away. Then, wanting to groan but biting the sound back, he rose to his feet and signaled for everyone else to do the same.

"*Vámonos,*" he said. "We must go faster. And tell the men to get their night vision goggles from their packs and keep them inside their shirts. We're going to need them tonight."

Brown Pass, Montana

Night had fallen again. Throughout the afternoon, they had watched to the east as the Bureau troops arrived and began to take up positions below. Once or twice, Tom had thought he'd seen Miriam moving among them, but he was too far away to be certain. Renate had nodded her approval at the troops' dispositions. By the time the sun fell, every position was thoroughly camouflaged, and the men vanished completely in the darkness.

When Tom looked up, he saw the moon shadowed by icy high clouds that only slightly dimmed its light as they came and went. There were two moon dogs, images of the moon created on the icy crystals high above. Never before had he seen two of them.

He pointed them out to Renate, who took a deep breath of appreciation. "This place is so beautiful," she whispered. "Perhaps the most beautiful place in your country."

At the moment, he was inclined to agree. They had eaten more soup and stew, and had been drinking melted snow almost nonstop. Gradually his headache and nausea had fallen away.

"It's almost time," he said.

"Yes. I will go back through the trees farther up the pass. We need to know when they come."

He nodded. "But how will you let me know?"

She smiled. "In my world, we come prepared."

Turning, she began to dig through his backpack. The next thing he knew, she was handing him a headset with a throat microphone, and a small transmitter that fit easily in his pocket. Then she donned a set for herself.

"We'll use these." She pressed her throat mike as she spoke, and he heard her in his headset, only slightly delayed.

"It works," he said, pressing his own mike to his

throat. She nodded, apparently hearing him in her headset, as well.

"We are ready," she announced, picking up one of the rifles. "I will let you know when I am in position."

Some vestige of male chauvinism reared its ugly head in Tom, telling him he ought to be the one heading back through the woods, but reality tamped it down. His leg was so stiff now that he was going to need a jolt of adrenaline the size of this park to make it possible for him to move with ease.

He reached out and clasped her gloved hand tightly. "Be careful, Renate."

She squeezed back, pulled up her hood and began to make her way back through the trees that lined the trail.

East of Brown Pass

Miriam glanced at her watch. It was nearly midnight, and the men were getting antsy. Part of it, she was sure, was caged adrenaline at war with mind-numbing cold. In a concealed cook tent, park rangers churned out chicken soup and hot coffee by the gallon, but eventually even that would fail to overcome the effects of lying motionless on icy ground in sub-zero temperatures.

"We need to do a last rotation," she told Kevin.

He nodded and toggled his radio. "Command One to Section Leaders. Rotate your men by threes to the warming tents. Ten minutes each. Confirm."

There was silence for a moment before the radio crackled.

"Alpha Section, copy."

"Bravo Section, copy."

"Charlie Section, copy. Command One, my men say they're fine and we're nearest the pass. Request we stay put and cover the rest."

"Negative, Charlie," Kevin said.

Miriam knew the highly trained SWAT team members were aggressive and confident, but all too often that could lead to complacency in taking care of the little details that kept a man functioning in difficult conditions. It was vital that Kevin take command and make sure the details didn't get missed.

Kevin keyed his microphone. "Charlie Section, I say again, negative on that. Rotate by threes to the warming tent. Confirm, Charlie."

"Charlie Section, copy," the voice said with obvious disgust.

Well, let him be disgusted, Miriam thought. At least disgusted he was alive. Miriam sipped a cup of soup and stamped her feet to keep the blood flowing. Kevin nodded to her, then stepped into as private a corner as they could find in the crowded tent. She followed.

"I know we're not alone on this mountain," he said, speaking almost too quietly to be heard. "I also know you're not going to confirm or deny that. I just hope he's smart enough to keep his damn head down."

Miriam simply nodded.

"I don't know what's going on here," he continued. "And I don't expect I ever will know. But I want you to know this, Miriam. If I'm right, I'm glad he's alive. And if you ever talk to him, tell him I'm sorry."

She nodded again.

"You're a fine agent, Miriam. Best I've ever seen. When the shit hits the fan, I want you here in the command center, helping me keep track of where it's flying. Not out there playing hero. Understood?"

"Yes, sir," she said.

She had no intention of staying in the command tent, blind to the tactical situation. She'd learned at Dos Ojos that a combat leader couldn't lead from the rear. But telling him that would only create problems. She would simply handle things her way.

Brown Pass

"They're coming."

Tom had found himself almost dozing as he looked up at the brilliant night sky. Renate's voice in his earphone snapped him out of his reverie. "How long?" he asked.

"Ten minutes," she said. "I'll let them pass, then join you."

"Copy that."

He turned and looked back through the trees to the west. Against the pristine white of the snow, through the light drifts that blew in the freshening wind, he saw a line of shapes approaching. But it was not the line he'd expected to see, with each man trudging blindly in the footsteps of the one in front of him. Instead, they were in an inverted V phalanx, weapons at the ready.

"They're in combat formation," Tom said quietly, knowing how sound carried at night, hoping the snow would muffle the sounds.

"Yes," Renate said. "Apparently they know your friends are waiting for them."

Shit, Tom thought. This wasn't going to be the simple ambush the Bureau had expected. If Dixon was forewarned, he would have planned accordingly.

Looking around, Tom took stock of the terrain and the situation, and tried to put himself in Dixon's shoes. He would have to descend the steep slope. There was no way around that. Nor could he outflank the ambush; the craggy walls of the mountains made that impossible. If Dixon's men had skis, they might rush down the slope faster than the SWAT team could handle and pass right through their positions. But how likely was it that a bunch of Guatemalans knew how to downhill ski? Not at all.

Still, Tom was sure Dixon wouldn't simply walk into the trap. Speed would be his ally. The faster he could get into the midst of the SWAT team's line, the better the chance his men could take advantage of the confusion and gain the upper hand.

"How are they moving?" Tom asked.

"Snowshoes," Renate answered. "Why?"

"Are they carrying anything with them?"

There was no answer.

Tom shifted onto his good leg and looked into the darkness. "Renate? Are you there?"

Still no answer.

Seconds turned to minutes that seemed like hours. He could clearly see Dixon's men now, trudging up the final slope, awkward in their snowshoes, but every eye alert. There was no sign that anyone had broken away to deal with a threat. And yet Renate was not answering.

"Renate?"

"Sorry." Her voice came in an almost inaudible whisper. "They passed within ten feet of me. And they have shields on their backs."

"Shields?"

"They look like little canoes."

"Dammit!" Tom said. "They brought sleds. Of course."

Dixon had known from the outset that his men might have to get away from trouble quickly. With men who were not trained for arctic maneuvers, what better way to be ready than to have sleds? They required little if any skill or training. Just hop on and let gravity and the frictionless ice work together to create velocity.

"I'm coming to you," Renate said.

Minutes later, Dixon's men had passed and Renate appeared wraithlike out of the blowing snow.

"We have to warn the Bureau," Tom said. "They don't know he knows, and they don't know he's prepared."

"We can't," Renate said, shaking her head. "And

don't even try to argue with me. We'll do what we can from here, but we can't expose ourselves."

"Bullshit," Tom said. "Miriam's down there."

"Yes, she is," Renate said. "But you knew the rules when you came with me. I'm sorry, Tom. This is how it has to be."

"There must be something—"

She put a gloved finger to his lips. "There isn't, Tom. I'm sorry. There isn't."

He turned away and watched Dixon's men deploy for battle, anger raging again in his heart.

32

"Charlie One, Command One. Targets in sight."

"Copy, Charlie One," Kevin said. "Give me the details."

"Looks like about twenty of them, Command One. But they've stopped at the head of the pass. Taking off their packs."

"Maybe they're admiring the scenery," Kevin said, turning to Miriam.

"Somehow, I don't think so. Something's wrong."

Kevin keyed his mike. "Command One, Charlie One. What else can you see?"

"Charlie One, I can't be sure. It's as if they're setting up camp. They're sitting down."

"Sitting down?" Kevin asked. "Say again?"

"Copy, Command One. Sitting down. It's hard to describe. They're rubbing their butts on the snow."

"Shit," Miriam said, turning toward the door of the tent. "I know what they're doing."

"Get back here," Kevin said.

"Tell them to get ready," Miriam said. "And tell them it's going to happen a lot faster than they thought."

With that, she left the tent and began to make her way up to the line.

If it hadn't been so deadly, Tom thought, it would have been comical. The Guatemalans shed their packs and laid out their small sleds, then sat on them and began to experiment with movement and balance. It was quite obviously a new experience for them, and a few immediately toppled over. But they quickly learned how to manage, and Tom felt as if he were watching a freight train bear down on an unwitting victim, unable to stop it or even cry out a warning.

After a few agonizing minutes, Tom saw Dixon look at his men and give a signal. The men leaned forward on their shallow, bowl-shaped sleds, their packs between their legs for balance, weapons at the ready, and headed down the icy slope.

Kevin took a step to catch Miriam, but then heard the radio erupt.

"Charlie One, Command One. Holy shit, they're on sleds. And they're coming fast."

Miriam had seen what was coming before it happened. And she was right. In this kind of fight, sitting in the command post was utterly useless. Kevin grabbed his rifle and headed out as the gunfire began.

* * *

Tom had a bird's-eye view of the developing battle. Muzzle flashes along the Bureau line revealed their surprise; they hadn't had time to switch on the powerful searchlights that had been intended to blind Dixon and his men. Worse, he'd seen Dixon's men donning night goggles. This was a far more even fight than the SWAT team had expected. And it was not going well.

Dixon's men swooped down the steep, icy slope as if powered by rockets, quickly passing through the prepared kill zone that the SWAT team had set up. In less than a minute, they were into the Bureau line and all hell broke loose.

Miriam reached Alpha Section just as the Guatemalans descended on them.

"Mark your targets!" she said, taking aim and squeezing off a round at the nearest approaching form. "Careful of our positions!"

The Guatemalan toppled as her rounds impacted, the sled shooting out from beneath him and up into the air. Miriam ducked as it whizzed past, and looked for another target. She ignored the distant thoughts that these men were no different than Miguel Ortiz, and focused on the task at hand. The manic chatter in her earphone told her that Dixon had achieved the surprise and confusion he needed. Now it was an even fight, their carefully laid plans disrupted and scattered like snow on the mountain wind.

A man beside her turned and loosed a ragged three-shot volley at a passing Guatemalan, and a cry erupted from the position to her left. It was what she had feared. Firing at fast-moving targets this way, it was all but impossible to avoid hitting their own.

The military called it "friendly fire," but there was nothing friendly about it when a 5.56 mm round ripped into a leg. It was pain and spurting blood and panic and terror, with the only "friend" the man beside you who stopped to clamp a hand over the wound.

The air seemed to be alive with bees, though Miriam knew better. Bullets were flying everywhere, in every direction, from every direction.

It was chaos, and men were dying.

"Goddammit!" Tom said, watching the melee below. He turned to Renate. "We could have warned them."

Deep within her snorkel hood, tears glistened on her cheeks. "No, Tom. We couldn't. We couldn't. We…"

For the first time since he'd known her, her composure shattered. He pulled her to him, squeezing her through the Nomex parka.

"You're right," he said. "We couldn't. And even if we had, it wouldn't have mattered."

"Damn this," she said. "Damn this job."

Tom couldn't disagree. After a moment, he pushed her away and looked in her eyes. "We can still help. Get your rifle. The Bureau people are still in their camoflagued positions. So whoever we *can* see is a live target."

"Yes," she said, nodding.

"The SWAT team doesn't know we're here," he continued. "They may shoot back."

"That's part of the deal," she said. "And they need our help."

He met her eyes for a moment, nodded and rolled into firing position. Sighting carefully, he began to look for targets.

Dixon whipped around, rolling off his sled and spraying fire into the hollow beside him. His heart tore at the thought of killing fellow Americans, and yet he owed a duty of command to his troops. If they were going down, they were going down together.

A white-clad FBI agent turned in the hole, trying to bring his weapon to bear, but Dixon fired first. A black hole opened on the agent's forehead, and he toppled back into the snow with a look of astonishment frozen on his features.

They would not survive this, Dixon knew. He had been in battle before, and he'd always known he would come out of it intact. This time, he knew he would not. But he could still die with honor, as a soldier.

He looked for another target and spotted a woman with an M-16, scanning the battlefield as she reloaded. He settled into the snow and took careful aim.

Miriam ejected one clip and rammed another home, pulling back the slide to chamber a round, her eyes flitting over the melee. Almost buried in the snow, she saw a man lying, facing her, the muzzle of his weapon pointed straight at her chest. She thought of Terry as she fought against time to shoulder her rifle and take aim.

Tom had spotted Dixon and fired, but the man had rolled off his sled just as Tom pulled the trigger. Before he could correct his aim, Dixon had turned to kill an FBI agent. And now he had another in his sights. Tom didn't need night vision goggles or binoculars to recognize the posture and movement of Dixon's target. It was Miriam.

He steadied his front sight on the side of Dixon's head, exhaled slowly and squeezed the trigger.

Miriam saw Dixon's head explode in the same instant she saw the muzzle of his weapon flash. She dropped to her knees and felt a tug at her parka, but no pain. Looking down, she realized the bullet had punched through the thick padding and missed her. She turned to see who had shot Dixon and saw the wink of another muzzle flash, high in the pass.

Tom.

She waved quickly, then returned to the deadly business around her.

"You saved her life," Renate said, calmly picking off a Guatemalan who rose up out of the snow. "Good job."

"It matters," Tom said, hardly realizing where the words had come from.

"Yes," she replied. "It matters."

* * *

Kevin fired three quick rounds into the back of a rebel who was trying to flee. And then it was over. As he walked around the bloodstained snow, the butcher's bill revolted him.

"Four of ours," Miriam said, joining him. "And three more wounded, though they'll be okay."

"And twenty-two of them," he replied. "Including Dixon. None of them even tried to surrender."

"Fool's courage," she said. "What a waste."

He looked at her torn parka. "You okay?"

She nodded. "Whoever shot Dixon saved my life. He must've flinched as he got hit."

"You were supposed to stay in the command tent."

"Look, Kevin—"

He put up a hand. "But you were right not to. You reacted to the tactical situation and tried to assert control of the battle from the only place you could. You did good, Miriam."

"Thank you," she said, looking around at the sprawled, leaking bodies. She ejected the clip from her rifle and worked the bolt to empty the chamber, watching the round spin through the air, brass glistening in the moonlight. Then she slung the weapon over her shoulder. "But you'll excuse me if I don't *feel* good about it."

West of Brown Pass

Tom winced at the pain in his leg as he strapped on his skis.

"You're sure we have to do this now?"

"They'll scour the area looking for evidence," Renate said. "We can't stay here."

With a final glance down at Miriam, he nodded and turned to follow Renate into the night toward Bowman Lake.

And invisibility.

Paris, France
March 18, 1314

Jacques De Molay watched from his cell as a spit was prepared in the shadow of the great Notre Dame. Today he would be roasted alive. He knew he should be terrified at the possibility, and yet he was not. Tonight he would be in heaven, with the Light. He only regretted that he had not been able to finish his work here first.

The Knights Templar had built well and quickly over the past two centuries. Aided by ancient wisdom, and cool, calculating financial minds, they had amassed much of the wealth of Europe in their coffers. Only a select few knew what De Molay knew, that the supposedly Christian Templars worshipped a far older religion and a far older goal.

The goal had seemed within his grasp. Perhaps he

had reached too far, too fast. Perhaps he had been overtaken by his zeal to be the Great Restorer, the Pharaoh-Aten, the Pharaoh of Light, who would once again bring the one true faith to mankind and renew the empire in which that faith had been born. So much had been gained. So much had seemed ready. And now it was lost.

An informant among them, among the select few. It was impossible, and yet there was no other explanation. Why else would Philip, that dolt of a king, have conspired with Pope Clement to declare the Templars heretics? And just when great plans had been laid for a fourth and final Crusade? French kings and Papal legates had longed for such for two hundred years, and yet, now that the opportunity had been created for them and served to them on a secret silver plate, they had turned on the very deliverers of that dream.

The only possible reason was that someone among his most trusted body had leaked the real reason behind this grand new adventure. Someone had told them that, if their armies succeeded, they would accomplish naught but to relegate themselves to the margins of power as New Egypt rose from the sands to rule again.

It had been so close. And it had come to ruin. Seven years ago, on Friday, October 13, 1307, Philip and Clement had destroyed the Templar order in France. But some had slipped away. The cleverest of the financial minds had melted into the darkness with the Templar fortune, ready and waiting to open the great banks that would once again put kings and princes in their debt and at their whim. And that would happen, De Molay knew. The power of the Light and the ancient mysteries was too great to be overcome by temporal powers. Sooner or later, his disciples would rise up and claim for their forebears a rightful place in the history of man, and the Light would become the one and only beacon by which all men guided their steps. It was only a matter of patience.

But De Molay would not see that day. Instead, he would die. And go to the Light.

Epilogue

Miriam curled tightly into Terry's arms and listened to his soft, meaningless words. In the past three months, the country had gone into a furor over what the press had dubbed "the Idaho Killers." The firefight had been front-page lead story news for a week. Guatemalan rebels in the U.S., killing FBI agents. Documents recovered from a buried bunker on the Dixon ranch confirmed that Wes Dixon, a West Point graduate turned right-wing renegade, had orchestrated the murder of Ambassador Kilhenny and the attempted assassination of Grant Lawrence.

It was mostly bullshit, of course. Miriam knew that. Whatever documents had been recovered had been modified to fit the story the Bureau needed to tell and the country needed to hear. Ominous rumors of vast conspiracies might sell in the tabloids, but deep down inside, people longed for clear, unambiguous justice. The Bureau's press reports gave them what they wanted: a crazed villain, an idealistic victim…and a courageous heroine.

She hated that part worst of all. She'd received a Presidential Commendation for her work in Guatemala, Idaho and Montana, and she'd answered more questions in front of more bright lights than she'd ever wanted to in her life. The simple fact was that Tom and Renate had done most of the work, including setting up the final ambush that destroyed Dixon's militia. Including saving Miriam's life.

She wasn't a heroine. She'd killed too many people in that frantic week ever to think of herself as a heroine. In her head, she knew she had done what was necessary. In her heart, she longed to sit down with Steve Lorenzo and find some measure of peace.

Lorenzo had disappeared into the jungle, along with Miguel Ortiz and the rest of the refugees from Dos Pilas. She had no idea where they were, and no inclination to look for them. Whatever secrets might lie in the depths of the Mayan past were probably better left buried. Lorenzo would see to that, or try to. Miriam had to trust that he would find a way to do what needed to be done.

At least Tom was alive. That seemed to be the only bright ray in the darkness that had begun settling over her life the day Grant Lawrence had been shot. Well, that and the fact that Grant was recovering and after a few months of physical therapy would probably be his old self.

If anyone could be his "old self" after surviving an assassination attempt. At least he and Karen could marry now, because a senator *could* be married to a homicide detective.

So it wasn't all bad. But Miriam's heart ached, anyway. When she remembered those she had killed, both in Guatemala and in Montana, Miguel Ortiz's face floated in her mind's eye. His and his sister's. Paper targets? No way. People. Real people. She wondered if she was ever going to be able to live with the ghosts.

And that left her here, in Terry's arms, the one place she felt even remotely safe. The musky hairs on his chest tickled her cheek as she snuggled against him. The rumble of his voice was soothing, even if she wasn't hearing the words.

"Honey?" he asked. "Are you listening?"

She lifted her head to look into his deep brown eyes, noting that his ebony brow was slightly furrowed. "I'm sorry, darling. What did you say?"

He chuckled and kissed her forehead.

"I asked if you would marry me."

The tears fell onto his chest as she nodded.

Rome, Italy

"Nice digs," Tom said, as he followed Renate into the office. Despite the tawdry and run-down appearance of the warehouse, the inside was an anthill of cubicles, maps and computer projection screens. "You guys live well."

"We get by," she said.

She led him through the maze, introducing him to her

colleagues, now his. Carlos Pitanza, former antidrug intelligence agent in Colombia. Peter Stone, former MI-6. Margarite Renault, ex-Sûreté. A dozen other names and faces blurred, although he knew he would learn them in time.

"There are another twenty or so in the field," Renate said. "Afghanistan. Saudi Arabia. Chechnya. Among other places. It's a busy world."

"Unfortunately," he said. "So where am I?"

"Right back here," she replied, leading him deeper into the warren of cubicles. "Next to me."

She stepped into her cubicle and returned with a thick red file. Three diagonal stripes crossed the cover, the office code for ultrasecret.

"Harrison Rice is going to get elected," she said. "Ed Morgan has disappeared, presumed dead. But we both know it's not over."

"The Frankfurt Brotherhood," Tom said, opening the file. "They'll own a U.S. president."

"Unless we find a way to stop them," Renate said. "But first, come with me. It is time you meet the head of our outfit."

He followed her between cubicles, down a freestanding hallway to a door marked Jefe.

"Chief?" he asked.

"You'll see why." She was smiling at him, and for the first time he saw a twinkle in her eyes. He hadn't known she could be tickled by anything, and the expression brought an answering smile to his own face. It had been so long since he'd really smiled that it felt as if ice were cracking on his face.

Then she threw the door open and said, "Chief? Our newest agent."

Tom stepped through the door but made it no farther. He stared in disbelief at the man behind the desk. "John? What the fuck?"

John Ortega, the man whose death Tom had grieved only two years ago, launched into his Cheech Marin patter. "I couldn't let my amigo weether in *de federales!* This bunch pulled me out of L.A., and next thing I know, I'm running the place."

An instant later, the two men were embracing and laughing, and slapping each other's backs.

Still smiling, Renate withdrew into the hallway and closed the door behind her, leaving them to catch up. Sometimes you lost everything to join this group. And sometimes you found something.

Her smile softened a bit and she murmured, "Welcome to Office 119, Lawton Caine."

Afterword and Acknowledgments

Wild Card is the first installment in an ongoing story, and as such it was an extremely challenging project. No work of this scope could be a singular enterprise, and we are indebted first and foremost to Leslie Wainger and Helen Breitwieser, our editor and agent respectively, whose unstinting confidence, support and patience gave us the courage—and the time, far beyond our deadline!—to undertake this project. You two are, quite simply, the best creative partners any writer could hope for.

This is a work of fiction. Yet what has come to be known as the Conspiratorial School of History offers a wealth of background from which a novelist can work. We do not endorse this theory of history, but we must acknowledge that it is an entrancing and deep mine of mythic potential.

Each of the flashbacks in the narrative is based on a documented historical event, although we have taken great creative liberties to weave them into the tapestry of this series.

An overview of the Conspiratorial School of History can be found in Jim Marrs's *Rule by Secrecy*.

For the history of Akhenaten and the Cult of Light, we have drawn primarily from Ahmed Osman's *Moses and Akhenaten*, and Erik Hornung's *Akhenaten and the Religion of Light*.

The enduring significance of the Battle of Actium is best described in Josiah Ober's essay "Not By a Nose," published in *What If? 2: Eminent Historians Imagine What Might Have Been*, edited by Robert Cowley.

The theory that Mary Magdalene may have been the wife of Christ, and have borne His child away to southern France, has been explored in many fictional and nonfictional works. We drew primarily from *Holy Blood, Holy Grail* by Michael Baigent, Richard Leigh and Henry Lincoln, *The Templar Revelation* by Lynn Picknett and Clive Prince, and *Lost Scriptures,* by Bart D. Ehrman.

Intriguing evidence for the existence of Christianity in pre-Columbian Central America can be found in Manly P. Hall's *The Secret Teachings of All Ages*, as well as Maggie Sypniewski's excellent telling of Aztec and Mayan poetry and the Quetzalcoatl myth on the Bear Clan Web site at Geocities.com.

While the United Nations does have an antiterrorism organization, whose mandate includes support of covert operations, Office 119, as well as its conspiratorial opponents, are complete fabrications.

Last, but by no means least, we are indebted to our

dear friend Rolf Winkenbach, whose endless patience with our questions about German culture, government, geography and other matters was essential in the creation of Renate Bächle. *Danke, Rolf; Sie sind ein Schatz!*
Rachel Lee
April, 2004

From the bestselling author of *Her Mother's Shadow* and *Kiss River* comes a haunting tale of dangerous passions and dark family secrets....

DIANE CHAMBERLAIN

Her family's cottage on the New Jersey shore was a place of freedom and innocence for Julie Bauer—until tragedy struck when her seventeen-year-old sister, Isabel, was murdered. It's been more than forty years since that August night, but Julie's memories of her sister's death still color her world, causing turmoil in all of her relationships.

Now an unexpected phone call from someone in her past raises questions about what really happened that night. Questions about Julie's own complicity. Questions about the man who went to prison for Isabel's murder—and about the man who didn't. Julie must harness the courage to revisit her past and untangle the shattering emotions that led to one unspeakable act of violence on the bay at midnight.

"Chamberlain adeptly unfolds layers of rage, guilt, longing, repression and rebellion, while gently preaching a message of trust and forgiveness. Complex, credible characterization..."
—*Publishers Weekly*
on *Her Mother's Shadow*

Available the first week of February 2005, wherever books are sold!

www.MIRABooks.com   MDC2146

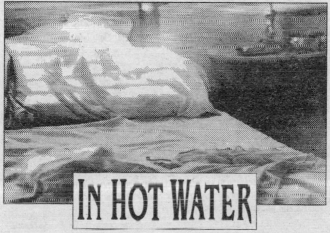

If you enjoyed what you just read,
then we've got an offer you can't resist!

Take 2 bestselling novels FREE!
Plus get a FREE surprise gift!

MIRABooks.com

We've got the lowdown on your favorite author!

☆ Read an excerpt of your favorite author's newest book

☆ Check out her bio

☆ Talk to her in our Discussion Forums

☆ Read interviews, diaries, and more

☆ Find her current bestseller, and even her backlist titles

All this and more available at

www.MiraBooks.com

RACHEL LEE

32004	SOMETHING DEADLY	___ $6.50 U.S.	___ $7.99 CAN.
66885	JULY THUNDER	___ $6.50 U.S.	___ $7.99 CAN.
66802	A JANUARY CHILL	___ $5.99 U.S.	___ $6.99 CAN.
66658	WITH MALICE	___ $6.50 U.S.	___ $7.99 CAN.
66554	SNOW IN SEPTEMBER	___ $5.99 U.S.	___ $6.99 CAN.
66173	A FATEFUL CHOICE	___ $5.99 U.S.	___ $6.99 CAN.

(limited quantities available)

TOTAL AMOUNT $ _____
POSTAGE & HANDLING $ _____
($1.00 FOR 1 BOOK, 50¢ for each additional)
APPLICABLE TAXES* $ _____
TOTAL PAYABLE $ _____
(check or money order—please do not send cash)

To order, complete this form and send it, along with a check or money order for the total above, payable to MIRA Books, to: **In the U.S.:** 3010 Walden Avenue, P.O. Box 9077, Buffalo, NY 14269-9077; **In Canada:** P.O. Box 636, Fort Erie, Ontario, L2A 5X3.

Name: _____
Address: _____ City: _____
State/Prov.: _____ Zip/Postal Code: _____
Account Number (if applicable): _____
075 CSAS

*New York residents remit applicable sales taxes.
*Canadian residents remit applicable GST and provincial taxes.

MIRA®

www.MIRABooks.com

MRL0205BL